ENDINGS:

KING ARTHUR AND HER KNIGHTS BOOK 7

K. M. SHEA

ENDINGS

Cover Art by Trif Book Design

www.kmshea.com

ISBN-10: 0692979913

ISBN-13: 978-0692979914

Created with Vellum

CHARACTERS

Adelind: Wife of King Pellinore—Queen of Anglesey

Agravain: The second son of King Lot and Queen Morgause of Orkney.

Ban: One of two kings who marched with Britt against Lot and his allies. He is from France, is well groomed, and is said to have a son who is an impressive knight.

Bedivere: A knight Britt met in London when she was crowned King. Britt chose him as her marshal on an impulse, without any input from Merlin.

Bodwain: Britt's constable and one of Merlin's Minions.

Bors: One of two kings who marched with Britt against Lot and his allies. He is from France, although he appears to be half bear. His two sons are said to be gallivanting around with King Ban's son.

Ector: The man who was selected to be Arthur's foster father. He has taken a similar role in Britt's life.

Gaheris: The third son of King Lot and Queen Morgause of Orkney.

Gareth: The youngest son of King Lot and Queen Morgause of Orkney.

Gawain: The eldest son of King Lot and Queen Morgause of Orkney.

Griflet: A young, ignorant knight who is related to Sir Bedivere and is close friends with Ywain.

Guinevere: The daughter of King Leodegrance whom Britt dislikes thanks to modern King Arthur stories and legends.

Igraine: Mother of the real Arthur. Uther Pendragon was her second husband.

Kay: Britt's seneschal and supposed foster brother. He takes Britt's safety seriously and is often seen writing in a log book.

Lancelot: The only son of King Bors whom Britt despises thanks to modern King Arthur stories and legends.

Leodegrance: King of Camelgrance, one of Britt's first allies.

Lot: King of Orkney and Britt's worst enemy. He rallied kings and knights and led them to battle before Britt and her allies overthrew him.

Maleagant: A duke and friend of King Ryence.

Merlin: Britt's chief counselor who is also responsible for yanking Britt back through time. He openly uses Britt to accomplish his dream of uniting Britain.

Morgause: Daughter of Igraine and Arthur's half-sister. She is married to King Lot of Orkney and has four sons: Gawain, Agravain, Gaheris, and Gareth.

Morgan le Fay: Daughter of Igraine, Arthur's half-sister and full sister to Queen Morgause and Queen Elaine. She is known to have magical powers.

Nymue: The beautiful Lady of the Lake who "gave" Excalibur to Britt.

Pellinore: A noble-looking king who attacked Britt with King Lot, King Urien, and King Ryence.

Percival: A Knight of the Round Table and the son of King Pellinore.

Ryence: A cowardly king who attacked Britt with King Lot, King Urien, and King Pellinore.

Tor: The son of a cowherd who is made a knight by Britt. He has a squire named Lem.

Ulfius: An older knight who once served Uther Pendragon and now serves Britt as her chamberlain. He is one of Merlin's Minions.

Urien: The brother-in-law of King Lot and a king in his own right, Urien fought with Lot, Pellinore, and Ryence against Britt but has since become Britt's vassal because he believes she holds his son, Ywain, hostage in Camelot.

Uther Pendragon: Considered to be one of the greatest kings of England. He is the real Arthur's father and died some years ago —leaving all of his lands and money to Arthur.

Ywain: The only son of King Urien. He swore loyalty to Britt after being captured by her men and has revered her ever since. Morgause is his aunt.

1

LOSS AND GAINS

Britt couldn't remember her mom's voice.

The realization struck her near the midnight watch, as she paced in the small, frost-covered queen's garden. The moon glowed overhead, casting silver light on the withered plants. Off in the distance a dog barked and soldiers greeted one another as the patrol shifts changed over…and for the life of her, Britt couldn't remember her mom's voice.

Her sister's face—a face she had seen every day of her childhood—was starting to grow hazy, too.

Britt could remember her mom's gusty laugh and the twinkle in her sister's eyes. Details like that were easier to recall, but everyday things—like faces and voices—were starting to slip from her memory. Instead, they were replaced with Merlin's sarcastic barbs, Kay's twitching mustache, Mordred's dimpled smile, and Gawain's clear eyes.

But while she treasured the new, her heart ached with the loss of the old.

"It's been three years," she whispered. "Just *three*! How could I forget them so quickly?"

Three years ago, Britt—an American from the twenty-first

century—had been pulled back through time while visiting England. Her time travel was the result of a spell forged by Merlin, who told her Arthur—the boy meant to be King of Britain—had run off with a shepherdess, and she was to take up his identity and rule in his stead.

Britt placed her hand on a stone pillar, seeking support. The stone was so cold it bit her palms, but she barely noticed.

"I'm happy," she murmured. "My knights accept me—the *real* me—Camelot is more beautiful than I could imagine, and we are at peace. But…how can I forget who I was, who I *really* am?" She took a shuddering breath.

"Milord?" one of her guards asked, shifting in the shadows.

Britt offered him a wan smile and waved his concern off. She resumed pacing, as if the exertion would help her recall the exact proportions of her sister's face.

She paused only when Merlin—his blonde hair white in the silver moonlight—popped around the corner of the garden. He held a sputtering torch, and his forehead wrinkled as he and Britt stared at each other from across the garden.

She forced herself to smile. "Good evening, Merlin." She used her grin to hide the stabbing pain in her heart.

The lines in his forehead grew deeper, and he took a step towards her. "Lass—"

"Merlin, My Love! Why do you tarry so?" Vivien—beautiful, blonde, and calculating—swept around the corner after Merlin. When she saw Britt, she planted a hand over her heart. "Oh, King Arthur!"

"Good evening, Vivien," Britt said, nodding.

"Good Evening, Sire!" Vivien smiled—a beautiful and cruel expression—and wrapped her hands possessively around Merlin's right arm. "It is rather cold to be outside, isn't it?"

Britt kept her eyes on Vivien. Smiling at the black magic user was easier than witnessing Merlin transform into a love-addled idiot before her eyes. "For some, but I dearly love winter."

Vivien wrinkled her nose. "But spring and summer are so much more romantic with the flowers and the quests you send your knights on! Wouldn't you agree, Merlin?"

Britt felt her control crumble as Merlin smiled down at the young woman and patted her hands on his arm. "Of course, Lady Vivien," he said. "But there are no flowers that can compete with your beauty." His expression was tender as he took one of her hands and kissed it.

Vivien giggled—a high-pitched sound that grated on Britt's nerves.

Britt knew Merlin's actions were a farce—an act meant to occupy Vivien, who was a very real threat to Camelot. But it still hurt to see him so affectionate.

She turned slightly, so she could stare out at the gardens instead of at the pair of them.

"If you'll excuse us, Your Highness," Vivien started. "Merlin was going to read poetry to me in his study."

"Of course! I hope you enjoy yourself, Lady Vivien," Britt said.

"I always do," Vivien hummed. "Come, Merlin." She tugged on Merlin's arm, then released her grip so she could swish her skirts properly.

Britt rubbed her forehead, feeling the pinching promise of a headache. She glanced up when she realized Merlin hadn't moved.

The light in his blue eyes was worried. He took a breath, as if to say something.

"Merlin? Come along!" Vivien called.

He briefly shut his eyes, then turned on his heels without saying a word.

Britt watched him go, feeling alone and abandoned, even though she knew he deceived Vivien for her sake.

For months, Britt had been in love with Merlin. It had briefly been a point of contention between them, until Britt got the maddening wizard to understand that her love for him wouldn't jeopardize Camelot and everything they had worked for. She thought friendship was the best she could hope for, but one early morning in summer, he had swept into her room and kissed her soundly.

By the time Britt processed the possibilities of what the kiss meant, Merlin had thrown himself into the role of pretending to be head-over-heels in love with Vivien.

"I just can't catch a break," Britt muttered.

"Milord?" a guard inquired.

Britt pushed another smile on her lips. "It's nothing," she said. "Well, men, are any of you up for a sword match, or shall we go rouse Mordred or Gawain?"

One of the guards—a big burly man with a thick Scottish accent who had the tendency to act like a nanny—suspiciously eyed her. "It occurred to me, 'Highness, that it is night, and you best sleep."

"I'm not tired," Britt said.

The Scottish guard folded his arms across his chest and looked unconvinced.

"Have you ever gotten a full night's sleep since you were made king, Milord?" another guard asked.

Britt scowled at her men. Most of them had been with her since she first arrived in Camelot, and *all* of them were hand-chosen by Kay, her foster-brother, to serve her. The long length of their relationship had naturally developed into a camaraderie —particularly given that besides the Knights of the Round Table, they were the only ones who knew her real gender. Unfortunately, the camaraderie had taken a decidedly *bossy* turn since Merlin started looking at Vivien with calf-eyes. They knew of her long-held tradition of pacing the walls late into the night—though they didn't know it was because even three years later she still missed her friends and family from her old life.

She planted her hands on her hips. "Have my sleeping patterns become your duty to safeguard as well?"

"They do affect your physical wellbeing, milord," the guard said.

She snorted. "What will come next? Will you be teaming up with the kitchen boys to make sure I'm eating right?"

"It's not a bad idea."

Britt whirled around at the new voice, a soft smile already spreading on her lips. "Kay! What brings you out here so late?"

Kay nodded to the soldiers as he joined Britt in the garden. "Merlin sent me," he murmured. Kay looked her up and down with concern, but his presence and words were enough to start soothing the fierce pang in her heart.

She shook her head to clear it, and smiled at her foster brother. "You don't have to look so worried. It's just..."

Kay was silent for a moment when she didn't continue. "You'll be glad to hear I received word from Father. He should return to Camelot in a few weeks."

Britt straightened, heartened by the news. (Kay's father, Sir Ector, had become Britt's foster-father since her arrival.) "Really? That's great! ...But is he okay? I thought he was going to stay in Bonmaison until spring."

"He's getting antsy, so mother decided a visit was in order," Kay said. "She'll be coming too..."

Britt and Kay chatted on. Her foster-brother was a steady and warm reminder: she wasn't alone, not really. Though she sometimes felt so, it was only because her heart was pulled between two times and places. She had her guards, Kay, and her other friends...and Merlin. Yes, Merlin couldn't break character, but yet he still managed to help her from the shadows.

"Her beauty shines like the sun, and parting from her fills me with such sorrow and longing!" Tristan, one of Britt's newer knights who had been sworn into the Order of the Round Table (and the secret of Britt's gender) some months ago with Mordred, sighed. "Iseult is the lady I wish to serve and do great deeds for. Our love is eternal, and there are none that can come close to the depth of our feelings!" he declared, passionately throwing his arms wide.

Britt studied the love-sick knight as she stroked Cavall—her apricot-colored mastiff. "Question: Didn't you meet Iseult when you were sent to pick her up in Ireland and bring her back to your uncle—who *raised* you—to be his bride?"

Tristan blinked and dropped his arms. "I did. She is my uncle's wife, now."

"And didn't you mention your love—which you called eternal, might I add—was brought about by a love potion you two 'happened' to drink?" Britt continued.

"Indeed," Tristan said.

"...And you don't see a problem with that?"

Tristan tilted his head and furrowed his brow in confusion. "No. Why would I?"

Britt stroked Cavall's velvety side, mostly to keep from smacking herself in the forehead from frustration. "Okay, it seems like we need a lesson in morals and blame-shifting. Lancelot, you better be paying attention—you need to hear this as badly as Tristan." She jabbed a finger in Lancelot's direction as she stood, her wooden chair scraping the floor.

Lancelot drew back in over-dramatized shock. "*Me,* My Lord?"

Britt barely managed to keep a sneer off her face as she met the handsome knight's green eyes. "Yes, *you.*" She shifted her gaze so she could address the rest of her knights.

They were gathered around the large, donut-shaped Round Table, each knight seated in his designated chair. Almost every seat was occupied, for it was winter and the knights only set out on quests and adventures in spring and summer. (Pellinore was the only knight missing, Britt noticed. He was probably tied to a chair back in Anglesey. It was the only way his wife could keep him from skipping out on his duties as a king and chasing off after the questing beast and recreant knights.)

Britt placed her hands on the scratched surface of the Round Table and leaned forward. "Married women are strictly off-limits." She took in the blank looks her knights gave her and adjusted her language. "What I mean is that marriage vows are holy. One must not seek love outside his or her marriage, and so as *chivalrous* knights, I expect you to honor the sanctity of marriage and refrain from loving a woman who is already spoken for."

Ywain—who had been in Camelot's halls since before Christmas, visiting while the magical spring on his lands was frozen and needed no protection—shifted uneasily. "What if she is a widow?" (Ywain had fought and killed a dishonorable knight, and then fell in love with and married his widow.)

"If she's a widow, it's fine," Britt said.

Ywain leaned back in his chair, looking relieved.

His close friend, Sir Griflet, thoughtfully rubbed his chin. "Are we still to help married women if they seek out our aid?"

"Yes," Britt said. "You should help anyone who needs it. I'm just talking about love. You are *not* to commit adultery with another man's wife—do I make myself clear, Lancelot?"

Lancelot ran his hand through his curly black hair that the ladies of Camelot were forever sighing over. "Absolutely, My Lord."

Britt was unconvinced, particularly because he accented his answer with a smile so flirtatious, she wanted to slap it off his face.

Though Lancelot was undoubtedly one of her most skilled knights, his very presence set her teeth on edge. Mostly it was because Britt knew the legends of the future—the ones in which Lancelot (King Arthur's best friend) and Guinevere (King

Arthur's wife) fell in love, had an affair, and were essentially responsible for the eventual ruin of Camelot.

Since a young age, Britt had disliked Lancelot due to those stories, which was why now—even though Britt marrying Guinevere, who knew Britt's true identity, was impossible—she still barely tolerated him. (Which was excusable given that he was a huge player and had a severely inflated ego.)

"But, Britt," Lancelot continued to her irritation. He said her name like it was some shared secret—as if *all* the knights of the Round Table didn't know it! "You have neglected to address one aspect of this unfortunate love affair over which Sir Tristan has no control: the love potion."

Britt straightened and brushed Cavall hairs off her chestplate. "Ahh, yes. The love potion. How exactly did that happen again?"

"Iseult was meant to give it to King Mark, but, alas, when we were partaking in a luncheon together on the ship, an ignorant servant mixed some of it into our drinks," Tristan said.

Britt quirked an eyebrow. "*Some* of the potion? There's a bit left?"

"Indeed. I brought it with me." Tristan pulled a crystal vial out of a satchel. When Britt held out her hand, he stood and deposited it in her palm.

She studied the amber liquid in the bottle, then discreetly glanced at Merlin.

Though they weren't publicly fighting, he had severely diminished his role in Britt's court as a way to wall off Vivien, so he wasn't forever opening his mouth and blasting Britt like he used to. However, she still needed his advice—particularly on matters of magic. Thankfully, they knew each other well enough that Britt could read the slant of his eyebrows like a book.

The pinched set of his lips and the haughty light in his eyes told Britt the potion was most likely a fake.

Britt swirled the vial so the liquid in it churned. "I don't know that I believe this is a true love potion, Tristan."

"But it must be, for the love I share with the beautiful Iseult sprouted the moment it touched my lips!" Tristan said.

She shrugged. "Then let's test it." Before anyone could stop her, Britt uncorked the bottle and took a swig.

Her knights shouted in protest as Britt swished the fruity liquid around her mouth and tried to place the sweet flavor. She swallowed it and glanced down at Cavall, fondly petting his head. "I assume—if it's real—it would make me fall in love with the first man I set eyes on, yes?"

Tristan made a strangled noise of affirmation.

Britt tugged on her cuirass—the armor piece that encased her torso. One of the leather straps that held it shut had slipped, and the buckle was stabbing her side. "Right. Then Mordred or Gawain, if one of you would oblige me."

A chair scraped, and Britt was about to turn in that direction —she thought it was Mordred who stood—when someone grabbed her chin and forced her face up.

Britt blinked as she stared into Lancelot's dreamy green eyes. A muscle in her cheek twitched in irritation—of course *he* would try to make her fall in love with him! Since the reveal of her gender, he had done his best to "seduce" her—which did little besides feed her flames of righteous indignation.

Rather than yell at him, as she normally would, she waited several long moments to be certain that the drink really was a fake, and not even a short-term love charm. (If it was, she would kill Lancelot the moment it wore off.) As her irritation and rage level didn't so much as budge, it was safe to assume the drink was harmless.

Lancelot, unaware of her inner musings, smiled handsomely and reached out to tuck a lock of her blonde hair behind her ear.

Britt whacked his hand away with a scowl. "Since when is your name Mordred or Gawain?"

"I was closer," he pointed out.

Britt rolled her eyes. "Woe befall my closest knights if I ask them to stand up. Go away." She poked him in the chest with a finger, prodding until he backed out of her personal space. She then turned to face Tristan. "I hate to break it to you, Tristan, but I think you've been duped. That was definitely apple cider."

Tristan shook his head. "How could that be? Lady Iseult said it was a love potion!"

"Then either she was duped as well, or she's purposely lying so she has an excuse to bat her eyelashes at you."

Tristan plopped down in his chair. "What do you mean?" he asked bewilderedly.

"She might have developed feelings for you and so badly wanted you to return her affection that she lied to you. You are, after all, astoundingly loyal to King Mark. If she hadn't fed you the line about the potion, I doubt it would have occurred to you to see her romantically." She set the crystal vial on the Round Table with a tap.

"Or perhaps she's an innocent party as well," she continued. "It's likely that whoever gave her the drink meant it to be a harmless way to help her feel better about her impending marriage to an unknown man. I know little of the plight of a genteel lady from these times, but based on what I *do* know, it's safe to assume she was afraid King Mark wouldn't like her, and her life would become unpleasant."

"My uncle would *never* treat a lady so shabbily," Tristan declared.

Britt ignored the comment and concluded, "I haven't met the lady in question so I could not say for sure which one it is. I would hope for the latter, but the former may be just as likely."

Tristan stared at the vial with a disgruntled expression. "It really is only apple cider?"

"Do I *look* overtaken with love for...*Lancelot*?" Britt spat the knight's name out with a shiver.

Tristan frowned, but Lancelot's cousin, Sir Lionel, hooted.

"Nope! You still look at him like he's a bat or a rodent of the night."

A smile tugged on the corners of Britt's lips. "And there you have it. If it makes you feel any better, it's very delicious apple cider." Judging by Tristan's troubled frown, it wasn't much of a consolation.

She glanced around the large chamber at the hundred or so knights who were present and planned her next move. They had nothing more to discuss, and she'd like to spare Tristan any further public display if she could, so she pushed her chair in. "I think we should end our meeting of the Order of the Round Table for now. As much as I long to continue our discussion and revel in our camaraderie, we all have responsibilities to see to." She smiled, pleased with her announcement. Though she still broke into slang and modern language occasionally, the flowery language most of the knights used was coming to her more naturally these days.

The knights gathered in clumps as the meeting disbanded. Sir Percival—the son of King Pellinore—and Sir Agravain—Gawain's little brother—patted Tristan on the back, doing their best to raise his flagging spirits.

Britt briefly considered joining her favorite trio, Sir Mordred, Sir Gawain, and Sir Kay. However, all three knights were eyeing the crystal vial containing the fake love potion. Judging by the quirk of Kay's mustache, Britt was willing to bet a lecture about consuming unknown substances was in her future, so she turned her back to them and pretended not to notice.

Lancelot gave her a smile as smooth as cream and started to approach her again.

"Nope!" Britt cheerfully said. She walked quickly—Merlin would have probably complained it was an unkingly pace—aiming for the giant doors that led out of the hall.

She successfully slipped out before Lancelot could catch her, almost bowling over Guinevere.

"Good day, Arthur!" Guinevere said in her sing-song voice. Her reddish-blonde hair glowed in the torchlight, and her smile was sappy but genuine.

Guinevere was the daughter of King Leodegrance, one of Britt's allies. While the old king was not unkind, he had made it clear he saw Guinevere's future marriage as a bargaining chip and was not opposed to wedding her to a less-than-savory character if it meant saving himself.

As a result, Britt had begrudgingly invited the silly girl to Camelot, even though she had long loathed Guinevere almost as much as she disliked Lancelot.

"Good day to you, Guinevere. I hope you weren't waiting for me too long," Britt said.

"Not at all! Besides, I knew if I didn't catch you now, I would be unlikely to get a moment with you all day. Sir Kay said today you are holding meetings to discuss what castle construction and expansion you will make when spring comes again!" Guinevere latched on to Britt's arm and leaned into her.

Britt, tipped off by Guinevere's clinginess, glanced down the hallway and caught sight of Vivien.

Though Britt initially had little patience for Guinevere when she first arrived, the young girl had become a great boon. She was one of a small handful of ladies who knew Britt's real gender, and she happily played the role of romantic interest for Britt to keep the general population assured, and also to keep females clear. One of those females was the wildcat Merlin was forced to moon over, Vivien.

Britt nodded to Vivien, who wore a magnificent velvet dress and jewels woven through her hair, but kept her attention on Guinevere. "I am honored you would take the trouble to learn my schedule," she said.

"Of course!" Guinevere chirped. "When do you think you will hold the feast for Sir Tristan, welcoming his return to the Round Table?"

Britt cringed. "I'm not certain…he probably doesn't much feel like celebrating at this moment."

"Why-ever not?" Guinevere asked with wide eyes.

Britt set a hand on Excalibur's hilt and considered her words.

"Merlin! I have so languished without you," Vivien proclaimed.

Against her will, Britt turned to watch the vile maiden greet Merlin.

Vivien's smile was victorious as she clasped hands with Merlin and leaned into his chest.

He chuckled and smiled down at her, making Britt's heart crack. "And I have missed you."

"Will you not stay with me for the rest of the day?" Vivien asked, her voice sickeningly sweet.

"If you wish it, I shall command it!" Merlin said.

Though she knew it was an act, a pang pierced Britt's chest like an arrow.

"Arthur?" Guinevere squeezed her hand, then smiled when Britt met her gaze. "Can we walk?"

"Yes, yes! Was there something you wished to discuss?" Britt forcibly turned her back to Vivien and Merlin, and she started walking arm-in-arm with Guinevere. She winced when Vivien's tinkling laugh nipped at her heels as she and Merlin fell in line behind them.

"Blancheflor, Clarine, and I ventured outside Camelot yesterday. The weather is finally settling, it was not quite so windy!" Guinevere chattered.

"I see," Britt said.

Behind them Vivien giggled. "Oh, Merlin. You are so handsome and so talented!"

"I am, aren't I?" Merlin said.

Britt realized she was clenching her teeth and forced herself to relax her jaw. "Did you ride or walk?"

"We walked. But I wanted to speak to you…"

Britt was only half listening as she tried to block out Merlin's and Vivien's conversation. "Hmm?"

"I've been outside Camelot several times this winter, and whenever I venture past the walls, I feel...watched," Guinevere said.

Britt honed in on Guinevere's words. "What?"

"My friends and I have heard horses in the woods, and Blancheflor even saw a man once. It feels unsafe."

Britt mulled over her words. Men in the woods? *Who would be so stupid to lurk so close to Camelot?* Due to the knightly practice of questing, most recreant knights had been cleared from the surrounding area.

Guinevere looked up at Britt with wide eyes. "I do not mean to burden you or bother you. Please, forget my words."

Britt winced again, this time bothered by guilt. When Guinevere had initially arrived, Britt had very little patience for her and did her best to avoid her at all costs. Her conscience had been bothering her about it ever since Guinevere happily consented to their act.

"No, I believe you," Britt said. "I'll speak to Kay about it and see to it that something is done."

Guinevere's slight frown was transformed into a bright smile. "Thank you, Arthur!" She hugged Britt's arm. Judging by the deepness of her sigh, the issue had probably been bothering her for a while.

Britt absentmindedly patted Guinevere on the hand, mentally adding the teenager's worry to her list of things to discuss with Kay.

Behind her, Merlin and Vivien laughed, an audible reminder that she couldn't turn to Merlin for help as she usually would. (Though Kay would probably fill the wizard in later.)

"MEN IN THE WOODS?" Sir Kay asked.

"That's what she said." Britt sat on a padded chair, crossing her legs at the ankles in as manly a fashion as she could. "She was pretty upset about it."

Sir Bodwain, Britt's constable, tapped his craggy nose. "Has anyone else received similar reports?"

The other men, Sir Ulfius—her chamberlain—and Sir Bedivere—her marshal—shook their heads.

"The commoners have not reported any problems, nor have the farmers," Sir Bedivere said.

Sir Kay smoothed his mustache. "The guards have not witnessed anything unusual, but they've only been out on their customary rotations."

"Perhaps it is a black-hearted man seeking out fair maidens, or perhaps even a faerie," Sir Bedivere speculated.

Sir Ulfius snorted. "Not likely. No faerie would bother us as our lands border the Lady of the Lake's, and she is the most powerful faerie in the area. And it would take a new brand of fool to drool over the women of Camelot from the shadows. Knights come and go at all hours of the day, exercising their horses, hunting, and training."

"I agree." Britt stared at the glowing coals of the cheerful fire that crackled in the fireplace. "I doubt there is such an intruder, but I want to take Guinevere's worry seriously. She's done a lot for me."

"I'll have the forest searched," Kay said.

Britt offered her foster-brother a smile. "Thank you, Kay. I'll mention it to some of the knights. They're starting to get rowdy after being stuck indoors for so long."

"They can earn their keep," Kay grunted. (Kay was somewhat famous for agonizing over the upkeep the knights cost Britt and was always happy to put them to use.)

"But what if whoever or whatever this shadowy figure is, is only after females?" Sir Bedivere asked.

"You mean because only women have seen any signs of it?" Sir Ulfius asked. "I wouldn't put much stock in it. You said so yourself none of the commoners have reported anything. There are plenty of commoner women who venture outside of Camelot during the day."

"Bedivere has a point, though," Britt said. "Yes, there haven't been many witnesses, but they're all female."

"Send Morgan out," Sir Bodwain suggested.

Kay frowned. "Why?"

"She is of the female persuasion, and she could blast any man who dares lay a hand on her," Sir Bodwain said.

"We would be poor hosts to ask our guest to risk her life," Kay said.

Britt raised an eyebrow, taking in his unusual interest in Morgan. Since summer, she had idly wondered if Kay felt more for the sorceress than he let on. She was beginning to suspect she was correct.

Sir Ulfius, on the other hand, was not bothered by Kay's darkening eyes. "It's hardly risking her life," he said. "All she will have to do is stand in the meadow."

Kay's brows lowered alarmingly, so Britt intervened. "I would prefer not to ask Morgan for help. First, because she is gone visiting one of her sisters and won't return for two weeks. Second, because it is well within our means to take care of this ourselves."

Kay nodded.

Sir Bodwain picked up a goblet of cider. "Whom, then, do you suggest we use?"

Britt smiled. "Myself, of course."

"No," Sir Kay said with a chopping motion.

"My Lord, you couldn't possibly put yourself in such danger," Sir Bedivere protested.

"It wouldn't be wise," Sir Ulfius added.

"And Merlin would have our heads." Sir Bodwain eyed the

empty wooden chair that Merlin, before he had to dance attendance on Vivien, used to frequently occupy.

"Did we not agree that there is no proof of any threat?" Britt asked coaxingly.

The knights exchanged looks.

"Yes," Sir Ulfius grudgingly said.

"Doesn't matter," Kay insisted.

"I'll be just outside Camelot," Britt said.

"You were just outside Camelot when Sir Damas kidnapped you last summer," Kay said.

"Yes, but that was an unusual circumstance," Britt said. She was quick to add, "and if you want to be angry at anyone over that event, Lancelot is the guy who deserves it."

Sir Bodwain pinched his eyes shut. "My Lord."

"He *stabbed* me. After I had already won the match!"

Sir Ulfius shifted in his chair and looked pained. "I suppose I could procure feminine clothes for you to wear—for you must leave Camelot in disguise. We wouldn't want anyone to recognize you."

She brightened. "Then I can do it?"

The three knights looked to Kay, who scowled. "I don't like it."

"The guards and knights can clear the forest first," Britt offered.

Kay sighed. "Very well. But I want a *week* for the knights and guards to search the surrounding area."

Britt, elated she had actually won for once, smiled broadly. "Of course! Though an entire week seems a bit overkill."

Sir Bedivere tilted his head. "Overkill?"

"Umm…overly protective."

"Considering the threat is probably nonexistent, yes," Sir Bodwain rumbled. "But it's just as well. It will make Merlin feel better."

"You'll tell him our plans?" Sir Bedivere asked.

"Of course," Sir Bodwain said.

Sir Ulfius took a slug of his drink. "I don't envy you."

"He has a week to adjust to the idea. I'm sure he'll be fine," Britt said. The rest of the knights looked unconvinced, so Britt thought it would be prudent to move on. "What is the next order of business?"

"Merlin wishes for us to discuss the threat from Rome," Sir Bodwain said.

Britt groaned. "Not again!"

"His fears are well founded," Sir Ulfius said. "Rome has frequently been a disease on our lands."

Britt was tempted to roll her eyes, but she kept her disdain to herself and forced herself to listen to her knights as they meticulously reviewed the case for expanding her kingdom.

2
THE RETURN OF DUKE MALEAGANT

Britt discreetly attempted to adjust the heavy fabric of her skirts as she lingered near the gatehouse of Camelot, standing just outside the walls.

For the first time since arriving in medieval England, she was dressed as a girl. Sir Ulfius had procured a warm, blue dress for her, and Guinevere had lent her a winter cloak lined with fur—though the back had Leodegrance's coat of arms embroidered into it.

The cloak was too short given that Britt fairly loomed over Guinevere, but it was warmer than the wool cape she had originally planned to use, so she was grateful for it.

Britt adjusted the hood of her borrowed cloak, her blue eyes fastened on the Forest of Arroy—the large, expansive woods that surrounded Camelot in a horseshoe shape.

She had been waiting for her guards to give the "all-clear" signal for several minutes now. *Perhaps they really did find someone?* Britt brushed off the concern. Kay had the woods searched thoroughly, and he wouldn't have let her wander outside—without an escort, horse, or her armor—if he thought there was even a remote threat.

Britt rubbed her nose and turned slightly when she heard horse hooves clopping through the gatehouse.

An armored knight mounted on his destrier bowed his head to her as he and his animal began to pass her. "My Lady," he murmured.

Britt smiled at him, though her eyes strayed to the lioness embroidered on his horse's barding. Before she could place the symbol, the knight snapped the visor of his helm up and hissed. "*My Lord?*"

"Ah, Ywain!" Britt grinned at the young man. "Aren't you on point today?"

Ywain's eyes bulged in his shock. "Why are you dressed so... so...so!" His deep voice was almost squeaky as he gestured to her dress.

"I'm running an experiment."

"A what?"

"Guinevere said she's seen men spying on her and her friends whenever they leave Camelot for a walk," Britt said. She shivered when a breeze rustled the hem of her gown and pulled her cloak closer. "Kay promises the woods have been cleared, but I want to be able to fully reassure Guinevere, so I thought I should test the area out."

"Dressed as a *woman?*"

"Well, Guinevere and her ladies are the only ones reporting any suspicious activity. An appropriate disguise seemed necessary," Britt said. After enduring her drafty skirts for this short amount of time, she wasn't exactly enthused either, but she wanted to show Guinevere she had taken her comment seriously.

Ywain removed his helm so he could scratch his jaw line. "Couldn't you have gotten one of the other knights to play the role? For you to do it seems like courting unnecessary trouble. What if you are found out?"

"No one will find out as long as I'm careful," Britt said. "Those who know me best and stand the greatest chance of recognizing me already know my, er, secret. As you showed," Britt said.

Ywain smiled broadly. "'Tis true."

"And anyway," she continued. "I didn't much fancy the idea of laying eyes on Kay or Gawain as a female impersonator."

"They would make poor women," Ywain admitted.

"Lancelot would be the most convincing in a big enough cloak, but only if he kept his mouth shut while prancing around Camelot—something I think impossible," Britt said. "But enough about my mission. What brings you outside of Camelot? You're not running home without saying farewell, are you?"

Ywain leaned back, making his saddle creak. "No, I won't return home for a while. I'm just exercising my horse."

Britt squinted up at him. "You're certain you don't have to return home yet? It would pain me to see you leave, but you *are* married."

"Oh, yes. I don't have to return home until early spring," Ywain said brightly. "My plan is to spend my winters with you, and my summers with dear Laudine, guarding the magic fountain!"

"...I don't think that's how marriage is supposed to work."

Ywain tilted his head. "But King Pellinore is rarely home, and his wife is just fine without him."

"Allow me to clarify, I don't think that's how marriage to Laudine works. I'm glad to have you in Camelot as long as you can stay, but I doubt that will make your wife happy," Britt said. Truth be told, Laudine was a bit of a sore spot for Britt. She didn't much care for her as the lady had made it clear she wanted Britt out of Ywain's life to free him from distractions outside their lands. (And she didn't even know Britt was female!)

Ywain swatted his hand through the air. "Laudine understands. I told her when we were first married just how much you mean to me."

"I see." Britt glanced out over the meadow and spotted a

mounted guard exit the surrounding woods. He waved once, signaling the all-clear. "That's my cue, so I had best move on. I'll see you at dinner?"

"I look forward to it, My Lord!" Ywain nudged his horse forward. The animal snorted and charged ahead, moving to loop around the castle and ride through the farmland that splayed out behind Camelot.

Britt watched him go, then began meandering around the meadow, zigzagging across it like a dog following a scent. She succeeded only in getting the hem of her dress soaked—the ground was wet and slick due to the winter precipitation.

After aimlessly wandering for an hour, she stood near the edge of the woods and peered around the meadow, which was a smear of green and brown. "Guinevere must have been mistaken. There's no sign of any sort of creepers or stalkers." She grimaced when her wet skirts sloshed against her ankle—an unpleasant jolt of cold. "Too bad there's no pepper spray in this century. Maybe Kay could lend her an attack dog?"

Britt heard a branch crack in the woods behind her. Thinking it was probably an overly fat squirrel or chipmunk, she lazily turned to peer behind her.

She was shocked to see a bushy bearded man dressed in shades of brown and green lunging for her. "Guards!" she shouted. She snatched up her only weapon—a small dagger fastened to her gold belt—and backed up. "Guards—attack!"

The man leaped for her. Britt dodged, but he managed to grab the edge of her fur-lined cloak. He yanked on it, dragging her towards him by her neck.

Britt fumbled to unclasp the throat latch. *I should have brought Cavall!* Cursing her disbelief in the potential threat, she threw the cloak off when she was finally free of it, throwing it in her attacker's face. "*Guards*!"

She tried to run and tripped on her wet skirts. Hissing in anger, she spun around, barely avoiding the man when he tried to grab her by the braid of her hair. She fixed her grip on her dagger and swallowed uneasily. If she couldn't run, she'd have to hold him off and hope her guards arrived soon. She could hear shouts echo from Camelot, so they were aware of her plight, but some of her guards were still posted in the forest. Why hadn't they come for her yet?

"Guards!" She struck out with her dagger, aiming for the attacker's shoulder. He fended off the blow with a metal arm gauntlet, though Britt had the satisfaction of making him grunt with the force of her strike.

She shifted her weight to one leg, intending to lunge forward and smash the pommel of her dagger into his neck.

Unfortunately, her dainty slippers had no grip to them, and she slipped on the wet grass.

The man grabbed her wrist and plucked the dagger from her grasp, tossing it away. Britt grabbed his shoulder with her free hand and kneed him in the stomach, knocking the breath out of him. He fell forward, into her, knocking them both to the ground.

Britt kicked off her useless slippers and scrambled towards Camelot, hope lighting in her heart when she saw mounted guards thunder from the gates.

The man grabbed her by the ankle and yanked her backwards, pulling her so roughly she smashed her jaw against the ground and bit her tongue.

Britt groaned in pain, and the man dragged her towards the woods.

When she regained her wits, Britt clawed at his eyes and bit an uncovered finger, but he successfully dragged her through the tree line.

"I have her," he said in a rough, gravelly voice.

"Excellent," another man said. "Now I shall finally have my revenge against Arthur."

Britt was unceremoniously spun around, giving her a glimpse

of a knight dressed in black armor and mounted on a red roan horse.

The man who attacked her clubbed her in the head, and Britt's last fleeting thought was that Kay was going to kill her for getting kidnapped on her own lands twice in the span of a year.

~

MERLIN DRUMMED his fingers on his worn workbench. He made certain he appeared calm—though in truth he wanted to start snapping out spells left and right.

"I should have taken more precautions." Kay's voice was dark with despair, and he clenched his hands into fists. "I never should have let her do it!"

Bodwain awkwardly patted the young knight's shoulder. "It is not your fault. We were acting on the word of three young, silly girls. No one else had reported anything foreboding; you had no reason to suspect she would be in danger."

"It does not matter," Kay said fiercely. "She should not have been put in a position where she *could* have gotten kidnapped—or worse."

"You can't keep her in a cage, Kay." Merlin shuffled maps on his workbench to keep his hands busy. "She's a dragon, not a dove."

Kay shook his head. Even his mustache drooped.

Bodwain scratched his graying beard. "The good news is that this kidnapping does bear some resemblance to the last time our king was snatched."

Merlin raised an eyebrow. "What do you mean?"

"Whoever has done this foul deed cannot possibly know who they have," Bodwain said.

Kay tucked his chin, but Bodwain continued. "She's the wrong gender to begin with. Whoever jumped her certainly had no plans to bag King Arthur."

Merlin narrowed his eyes and stared at his bookshelves. "We must assume, then, that the target was a genteel lady—for it was only Guinevere's group who saw anyone." He blinked when he realized someone had placed a scarf on his stuffed owl—Britt, probably. She was likely spoiling for a fight. Since he spent most of his waking hours occupied with Vivien and stayed away from Britt for her own good, they hadn't been able to exchange gibes lately.

"Could the target have been Guinevere herself?" Kay asked.

"Only a blind halfwit would mistake Britt for Guinevere," Merlin said wryly. "Britt fairly looms over her."

"Yes, but Guinevere lent Britt her cloak," Kay said.

"So?" Merlin asked. Kay and Ulfius were the only beings in the castle who kept meticulous record of Britt's clothes. A cloak was a cloak; who cared who owned it?

"No, Sir Kay is right." Bodwain cocked his head. "Lady Guinevere's cloak has King Leodegrance's coat of arms embroidered on the back."

Merlin paused. "Oh."

Bodwain offered him a smile. "You couldn't have known—you didn't see our king in her disguise. Looked like a proper lady, she did. Though a bit tall."

Merlin kept his mouth shut and his expression bland. He *had* seen Britt garbed up in the cloak and dress. Vivien had dragged him through lower Camelot for a brief stroll/shopping trip while Britt sat outside the gatehouse, waiting for the forests to be searched.

He only caught a brief glimpse of her, garbed in a cloak and a blue dress that made her eyes brilliant, as Vivien dragged him across the street.

It was shocking to see Britt dressed so. Even when she first arrived, Britt Arthurs was clothed in pants. He had always known she was female—by the heavens, he had *kissed* her, and that moment was forever branded in his brain. But seeing her, carefree and smiling…he had almost forgotten himself and called out to her.

Vivien thankfully hadn't noticed Britt, or Merlin's inattention, as they sailed past the gatehouse.

Bedivere barged into the room, throwing the door open with so much force its hinges shrieked in protest. "There is hope," he said as Gawain, Mordred, and Lancelot filed in behind him. "Whoever snatched our king left a trail behind. We can track them and recover her."

Bodwain brightened. "Excellent news! That already puts us far ahead of the last time she was taken!"

"Do we know for certain the trail follows the blackguard who has her?" Kay asked.

"Why of course!" Lancelot puffed up with pride. "I followed the tracks for some time myself! I can assure you it is the right one."

Mordred held up a scrap of blue cloth. "The rogue is leaving a deliberate trail. It seems he *wants* us to find him."

"If he does not know who he has," Merlin started, "he probably means to call Arthur and the Knights of the Round Table out."

"Then he has succeeded," Kay growled.

Merlin returned to drumming his fingers on his workbench. "A small party should follow the trail with all haste and be prepared for a fight. The rest of the knights should make ready for battle and assemble the army."

Bodwain squinted at him. "You would rally the army when we don't know who is behind this event? It might be a small issue—just a blackguard knight seeking a fight."

"There is logic to your argument, but it is a risk we cannot take," Merlin said. "Rome is at large, and Scotland and Ireland have no allegiance to Britt. There are too many players in this game who would love to witness her demise."

Bodwain slowly nodded in acceptance, and Merlin mentally

congratulated himself for supplying a decent reason on such short notice.

The truth was Merlin would have rallied the army for Britt no matter how little the threat was. She had pushed and shoved her way past all his defenses into his affection. He would not take any chances in rescuing her.

"The scouting party—which, with God's mercy—will also become the recovery party, will have to be small," Gawain said, getting down to the logistics.

"I'm going," Merlin said.

Gawain and Mordred nodded, but Bodwain murmured in a lowered voice. "Can you leave Vivien that long? Won't she find it surprising?"

"I'm still Britt's chief counselor. I would think she would be more surprised if I did *not* go," Merlin said.

As Bodwain nodded, Percival—King Pellinore's oldest son—knocked on the cracked door and shyly leaned into the room. "If you are taking volunteers, I would like to join," he said.

Ywain, lacking Percival's discreetness, threw the door open. "Naturally, I'm coming as well."

Merlin pointedly stared at the door. "Has your new wife done away with the concept of *private meetings*, Sir Ywain?"

"Nah," Ywain said. "I put my foot in the door when I saw Sir Bedivere, Sir Mordred, and Sir Lancelot enter, so it stayed cracked. So, who else will join us?"

"I will come! Our King needs rescuing, and I shall answer the call," Lancelot declared.

Kay glared at the flashy knight. "Last time you came to her rescue, you stabbed her."

Lancelot made a tisking noise. "You are just as bad as our king herself in endlessly bringing that accident up."

"It was no accident," Kay insisted.

"Yes, but it made her come clean before us knights, and now look how happy we all are," Lancelot breezily said.

Merlin, judging that the conversation would take more time than it was worth, made his exit. "Sir Kay will be in charge of the search party," he said.

"Where are you going?" Bodwain asked.

"To make preparations." Merlin slipped out the door—taking care to close it securely behind him—then set out down the hallway, making a mental checklist of what he would need to bring. (Roen, Britt's charger, and Excalibur, her magic sword, were at the top of the list. She would pitch a fit if they showed up without them.)

He made it all the way down to the main floor of the keep before Vivien found him.

"Merlin," she said in a voice as sticky as honey. She smiled as she clasped his arm and joined him. "The castle is in an uproar. What has happened?"

"Arthur has gone missing," Merlin said, keeping his words deliberately vague. (If they were lucky, whoever kidnapped her would *never* realize who they had.)

Vivien gasped. "How terrible! Whatever shall you do?"

"I'm joining the search for him." He forced himself to smile at her, as if this entire ordeal didn't much bother him.

Vivien jutted her lower lip out in a pout. "You're leaving me?"

Merlin stifled a shiver; he could feel her activating her black magic. It felt clammy and tarry, and slithered through his magical sense like something foul. It was designed to ensnare his mind, but Merlin carefully misdirected it and played the love-addled idiot. "It will be a trial," he said with a sigh. "I shall miss you every moment—for your beauty...*shines* so. But I'm afraid the search party is no place for you."

Vivien peered up at him, judging his expression.

Merlin patted her hand. "It should only be for a short time. I would get out of it if I could, but I *am* Arthur's chief advisor."

"Yes, you are terribly important," Vivien said with great satisfaction. "I suppose I can spare you. But then you must talk with me, and tell me your clever plans for taking Scotland and Ireland."

Merlin resisted the urge to roll his eyes, a gesture he had learned from Britt. *Idiot girl. She could not betray her true goals any more clearly.* Through his network of sneaks and spies, Merlin had confirmed that Vivien was an ally of Rome and had been sent to weaken Arthur. When Britt proved to be utterly unresponsive, she had decided it was Guinevere's fault and had nearly killed the visiting princess.

Merlin thought it was best to step in then. It was not a bad arrangement. Though he was not Vivien's original target, she was satisfied because she thought she had a major member of Arthur's court under her control, and it gave Merlin the chance to feed bad information to Rome.

The only downside was that Vivien constantly inflicted herself upon Merlin—and he still didn't relish the idea of a black magic user wandering about Camelot.

And it affected Britt.

He held in a sigh. "Yes, when I return we can speak of Ireland and Scotland. I will surely tell you everything," he said.

"Indeed." Vivien smiled and shifted her hold on his arm. She chattered on, but Merlin only half listened.

It took every scrap of his self-control to keep from shaking Vivien off and demanding that the search party leave that instant.

Britt.

His heart beat her name. He had fallen for her in a million ways without his knowing—or her knowledge. It was the moments like this—when she was gone and he feared for her safety—that he felt the true depths of it.

"Merlin, are you listening?" Vivien asked.

"Of course," Merlin said. "I was merely awed by your beauty and charm."

Vivien giggled.

A half sigh leaked out of Merlin, as he made himself concentrate. It would do no good to be wistful in a time like this. They needed to move…for who knew what sort of scrape Britt was in.

BRITT FOLDED her arms across her chest and stared at the door of her makeshift prison cell.

Yesterday, after being kidnapped, she'd woken up on the saddle of the knight in the black armor riding his red roan horse. She fought him, kicking and elbowing him—she would've bitten him if he wasn't wearing armor—with such exuberance that the knight gagged her, tied her up, and tossed her in the back of a wooden cart. They arrived at an unknown castle shortly after sunset, and Britt had been unceremoniously dragged up a tower and stuffed into a small bedroom.

She was locked in, and no one had visited her since dumping her on the straw mattress the night before.

Britt's stomach growled, and she rubbed her arms as a light breeze from the small window chilled the air. She scowled at the door, then edged towards the window and peered outside. Her tower bedroom was only on the second floor, but even though Britt suspected she could have safely jumped from the window without breaking anything, it was no use. The window was too small for her to fit her shoulders through—she'd already tried. Outside the courtyard was abuzz with activity, like a child's ant farm. Guards and commoners alike swarmed the area, going about their daily business as she watched longingly.

She leaned against the stone wall, resting her forehead on the cold rock. "It's safe to assume they believe I am a lady, not a king in disguise, or I don't think they would've put me in a bedroom."

The last time Britt had been kidnapped, she'd woken up in a dungeon. The bedroom, though small and unadorned, was a significant upgrade from the dank prison cell. It was a great encouragement, for Britt would much rather they underestimate her and remain ignorant of her role in medieval England than understand exactly who they had in their clutches.

But the whole experience was rather alarming. "I feel like I was targeted, but I don't think it's because I'm Arthur." She turned away from the window and scowled at the door again. "But who would go around kidnapping ladies from Camelot?"

The black armored knight's unconfirmed identity ate away at her. She vaguely recalled seeing similar armor, and a red roan horse, but she couldn't place where...

As if on cue, the black knight flung open the door and strode inside. He closed the door behind him and stood between it and Britt, cutting off her only exit. "Guinevere, I assume?"

Britt blinked, surprised anyone would mistake her for Guinevere. (Not only was Guinevere's hair more of a red gold, and Britt's a true blonde, but Britt had several inches on her, not to mention pounds of muscle the dainty princess lacked.) But, it was likely in her best interest to play along, so she tilted her head and asked, "And whom am I addressing?"

The knight removed his helm, revealing dark, narrow eyes and dirty blonde hair. "It is I, Duke Maleagant." He smiled so sharply, it was more of a leering grimace.

Duke Maleagant. Combining his name with the memory of his armor and unusually colored horse, Britt finally recalled the circumstances of meeting the unpleasant man. Duke Maleagant was the rogue noble who had attacked King Leodegrance and demanded Guinevere's hand in marriage. Britt, acting as Guinevere's champion, had defeated him twice before running him off Leodegrance's lands.

Britt growled. "You."

Maleagant's smile turned into a smirk. "Yes, me." He squinted at her. "But you really are Guinevere?"

The question caught Britt off guard. She would've thought that Maleagant, having demanded Guinevere's hand in marriage, would have known she was not the beautiful princess. It seemed, however, that luck was on her side. Copying a gesture she had seen Guinevere perform multiple times, Britt placed her hand over her heart. "How can you fail to recognize me? Don't you recall? You saw me when you invaded my father's lands."

Maleagant shrugged. "I do not waste my time on silly girls."

"You wanted to marry me!" Britt squawked.

"I wanted your lands that come with you as a dowry," Maleagant corrected. He sneered, an upper lip curling. "You mean nothing to me."

"If that is so, why have you kidnapped me?" Britt moved to put the bed between them as she eyed the unpleasant man.

"Because you are Arthur's love. I have a score to settle with your wretchedly righteous king." Maleagant's smile made its second appearance. "With you in my clutches, he will not fail to come to my lands."

Britt tugged on the end of the braid in which her hair was secured. "You seem to mistakenly think he would come here alone. Don't you know that by kidnapping me, you will have brought the wrath of Camelot down upon you?"

The statement was truer than Maleagant knew. Britt was certain that Kay and Merlin were amassing an army to bring her back home.

Maleagant hooked his thumbs on his sword belt. "It does not matter how many men Arthur brings with him. My fight with him is a matter of honor, a battle between two men."

He's probably still ticked about being beaten at Camelgrance. Sore loser. "What makes you so sure Arthur will agree to fight you again? He's already beaten you twice. There's no need for him to prove his superiority to you a third time."

The verbal blows seem to needle Maleagant, as she had intended. He growled under his breath, then snarled at her. "He is not my superior. And if he loves you as much as it is claimed, he will fight. Or I will marry you."

The threat did more to cow Britt than he could have known.

"You still seek after my lands?" They were Guinevere's lands, really, but she might as well play the part if she was going to let them think she was the princess anyway.

Maleagant meticulously smoothed his hair. "Of course. After my honor, my main concern is expanding my kingdom."

Britt blinked. "But you're a duke, not a king."

Maleagant angrily frowned, his dark eyebrows furrowing into a tight V shape. "Arthur must be a spineless mongrel of a man if he is so deeply in love with you—a shrew with the tongue of a snake."

"He still beat you in combat, twice," Britt reminded him.

She regretted her words when Maleagant drew his sword from its scabbard and chopped down on the wooden bed frame. His shoulders heaved with anger, and he seethed. "You are lucky I need you alive to lure in Arthur. But remember...I will beat him and be the victor in this final battle. Then you will become my bride. You would do well to mind your tongue, if you wish for our marriage to be a pleasant one."

Maleagant swept from the room, slamming the door shut behind him and locking it before Britt could react.

She listened to his footsteps stomp down the hallway and shivered. *Lesson learned. I probably shouldn't push him again until I'm out of his reach or confront him as Arthur.*

Still, his visit had somewhat heartened her. If he didn't plan to do anything until "Arthur" showed up, as long as she didn't run her mouth too much, she'd be safe. All she had to do was wait to be rescued by her knights.

The thought didn't sit too well with Britt—she hated to sit around and wait for help when she was capable of doing something herself—so she was still stewing over her options when a male servant opened the door and put a tray of food on a small end table. He didn't even glance at her or seem concerned that she might bolt from the room while his back was to her.

Britt waited until he left before she snatched a hard roll off the tray and began sampling the dishes. *So, they don't see me as a threat, do they? Then this damsel should be able to cause some serious distress...*

~

MERLIN STROKED THE SLEEK, glossy shell of the strange machine Britt called an iPod. She'd given Merlin the apparatus many seasons ago, and though Merlin had spent hours studying it, he found it as confounding as its previous owner.

Still, he found reassurance in clenching it as he stared at the backs of his horse's ears and followed the knights leading the way.

I wonder if Britt could tell me what strange materials were used to make this contraption.

Merlin's thoughts were interrupted when Ywain turned his horse in a circle and announced, "I'm going to part ways with you all for a bit. We're so close to my lands, I feel I should stop and check in with Laudine."

Merlin adjusted his hold on his reins and eyed the young knight. "Do you care to share why you fought, fussed, and kicked up a mess to make sure you were included in this group, only to abandon us before we reach our goal?"

"I would never abandon My Lord!" Ywain said indignantly. "Actually, I'm stopping only because Britt instructed me to. It's been some weeks since I've seen my wife, and My Lord suggested I return home to make sure all is well. Laudine is quite skilled at running the lands, so I am certain it will be a short stop."

"Of course it will," Merlin griped.

Ywain didn't seem to hear him as he turned his charger in another circle.

"Safe travels," Percival said. "May all be right with your home."

"I'm certain it is. I will catch up with you all before you reach the blackguard who has kidnapped our king!" Ywain departed, nudging his horse off the path and charging into the woods. He raised his hand in farewell and swiftly disappeared into the trees.

Gawain watched his cousin go before returning his attention to his conversation with Kay. "You believe we will find her soon?"

"We are close to their camp, if not the place in which they are holding her." Kay smoothed his mustache as he considered the dirt road on which they traveled. "Based upon the time at which they left yesterday, I believe they would've run out of sunlight at this point in their travels."

"Can you be certain?" Percival directed his horse so it walked shoulder-to-shoulder with Gawain's. "We don't know how fast they were traveling."

"Ahhh, but we do." Merlin smiled wryly. "If you recall, Lancelot found tracks that indicated whoever kidnapped Britt eventually joined this road with a cart. As carts are not made for speed, it is safe to assume they were not able to move much faster than a quick walk or trot."

Gawain stroked his horse's glossy neck. "Using that logic, wouldn't the cart indicate they were bound for a destination, not a camp?"

"That is certainly my hope," Merlin said, "for it would mean she cannot be too far."

The conversation reached its natural conclusion when the sound of pounding horse hooves drew the party's attention. Up ahead, Lancelot and Mordred thundered down the road on the backs of their warhorses.

"Trouble!" Lancelot shouted. "Trouble, ahead."

Kay's hand strayed to his sword. "What sort of trouble?"

Mordred halted his horse, which pawed at the ground. "The sort that wears uniforms and carries weapons," he said grimly.

"Soldiers?" Gawain asked.

Lancelot and Mordred nodded.

Merlin tucked Britt's iPod into a pocket of his tunic. "Show us."

IT WAS JUST as they promised. Not a mile up the road—and a short ride off the trail—soldiers swarmed a meadow. The orange and green banding of their uniforms made them look like pox marks dotting the area. Several flags fluttered in the wind, declaring their allegiance.

Gawain peered around a tree trunk. "Those are King Ryence's colors and coat of arms."

"Perhaps," Merlin said, "but those are not British soldiers." He squinted, making out the short, squarish shapes of the swords the soldiers carried. The breeze carried some of the guards' shouts to his ears. Recognizing the foreign tongue in which they spoke, dread hit Merlin like a hammer. "Those are Roman centurions."

Kay sucked air in between clenched teeth. "You are certain?"

Merlin shifted from a crouch to a kneeling position. "I'd stake my life on it."

"Perhaps our little king is in more trouble than we initially estimated," Lancelot said.

"Or perhaps the soldiers are unrelated to Britt's kidnapping," Mordred said.

Merlin tore his gaze from the blot the soldiers made on the landscape and raised an eyebrow at the young knight. "What makes you say that?"

"Because we are about to enter King Bagdemagus's lands, and though he is not allied to Camelot, he is famous for his hatred of foreigner legions."

Gawain straightened, alarmed by the realization. "King Bagdemagus? Is he not the father of Duke Maleagant, the, the..."

Merlin rubbed his chin. "The rogue Britt beat to save King Leodegrance, Guinevere, and Camelgrance? Yes, that would be him. Come, it would be wisest if we didn't pause to discuss the dangers of this new revelation this close to the enemy."

Merlin and the knights, hidden by the underbrush of the

forest, stole their way back near the road, where Percival waited with their mounts.

"Was it an army?" Percival asked.

"Yes." Merlin took the reins to his long-legged gelding. "A Roman one."

Percival swore under his breath and shook his head. "This is an awful time for our king to be missing."

"Awful and dangerous," Kay said as he swung up into the saddle.

Gawain offered Percival a wan smile. "I hope your watch was an uneventful one?"

Percival handed off the last horse, a flighty dapple gray, to Lancelot. "Yes, though I believe I heard something that might encourage us all."

"And what might that be?" Mordred asked.

Percival brandished a finger in the air. "A cart."

"What are we waiting for?" Lancelot demanded. "That may be the very same cart that transported our dear king. After it!" He nudged his horse, who took off down the road in a great blur.

The other knights hurried after him, but Merlin took a moment to gather his reins before following. "I'm beginning to see why Britt is always so eager to kick him out of Camelot."

It took only a few minutes to catch up with the cart, which was a large vehicle of conveyance made with rough, rickety boards that were dubiously nailed together. When Kay confirmed that it was the approximate size of the cart that may have carried Britt to her destination, Lancelot lost no time in prancing up to the farmer driving it and smiling.

"Greetings to you, good man. On the day of yesterday, did you happen to take on a passenger? A beautiful young lady, by perchance?"

The farmer, a swarthy fellow who looked old enough to be Lancelot's grandfather, frowned. "What?" He shouted above the rumblings of the cart.

Lancelot, his smile still in place, spoke louder. "Last night did you transport a young lady?"

"What?" the farmer shouted again.

Lancelot yelled in return. "Last night! Young lady! Did she ride in your cart?"

The farmer shook his head. "I can't hear a thing over this cart. If you want to gab, you'll need to hop on."

The fashionable knight gaped at the farmer in horror, but rallied enough air to his lungs to shout, "Can you not pull over?"

The farmer shook his head. "Fraid not. I've got to get this hay to Gorre, and I won't make it tonight if I stop."

Lancelot almost recoiled in horror and balked at the farmer's refusal. "I-I…" he stammered.

Merlin rolled his eyes. *The Romans can invade, and King Arthur herself can go missing, but God forbid Lancelot lower himself to the dishonor of riding in a cart.*

All the other knights were already moving to dismount their horses, but Merlin was the fastest. He popped off his slender gelding, tossed the reins to Kay, and hopped up in the cart before Lancelot had the chance to look ashamed.

"Good day to you, master farmer," Merlin began. "Can you tell me, were you in these parts yesterday?"

The farmer nodded and adjusted his scarf and cloak. "Sure was. This area is short on hay. I've been driving it in every day from other lands."

"Did you happen to see a young lady clothed in a blue dress? She was likely in the company of a knight," Merlin said.

The farmer draped his reins so they brushed the rumps of the furry mules that pulled the cart. "Indeed, I have. I saw such a lady traveling with Duke Maleagant. He had me cart her back to his father's castle."

Merlin almost stooped with relief. "Did she look well?"

The farmer considered the sky. "Well enough, though she

must've fought like a bear. He had her trussed up, and he warned me she scratched. And kicked."

His relief swiftly turning into glee, Merlin smiled broadly. If Britt felt well enough to put up a fight, she was likely doing just fine. "Are you certain she remained at Duke Maleagant's castle?"

The farmer leaned close so he didn't have to shout over the rumblings of the cart. "Can just about guarantee it!"

"Excellent!" Merlin clasped the farmer on the shoulder. "Thank you for your assistance. I wish you well on your excursion."

The farmer shrugged as Merlin hopped out of the cart and swiftly mounted his horse again.

"Well?" Percival asked.

"It seems this is all Duke Maleagant's work," Merlin said.

"Then we must be nearly at the end of our journey," Gawain said. "For his lands aren't far from here."

Kay nodded in agreement.

"What are we waiting for? "Lancelot asked. "We must charge forward, for our king!" Once again, he heeled his horse into a canter, quickly overtaking the farmer and his cart, and galloping down the road.

"He can certainly move fast when it suits him," Kay grunted. He shook his head, then chased after the knight, Mordred and Percival on his heels.

Gawain lingered with Merlin. "Are you…all right, Merlin?"

Merlin, who'd been pondering what sort of punishment he should allot Duke Maleagant, shook himself from his pleasurable musings. "I am quite fine, thank you. Come, we wouldn't want to let Lancelot get too far ahead of us."

Gawain nodded and nudged his horse after the other knights. Merlin was only a step behind him, though his thoughts were still dark.

If Maleagant harms her at all, I will burn this land to the ground.

3
MOVED BY ROME

Dusk settled on the horizon, and Britt pressed herself against the wall, crouching so she would be hidden behind the door when it swung open.

She was waiting for the servant to deliver her dinner.

Given her current situation—and her history as a captive—Britt discovered that she was surprisingly well cared for as Duke Maleagant's hostage. Servants delivered food at regular intervals and frequently asked if she needed anything. (Already they had delivered two additional blankets and a drapery to hang over the drafty window.)

Given that they had been so kind, Britt was feeling a little guilty as she squatted, waiting to ambush whatever poor soul came to feed her.

Her guilt left her when the door clanked, then creaked as it was pushed open. A male servant shuffled into the room, carrying a tray of food. As soon as he cleared the doorframe, Britt slammed the door shut behind him. He set the food down and twisted to face her, but Britt caught him off guard and grabbed his shoulder, tossing him over her knee.

He made a wheezing noise when he hit the ground and the air

was slammed out of his chest. His fingers twitched, and he coughed.

"Sorry about this." Britt approached him, the shredded drapery in her hands. "But your master is a sexist pig." She wasted no time in stuffing a wad of the ripped-up drapery in the servant's mouth, gagging him.

She stripped the servant of his tunic, though she left his underclothes and cloak for him, then secured his hands and feet with the drapery. Biting her lip, she surveyed him, then wrapped a strip of cloth over his eyes.

Merlin would have massive heart failure if I didn't make some attempt towards modesty.

Her adrenaline pumping, Britt quickly changed out of her dress and slipped into the servant's scratchy tunic. "Just beautiful." She peered down at her legs. "This might work. I'm hairy enough to pass off as a dude. Still, this is pretty drafty."

Britt eyed the servant's stockings—chauses, Merlin insisted on calling them—but settled for grabbing his cloak. (Not wanting to be totally heartless, she wrapped one of the extra blankets from her bed around the poor man.)

Nodding in satisfaction, Britt dusted off her hands then slowly approached the door. She carefully opened it, warily poking her head out into the hallway. Not a soul was outside, not even a guard.

Britt slipped into the hallway and closed the door behind her. *Maleagant might be a sexist pig, but at least it's making this misadventure easier!* She twitched her shoulders back and sailed up the hallway, doing her best to appear confident. Her first goal in her plan to escape was to find a helm to hide her face.

The armory of Camelot was on the bottom floor of the keep. For technical reasons, Britt was betting it was the same in Duke Maleagant's castle. So she scuttled down the first staircase she found.

As she wandered the back halls of the main floor, she could

hear faint chirps of music and boisterous shouts muffled by the stone walls. *Maleagant must be holding a feast.* Wary of this fact, she did her best to stay far away from the sound. She did not want to chance Maleagant finding her. She also wanted to avoid other servants as much as possible, for they would surely recognize she was not one of them.

She began conducting a random search of a back hallway—opening the doors and peering inside. In her examination, she found a surprisingly well-stocked library, a study, two storage rooms, and what passed for a medieval bathroom. Her curious nature fled, however, when she heard voices moving down a hallway that intersected with the one in which she was standing.

Britt made an abrupt U-turn and darted back down the hallway she'd been working her way up. She slipped around the corner and leaned against the wall, waiting for the talkers to move on. Unfortunately, the voices turned down her hallway and continued to draw closer.

Biting her tongue to keep from making muffled oaths, Britt fled, hustling down the new passageway. She glanced at the doors as she ran, looking for a place to hide. She skidded to a stop and backed up when she saw a large, promising door that had Duke Maleagant's coat of arms burned into it.

She nudged it, grinning when it slowly swung open and revealed a darkened interior. She hesitated, wondering how smart it would be to plunge into a dark room, but the voices hadn't stopped or grown faint, so she slipped into the room, taking care to close the door softly behind her.

She took a few shuffling steps inside, almost cursing when she walked into some sort of crate and bashed her shins. The crate rattled, making a metallic clang. Britt held her breath, but the passersby didn't seem to notice and kept walking. She exhaled only when their voices faded from hearing, then cracked the door open and heard only silence.

"Apparently, though I make a decent knight, I would be a

terrible ninja." She rubbed her smarting shins as she threw the door open wide, letting the hallway torchlight brighten the room. Sharpened edges of polished swords glittered, and pieces of suits of armor gleamed in the dimly lit room.

Britt smugly smiled, pried one of the hallway torches from its post, closed the door, and set up shop in the armory.

Finding enough pieces of armor that fit her reasonably well proved to be more of a challenge than she expected. When most of the male chestpieces proved to be too large through the shoulders and torso, she tried switching to what was clearly armor meant for squires learning knightly arts. Those, unfortunately, were too short through the torso and chest.

In the end, she was forced to take a cuirass that was too big for her; she stuffed it with rags and padding to make it more comfortable. Finding a throat guard was far easier, as was securing a helm. Unfortunately, most of the helms smelled like something died in them, and the only helm that fit Britt's head and had a visor to cover her face smelled terribly of sweat.

Britt grimaced as she unbraided her hair—it was making the helm sit oddly—and pulled her blonde locks back in a low ponytail. "Maybe having Lancelot in Camelot is worth the trouble and irritation. His fastidious hygiene habits have worn off on all the Knights of the Round Table."

Cringing, she slipped the helm over her head. The helm's sour stench assailed her, but she shut the visor, feeling far more secure dressed in armor and with her face hidden.

"I better grab a weapon." She turned to the rows and racks of swords, axes, shields, and maces neatly arrayed along the walls.

The swords were well-balanced and well made, though none of them fit her hand half as well as Excalibur. It took her a few minutes to find a sword length and weight that suited her, but by the time she was properly geared, she felt quite giddy.

"All I have to do is snag a horse, then I'm home free! Not bad for rescuing myself." Britt slipped out of the armory and once again wandered the confusing maze of hallways. She eyed the barren, unadorned walls, and wished that Duke Maleagant had shown a little more predisposition towards decorating. *It would make navigating this place so much easier*!

She crossed paths with two female servants, who scurried past and did not question her presence in the back hallway. Her glee grew as she heard the faint whinny of horses. She followed her ears and found an open air corridor that popped out into the castle courtyard.

She almost skipped down it when a man called out after her, "You there! Halt!"

Britt's stomach dropped to her toes, and she slowly turned around.

Duke Maleagant, flanked by five soldiers, strode in her direction. Maleagant rested a hand on the hilt of his sword and narrowed his eyes. "Declare your name, knight," he ordered.

"Um..." Britt floundered, her mind racing as she tried to come up with a reasonable name. She couldn't use her usual alias, Sir Galahad, for his name was too easily associated with the Round Table. "No."

Maleagant smirked. "Remove your helm."

Britt shifted her gaze from Maleagant to the soldiers behind him. *Unless he's practiced like crazy, I can handle Maleagant... But fighting five soldiers on top of that? And even if I did, by some miracle, beat them all, they would still raise the alarm.* She sighed, her shoulders caving with disappointment. She was caught. Even worse, it was very likely Maleagant wouldn't make the same mistake twice and would now have her better guarded. "Hopefully he won't throw me in a dungeon. If the helms smell this bad, I don't want to imagine what that place reeks like," she grumbled as she began to remove her helm.

Her low ponytail spilled over her shoulder as she rested the helm against her hip and raised an eyebrow at Maleagant.

Maleagant's smirk grew, and he flashed his teeth in an almost canine manner. "I knew you would come, Arthur."

Britt froze, awestruck by Maleagant's stupidity. *Is he really so unobservant that he wouldn't realize I'm the girl he thought was Guinevere?* It didn't matter much if he knew she was Arthur; Merlin was most likely bringing a company of knights and an army to take her back anyway. The bigger problem was that Maleagant's servants were probably not as thick-headed as he was. There was a fairly certain chance they would notice that "Guinevere" and "Arthur" looked suspiciously like twins. There were several possible outcomes if they reported this fact to Maleagant. None of them were situations Britt particularly wanted to experience, and the majority of them would very likely cause everyone in Camelot to foam at the mouth.

Unaware of her inner musings, Maleagant continued, "You may have successfully freed your dear Guinevere, but it matters not. *You* are now my captive."

Ahh, they must've found the servant in my room. Warring between pity for his low IQ and worry for her dim future, Britt pitched her voice a little lower than usual and glared at Maleagant. "What is it you want?" She already knew he wanted to fight her, but at the moment it was in her best interests to attempt to placate him.

"I wish for a rematch, to cross swords with you again." Maleagant drew his sword from its scabbard. The blade glowed golden in the setting sunlight that streamed in from the entryway.

Britt flicked her ponytail over her shoulder. "Why? Do you really think you can beat me this time?" She tilted her head and studied him. "You said so yourself, I have successfully smuggled Guinevere out of your own castle without raising your notice."

"I care not what has happened to Guinevere," Maleagant snorted. "She was a lure to draw you here. My intent all along has been to fight you and restore honor to my name. Besides, I can easily track her down again."

Britt scratched her chin and considered him. Perhaps he was not as dumb as she thought and was only incredibly focused… much like a certain wizard she knew. Or maybe he was super near-sighted. Aloud, she said, "Honor? You never had much of that to begin with. Your actions at Camelgrance were deplorable, and I had to defeat you not once, but twice *and* bring in my knights to make you live up to your word."

Snarling, Maleagant raised his sword. "You insult me?"

"No. That was more of a reminder."

Maleagant roared. "Draw your sword!"

Britt cast a wary eye at the soldiers guarding Maleagant's back as she reluctantly slid her stolen/borrowed sword from its scabbard. She missed Excalibur, but she was mostly regretting not having its scabbard with her as well. Excalibur's scabbard was infused with magic and could keep a person from bleeding. *Which would be extremely useful if his soldiers intend to riddle me with holes after I beat their master.*

She tossed her helm aside, since Maleagant did not wear one either, and adjusted her stance, preparing to swipe at him. But the duke surprised her by darting into a lunge immediately. He struck her straight on and with such force she had to move backwards to stay on her feet.

He tried to slam his head into hers, a move that would've sent her to her knees, but Britt managed to disengage their blades and sidestep him.

Before she could press her advantage, Maleagant took a backhanded swing at her. It was clumsy and didn't have much force as he was swinging up behind himself, but it kept Britt from striking his open side.

Adjusting, she held her sword so he chopped down on her blade. She pushed up, forcing Maleagant to either move away from her or to bend his arm at an unnatural angle.

He chose the former, and took three long strides away before spinning around. He pivoted on one leg and whirled his blade in a circle to gain momentum.

Someone's been practicing. Britt dodged the strike and stabbed at his open side. Her blow landed, but Maleagant's armor stopped it from doing any major damage. What was more unsettling was that Maleagant did not budge with the blow.

Realizing she'd adopted a rather cocky attitude towards the furious duke, Britt carefully modified her stance. He had vastly improved since the last time she fought him, and while from a technical point she could still beat him, she was positive his stamina would outlast hers. She had to be cautious, or his forceful blows would sap her strength before she had the chance to knock him down.

As if he read her mind, Maleagant chopped his sword straight down at hers, making her arm vibrate with the force of the blow.

Britt glanced behind her, then began retreating down the open-air corridor that led into the courtyard.

Maleagant stalked after her, lunging forward with a stab aimed at her heart.

Britt danced backwards, avoiding the blow and watching how he moved and distributed his weight.

He turned his stab into a swipe that would've run diagonally across her chest. Britt parried it, though she gritted her teeth and had to plant her legs at the strength behind his attack. He took a tiny step backwards to give himself enough room to maneuver another wide blow at her.

He's mostly been using sweeping blows and large distances to complement his strength. If I move the fight close, I should be able to get past his defenses. She inhaled deeply, adjusting her weight from her heels to the front of her feet. She blocked his lunge to her left side. Her arm muscles burned, but she stiffened her shoulders and feinted a tackle at his waist.

True to his style, he took a step back to make room for another wide, glancing blow. Britt moved just enough to dodge the worst of it. His carry-through strike was so close, it actually made a shallow slice on her cheek. Britt didn't even notice the pain as she lunged upwards, popping her sword, hilt first, above her.

She slammed the hilt into Maleagant's face. She heard bone crunch, and Maleagant shouted and sank to his knees as blood dribbled from his nose.

Maleagant struggled to hold his sword with one hand and his bleeding nose with the other. He removed his hand from his nose long enough to cast off his gauntlet, and Britt could see she had nailed him a good one. His nose was crooked where before it had been straight.

The sound of swords sliding free from scabbards made Britt whip around and face Maleagant's previously forgotten soldiers. All five of them slowly descended upon her, moving like sheep-dogs as they tried to back her away from Maleagant.

"My Lord, are you all right?" one of the soldiers asked.

Maleagant groaned and still clutched his nose.

Britt moved to put Maleagant between her and the soldiers. "I won't hurt him. Well, I won't hurt him *more*."

The soldiers did not answer her and continued to slink closer.

Though the chilly winter air gusted down the corridor, sweat beaded on Britt's brow. She could try running, but the soldiers would be on her tail, and she wasn't likely to get very far. Her arm muscles ached, protesting the vigorous workout she had just put them through. However, after breaking Maleagant's nose, Britt doubted she was going to get the same treatment she received as Guinevere.

Two of the soldiers knelt at Maleagant's side, the other three moved around him, stalking towards Britt with their swords extended.

Britt set her jaw and slowly raised her sword.

"That is enough!" A man shouted behind her.

Britt swiveled, putting her back to the wall, and watched the newest member of the drama storm down the corridor towards them.

He wore a suit of armor, which was well made, though it did accentuate the slight puff of his belly. His hair and beard were graying, but Britt could see the smile lines worn deep into his face.

He narrowed his eyes, which were as dark as Maleagant's. "Gold hair, a tall bearing, and a face too comely to be mortal." He shifted his gaze to Maleagant. "My son, thoroughly thrashed."

Britt's heart sank as the man, assumedly Duke Maleagant's father—whom Merlin had surprisingly never thought to mention—frowned at her.

"You," he said, "must be King Arthur."

Though she was surprised by the revelation, Britt pushed her shoulders back and raised her chin. "I am." She glanced uneasily at Maleagant, wondering how badly his father would hold his injury against her. "I came here to save a girl who was under my care, the Lady Guinevere, daughter of King Leodegrance of Camelgrance. She was taken—against her will—from Camelot by your son."

Maleagant's father raised his bushy eyebrows. "Based on the state Maleagant is in, I assume you succeeded in freeing her." He walked past her and joined the soldiers kneeling at Maleagant's side. "Is it just your face?" He asked his son.

Maleagant nodded, though he glared at Britt over his father's shoulder.

"Let me see." The older man took Maleagant's hand and peeled it away. He inspected the broken the nose with a surprising amount of tranquility. "It seems it is broken. I believe it would be wisest to have someone look at it." He slapped his son on the shoulder, then returned his attention to Britt. "It is fortuitous you are here, King Arthur. For I have just returned from inspecting my lands, and I have witnessed a rather disturbing sight."

Britt suspected the disturbing sight was most likely a company of knights from Camelot, but she refrained from making any sarcastic observations. "Oh?"

"Indeed. Romans."

Britt dropped her defensive stance for the moment, surprised by the news.

Merlin had always rambled on about Rome being a serious threat. She had never really believed him. She thought he was using it as an excuse to pick fights with other kings.

"Romans? Here in Britain?" She asked.

Maleagant's father stood. "I'm afraid so. Ghastly rogues, trampling all over our lands and attempting to take what isn't theirs." He grimly shook his head. "In light of this revelation, I would like to conduct a meeting with you to discuss the defense of Britain."

His announcement of Romans in Britain surprised her less than this second offer.

She narrowed her eyes. "You wish to discuss fighting Romans with *me*?"

Maleagant wiped a bit of blood off his nose, groaning loudly when he prodded it.

"I do. Though I would like a change in locations first. We may as well be reasonably comfortable while discussing such a grim topic, and someone really should see to Maleagant's nose." Maleagant's father swiveled so he faced the soldiers. "You three, see King Arthur to my personal study. We will join you shortly, Arthur."

Britt watched the father and son troop down the hallway. Before they were out of hearing distance, Maleagant's father flicked his son in the head. "If you continue to get into scrapes whenever I leave, I will put a collar on you and drag you with me like a pet dog."

Maleagant muttered something that sounded like a muffled variation of, "Yes, Father."

Unbalanced by the surprising news, and still a little distrustful, Britt turned to the guards and raised an eyebrow. "Tell me, is his personal study code for the dungeon?"

The guards, seeming to lack the good humor of the soldiers who frequently guarded Britt in Camelot, stared at her. "This way, Your Highness," one of them said, indicating the path that led deeper into the keep.

Britt sighed. "Into the rabbit hole then."

~

BRITT FURROWED her eyebrows as she took careful inventory of the study where the soldiers had dumped her. (It was one she had viewed previously while looking for the armory.)

It was different from Merlin's. It had far fewer scrolls and books, but more castle models and tapestries of battles. It smelled of smoke and leather, whereas Merlin's always held a faint whiff of exotic spices.

She placed her back to a wall and glanced nonchalantly at the three guards, who were lined up by the door and staring at her. She tapped her fingers on the hilt of her sword—which, surprisingly, the soldiers had not taken—and straightened her stance when the door swung.

Maleagant stomped into the study, a green paste smeared on his swelled nose. Already he was showing signs of two glorious black eyes—complete with dark circles and swelling.

A bark of laughter almost exploded from Britt's mouth, but she turned it into a croaking cough at the last moment. Based on Maleagant's glowering expression, he knew she was chortling anyway.

Maleagant's father was two steps behind him. He raised his eyebrows when Maleagant planted himself against the wall—his hand on his sword—then hefted his eyes to the heavens and slightly shook his head. "Come, sit, Arthur." He seated himself on a wooden chair positioned in front of the cheerfully flickering fire.

Britt approached him, but after glancing at Maleagant—who tightened his grasp on his sword—she stood behind her chair, resting a hand on the back of it. "What is this about, sir…" she trailed off.

"Ahh, yes. While you are acquainted with my son, I don't believe we have ever met. I am King Bagdemagus. I rule these parts." King Bagdemagus nodded to her. "To be frank, Arthur, I would like us to join forces."

Though she was shocked by the offer, Britt kept her reaction minimal. "Why?"

"When the Romans move, any land standing alone will not survive." Bagdemagus folded his hands on his lap. "I have a few allies, but even if we band together, I don't think it's likely we will last long." He tilted his head slightly and studied Britt. "You, however, have the most alliances, the best organization, and the highest position in Britain. If you call, your allies will answer. With all those resources at your disposal, I believe you and your alliances will survive."

"*Father!*" Maleagant growled.

*I wish Merlin were here…*He always handled the political maneuverings. It made her nervous to be doing it solo. "We have been preparing for the threat of Rome for some time," Britt said carefully. "But I admit I find your sudden offer…surprising."

"You mean because I haven't been your supporter?" King Bagdemagus grunted. "I never saw much use for your wizard's decree of a High King who ruled over all of Britain, but the current situation has changed my mind. Divided, we won't last. I will take an oath to you if it means saving my lands."

"You cannot mean it, Father!" Maleagant protested. "He has insulted my honor."

Bagdemagus scratched his graying beard. "I'm afraid you did that yourself when you kidnapped a lady of noble birth."

Maleagant tucked his head and glared at Britt.

Bagdemagus continued, "You must understand, son, that being a leader means doing what is best for your people. Personal honor is important, but it doesn't feed your army or protect your land. It is our duty to care for those in our charge, and that is far more important than any petty personal squabble."

Silence ruled the study for several moments, and Britt awkwardly scratched the back of her neck. "I appreciate your frankness…"

"But you are hesitant," Bagdemagus said when Britt spoke no further.

"It's only," she faltered, failing to think of a flowery way to speak her mind. Finally, she blurted out, "look, I know you're friendly with King Ryence. He's my sworn enemy, and I don't see that changing anytime soon."

Bagdemagus leaned back in his chair, making it creak. "That was the most disturbing part I failed to mention. The Roman soldiers in the area? They are all dressed in the colors of—and uniforms belonging to—King Ryence. I'm sure they mean for it to be a disguise, but only a buffoon would actually fall for it."

"Is it possible they stole the uniforms as a ploy?" She asked.

"No," Bagdemagus said with the bark of laughter. "There are far too many of them for that to be a plausible excuse. No, I'm afraid King Ryence has betrayed his own country and is helping the Romans of his own free will."

"I see," Britt said. When she was first crowned king, King Ryence had been the smallest threat to her throne. Ironically, he'd become the biggest pain of the century.

"Moreover, King Ryence and I have recently had a…parting of sorts." King Bagdemagus glanced at Maleagant. "I was not thrilled when Ryence, some seasons ago, convinced Maleagant to attack Leodegrance while I was in Ireland visiting my wife's relatives for the summer."

"I told you, Father, it was to expand our kingdom," Maleagant argued.

"Yes, I'm sure that's what he told you and what you focused on," Bagdemagus said wryly. "The truth is, Ryence has had an ax to grind with you, Arthur, and your allies since you were crowned. I think he became especially bitter when you rallied King Lot and King Urien to your side."

Britt snorted. "Rallied might be a strong word."

"Either way, Ryence's abuse of both my absence and of Maleagant's hard-headedness put a strain on our nonaggression pact. But inviting Romans into our country, hiding them so they may, assumedly, take over?" Bagdemagus shook his head. "I'll not align myself with traitors and backstabbers."

"Yes, that certainly does change things." Britt smiled. "I am extremely interested in welcoming you as my ally; however, I'm afraid I must return to Camelot and share this news with my men. We'll move against the Romans, but I cannot commit to any sort of action without knowing more."

Bagdemagus nodded. "I imagine you would like to talk to your allies and gather more information. If I might be so bold, may Maleagant and I call upon you in Camelot? I'll send out my men to flush out more Romans and gather as much intelligence as possible before we join you, of course."

Britt pondered the offer, trying to decide if there were any hidden threats to it. She was about to agree to it, then Bagdemagus added, "When we arrive, I will make certain that Maleagant apologizes to the Lady Guinevere. His conduct has been most dishonorable."

"But Father," Maleagant interjected. "He acted in dishonor towards me first!"

"Defeating you at swordplay and jousting has nothing to do with honor, and everything to do with being the better knight. It is high time you learn this." Bagdemagus scowled at his offspring.

"A personal apology is absolutely unnecessary," Britt said,

anxious to kill the idea before it settled. (Even if Maleagant was as observant as a blind mouse, it was doubtful he would fail to notice Guinevere was not the girl he had kidnapped.) "I will pass along your apology to Guinevere myself. I'm sure she will be very happy to receive it. There is no need to call upon her when you visit Camelot."

"As long as all is well between us," King Bagdemagus said. He stood, groaning slightly as he rolled his shoulders back. "God surely brought you here today, Arthur. Thank you for hearing me out, and I look forward to a long-lasting friendship between our lands."

"I as well," Britt said.

"I imagine you wish to set out for Camelot as swiftly as possible, but I must encourage you to spend the night with us. The sun has already set. A night here should not delay you much. In the morning, we can see you off with a horse and proper provisions." Bagdemagus looked pointedly to his son. His eyebrows furrowed when Maleagant stared at his feet and said nothing.

Catching on to his father's ire, Maleagant said utterly unconvincingly, "Yes, please spend the night. It would bring us such joy."

Britt rubbed her nose to hide her grin. "I thank you for your offer, and I believe I will take you up on it."

"Excellent!" Bagdemagus smacked Maleagant on the shoulder. "Then tonight, to celebrate our new friendship, we will feast! Come, I'm starved enough to eat a bear."

Britt followed her hosts from the study. Feeling smug, she almost leaped with glee. *Not only did I manage to free myself from capture, but I snagged a new ally to boot!* The reminder of the Romans dimmed her joy, but Bagdemagus's change of heart gave her hope.

If he was willing to stand with her to stop the Romans, perhaps Merlin's vision of a unified Britain was not too far off.

4
REUNITED

The following morning, Britt set out on her trip home feeling excessively smug. She smiled as she leaned forward and patted the neck of her borrowed gelding. The sun shone brightly overhead, and the air, though still chilly, held the promise of spring. She was so happy, she was almost tempted to start whistling.

Instead, she chortled to herself and glanced over her shoulder. "Come, Maleagant. You can't be a good guide if you ride *behind* me."

Maleagant glared at her from the back of his red roan horse. "I don't care what Father says, you must know how to get home. How else did you find your way here?"

"It doesn't really matter, does it? Your father said you had to come with me to the borders of my lands. Just think, this will be such a good bonding experience!" She chirped.

Maleagant nudged his horse into a trot and passed her. He scowled unhappily, amplifying Britt's pleasure in their ride.

"Perhaps I should thank you for kidnapping Guinevere—though should you attempt to repeat that exercise, you will find the outcome far less pleasant." Britt peered at the sky.

Maleagant, forgetting his injury, snorted through his nose. Immediately, his face stiffened with pain, and he gritted his teeth.

Britt didn't bother to hide her smile. "In any case, if you hadn't kidnapped Guinevere, I would not have so swiftly met your father and forged this new alliance."

Maleagant's eyes narrowed into slits.

"Really, you are responsible for this budding relationship between our lands." Britt would've continued; she was mildly curious to see how far she could push him, and she was still irritated enough with him for the kidnapping escapade it seemed only right. But her fun was interrupted when the pounding of hooves reached her ears.

"Arthur! I say, Arthur!"

Though her soon-to-be rescuers were still out of sight, Britt felt confident enough they were her knights. She turned to Maleagant and gave him one last smile that was as innocent as a summer sky. "It seems my men have followed me here. If that is so, I regret to say your guidance back home will be unnecessary."

Before Maleagant could respond, a man on horseback broke through the edge of the trees.

Taking in the blue and white barding on the dapple-gray horse, Britt scowled. "I've changed my mind. Take me back to your father. I'd rather be a captive than go home with *him*."

"Arthur!" Lancelot shouted. "I have found you!" He pulled his horse back into a walk as Mordred, his gelding moving at a much more controlled pace, exited the forest at the same spot Lancelot had.

"Yes," Britt said with zero enthusiasm. "I have already freed Guinevere. I'm certain she's back in Camelot by now."

"Guinevere?" Mordred asked as he joined their little clutch.

Lancelot shifted his gaze from Britt to her traveling companion and wrenched his sword from its scabbard. "You are Duke Maleagant! You dared to lay a hand on—"

"Guinevere!" Britt forcibly inserted. "And he did, but his

father regrets Maleagant's actions very much, and we are now allies."

Lancelot's brows shifted from being pinched with anger to furrowed with puzzlement. "Allies?"

"Br—Arthur!"

Britt's smile returned as she saw Merlin—followed by Percival, Gawain, and Kay—gallop out of the trees on horseback. (Roen, Britt was thrilled to see, was tied to Percival's saddle.) "Greetings, my closest companions!"

Merlin trotted his horse in a circle around Britt and inspected her from head to foot. "You're uninjured?" He glanced at Maleagant's magnificently bruised face.

"I'm fine. Maleagant found me after I freed Guinevere, but it was just as well," Britt said.

All the knights in Britt's rescue party blinked confusedly at her.

"I am glad to hear Guinevere is safe. I assume she is already on her way home to Camelot?" Merlin asked.

"Indeed," Britt said.

Kay halted his horse so close to Britt they almost collided. He gazed suspiciously from her to Maleagant. "What is this all about, Arthur? Why do you ride with *him*?"

Britt sighed. "I'm afraid it's a long story. But let me preface it with some bad news: there are Romans in Britain."

"We know," Gawain said.

"We stumbled upon a squadron of them as we made our way here," Percival added.

"Were the soldiers dressed in King Ryence's colors?" Britt asked.

The knights nodded.

"Then you will understand why I made a pact with King Bagdemagus, making him our newest ally," she said.

"You what?" Merlin said.

"You made a pact with the father of the man who kidnapped…Guinevere?" Kay asked.

Maleagant kept his silence throughout the ordeal but angrily stared at the fringe of his horse's mane.

"Bagdemagus made a very convincing argument, one I believe you will approve of, Merlin." Britt slipped off her borrowed horse and approached her trained charger. Roen pressed his velvet muzzle to her cheek. "He said a divided Britain will fall before Rome. Moreover, he is quite angry with King Ryence for betraying our country. He requested that we become allies so we might stand against Rome together."

Percival untied Roen's bridle and handed it to Britt with a smile.

Merlin pressed his lips tightly together. "I'm glad he sees the wisdom in it, though I still reserve judgment." He turned his attention to Maleagant. "I assume Bagdemagus must have your cooperation, however unwillingly it is given?"

"I will not bow to your beardless-youth-King," Maleagant snarled.

"This 'beardless-youth-king' trounced you twice on the battlefield," Gawain said.

"And again, it seems, more recently," Percival nodded at Maleagant's face.

"Perhaps he needs to go a few rounds with us knights as well, so we might remind him what chivalry and honor are." Kay's eyes glittered with barely reined in rage as he stared the duke down.

"Now, now," Merlin said. "There's no sense fighting between…friends."

"If I might speak up on behalf of King Bagdemagus," Mordred said, the calmest of the bunch. "He is an honest and rational man. You can trust in his offer of an alliance."

"Oh? Is he acquainted with your family?" Merlin asked.

Mordred smiled enigmatically. (Merlin had been trying to

weasel the secret of his birth and family out of the affable knight since he first came to Camelot.)

Merlin rolled his eyes, then slipped off his horse and joined Britt at Roen's side as the rest of the knights continued to eye Maleagant. "Do you trust this offer of friendship?" He murmured.

"He seemed genuine, and he had no reason to lie. He caught me right after I pounded in Maleagant's nose. He could've easily thrown me in the dungeons instead of playing politics," Britt said. "Besides, I trust Mordred's word."

Merlin nodded and rubbed his clean-shaven chin. "Your observations ring true with what I have heard about Bagdemagus. And if the Romans come, we will need every ally we can get."

Britt grinned. "I thought for sure you would claim this is just one more step to unifying Britain."

"That, too," Merlin said. His brilliant blue eyes grew soft as he again inspected her. "Are you truly uninjured? You didn't suffer at Maleagant's hands?" He motioned to her scratched cheek.

Britt shook her head and whispered, "The worst he did was mistake me for Guinevere and stuff me in a bedroom."

He chuckled. "That certainly is a mistake." He extended his hand, as if to reach out and brush her cheek, then stepped back and turned to look at Maleagant. "I am grateful, Duke Maleagant, for the hospitality you have provided to our king. Moreover, I look forward to seeing you in Camelot. May I assume you and your father will be joining us there soon?"

Maleagant shifted in the saddle, but it was Britt who responded. "We've already made plans for them to come in a fortnight or so. Bagdemagus wanted to begin the process of rallying his troops and knights first."

"Well planned!" Merlin clapped his hands in genuine satisfaction, then paused. He made a show of rubbing his chin and considering Maleagant. Britt could sense his mood change as he continued. "It is not my duty to judge the actions of nobility, but perhaps you are due for a warning before you come to Camelot. You see, there is an order in Camelot, the Order of the Queen's Knights." He sighed, as if apathetic towards the situation, and ignored Britt's strangled grunt. "I'm afraid kidnapping Guinevere did little to endear you to them. I advise you to be on your best behavior, else you might find a sword—or a bit of magic—at your throat." His words sounded solicitous enough, but his eyes were dark and tumultuous like a storm.

Britt frowned slightly, surprised he would risk enraging their new ally.

Maleagant shifted in his saddle, and his eyes nervously rolled from Merlin to the other knights and back again.

Unconcerned, the wizard smiled brightly. "Off with you, then! Take Arthur's borrowed horse with you, and please pass our greetings along to your wise father."

Britt patted Roen's neck, then sauntered her borrowed horse back to Maleagant, handing off the reins to him.

Maleagant swiped them from her and wasted no time turning his horse towards his father's castle.

Britt watched him trot off as she retreated back to Roen's side. "I'm surprised you let him go. I thought you would insist he come to Camelot with us right now to serve as extra encouragement for King Bagdemagus to come."

"There's no need for it. If King Bagdemagus made arrangements with you, I'm certain he will come," Merlin said.

Britt open her mouth to argue, but Kay dismounted from his horse, approached her, and then embraced her. Kay's hugs were a rare thing, and Britt couldn't recall the last time he'd given her one publicly. So, she happily hugged her foster brother back, and briefly rested her chin on his armor-covered shoulder. "Thank you for coming for me."

When Kay released her, she met the gaze of the other knights. "I mean it: thank you."

Gawain smiled. "We will follow you wherever you go, My Lord."

Britt returned the smile with her own grin, a true one, not the professional one she used when playing Arthur.

"It is our honor to serve you." Percival blushed and fussed with his horse's reins.

"As the Queen's Champion, of course I shall always ride to your rescue," Lancelot said, ruining the moment.

Britt's eyebrow twitched in irritation, but she ignored the mouthy knight. "So, what game are you playing, Merlin? I know you didn't send him back for the fun of it." She groaned a little as she put her foot into the saddle and mounted Roen.

"We need more information on the Romans," Merlin said. "I didn't particularly want to conduct our search with Duke Maleagant leering over our shoulders."

"I agree more information is needed," Kay said. "However, our first priority should be returning Arthur—Britt—to Camelot."

Merlin narrowed his eyes and shook his head.

"We could always split up," Gawain said. "Sir Kay and I could see the king back to Camelot and alert your spy ring, Merlin."

"We haven't the time," Merlin said. "The Romans are moving now. They obviously are not aiming to attack anyone in the next few days, but they are moving somewhere. I wish to learn their plans now, before they have the chance to cook up something particularly nasty."

Kay frowned as he mounted up his horse. "Are you really so worried we don't have the time to take Britt back?"

"I did not predict King Ryence would side with the Romans," Merlin said grimly. "So yes, time is of the essence."

"Suits me just fine," Britt said. "I'd like to see these Romans everybody's talking about. Are they wearing the stereotypical breastplate and little skirt things?"

Percival scratched his chin. "Skirt things?"

Merlin crinkled his forehead. "I have no idea what you are

referring to, but they are dressed in King Ryence's colors and uniforms, as you may remember."

"Oh, yeah. So we'll skulk around and scout out the Romans for a few days before heading back to Camelot? Sounds great to me."

Kay's frown deepened so much, even his mustache could not hide it.

"A day or two is all we will need, lass," Merlin said. "Then your overprotective seneschal will be granted his wish of dragging you back to Camelot."

"That's no fun," Britt said.

Kay, on the other hand, nodded in agreement.

"We must begin our scouting and spying with all haste," Merlin announced.

Lancelot placed his hand over his heart. "Of course! Fear not, for though I am the best knight in Camelot, I am also quite skilled in matters of subterfuge."

"You only think you're the best knight because Gawain was not present for the tournament last summer, and Kay and Bodwain were not allowed to enter," Britt growled.

"Should we separate for this task?" Gawain asked.

"It would allow us to cover more ground, and you did say time is of the essence," Percival piped in.

Merlin adjusted his cloak while the wind brushed through his fine blonde hair. "Yes, my plan is for us to split up in pairs."

"Great!" Britt chirped. "I'm with you or Kay, I assume?"

Merlin's smile crawled across his face and dripped with smugness. "No, I'm afraid not."

Britt collected up her reins. "Then Gawain? Percival?"

Merlin shook his head.

Britt dropped her good humor like a rock. "You can't!"

"I'm afraid I must," Merlin said. "For you must pay for the great worry you caused me."

"But it wasn't my fault!" Britt protested.

"You should have thought of that before you spent the night in the castle and refrained from checking to see if we were in the area. That was a whole extra night my tired nerves had to suffer through." Merlin sorrowfully shook his head.

"I'm sorry. Truly. Really." She did her best to grovel from horseback, though Roen was taller than Merlin's mount. "I'll do anything! Just please don't pair me with..."

"EVERY TIME! Every time he's angry with me, he sticks me with *you*." Britt muttered at the road, her mood too foul to even look at her search partner.

"It is my honor to be consistently paired with you, Britt," Lance said with his odiously charming smile.

"That's Arthur to you. And it's an *honor* I wish Merlin would not bestow upon you so often," Britt grumbled. She glanced up at the cloudy sky and strained her ears for the telltale noises of the Roman army—the neighing of horses, the jingle of tack, or the clang of armor.

Britt and Lancelot had been sent north of King Bagdemagus's lands. Their objective was to estimate the number of soldiers in the area and see if they could deduce in what direction the Romans were marching.

Britt didn't hear any sign of them yet, but Percival had said they were traveling on the main roads.

"I'm afraid I don't understand why it is such a punishment for you to ride with me," Lancelot said. "I am the best knight in Camelot, your champion, and your most loyal subject."

Britt snorted. "You are *not* my most loyal subject. I'm not even convinced you're loyal to me at all."

"How could you say such a thing?" Lancelot protested. "I took my oaths to you with great seriousness." He patted his horse when it shook its head.

"Do you really want me to recite the list?" Britt shifted in her saddle so she could flatly stare at the charming knight. "Because, let me remind you, at the very top of it is the fact that you stabbed me in the shoulder!"

Lancelot lazily swapped his hand through the air. "That was long ago."

"That was *last summer*!"

He ignored her correction. "Since your gender was revealed, I feel I have been quite helpful. After all, it was I who spoke out to the rest the Knights of the Round Table when they questioned you as our king." He smiled benignly.

Britt, not trusting his pretty face and smile, raised her eyebrows. "If you have helped me, it is only because it has served your need at the time."

"All I want is your affection and approval," Lancelot said with false innocence.

Though he used pretty manners, Britt was not fooled. Merlin might think her paranoid, but ever since Lancelot asked to be called the Queen's Champion and secretly established the Order of the Queen's Knights, Britt knew Lancelot had to have a sneaky agenda he was aiming to achieve. If he really wanted her to like him, she knew it was not merely because he wanted them to be friends.

She pressed her lips together to keep her sharp observations in. "If it is my affection you are seeking to secure, let me assure you you're going about it all wrong."

"Yes, I recently realized that as well." Lancelot smiled at her, but it was more of a smirk than his charming grin. "It occurred to me that if I really want your affection, I would be wisest to act like Merlin."

Britt turned Roen so sharply he almost ran into Lancelot's dapple gray horse. Lancelot's smirk grew as Britt clenched her teeth. "Lancelot," she growled.

They were interrupted by the pounding of horse hooves.

Britt and Lancelot twisted in their saddles to see four mounted soldiers pop out of the woods that surrounded the road they traveled. The soldiers spotted them and pulled their horses into an abrupt halt.

Well. So much for subtlety.

Britt made her stiff irritation with Lancelot drain away. She smiled lazily, her eyes at half mast, as the soldiers corrected their course straight for her and Lancelot. Her nerves buzzed with their approach.

It was likely the soldiers were scouts sent ahead of an army. If Britt and Lancelot could not convince them they were harmless, they would probably have to fight their way out. She didn't think four soldiers would be a problem, particularly if she and Lancelot worked together. The bigger issue would be the army would then be alerted to their presence.

"Hail, sir knights," one of the soldiers called out.

"Greetings," Britt chirped. She was quite proud that her voice did not quiver.

Lancelot, never to be outdone, added, "How fare you soldiers this fine day?"

Three of the soldiers frowned and looked up at the clouded, gloomy sky. The fourth drew his horse closer to Britt and Lancelot. "Quite well, thank you sirs. Whom do I have the pleasure of addressing?"

Though Britt kept her expression bland, she did not miss the way the soldier's hand crept towards the daggers attached to his sword belt.

Lancelot, however, smiled. "I am Sir Lancelot of King Arthur's court."

Britt fought the urge to reach out and shake Lancelot until his brains were jostled. What kind of an idiot announced his name on a mission of secrecy? "And I am Sir Galahad," she was quick to add, lest he thoughtlessly oust her as a king.

The soldier narrowed his eyes, and behind him his companions stirred, all reaching for various weaponry. "What are King Arthur's knights doing in these parts? These lands belong to King Bagdemagus, and he is no friend of Arthur's."

"Actually..." Lancelot began.

"We are here on a quest," Britt blurted.

The soldier raised an eyebrow. "A quest?"

"Indeed," Britt said, racking her mind for a possible mission. Unfortunately, no ideas were forthcoming. She frantically tried to recall any sort of King Arthur legend she'd heard in the twenty-first century—any movie or TV show even! "We are here, searching for the famous, hallowed, legendary...Holy Grail." It took all of her experience of acting as a boy king to keep her eyes from bulging at her lie.

The soldier's other eyebrow joined the first half way up his forehead. "You search for the Holy Grail?"

"Yes, yes we do." Britt nodded. She flashed him a smile and hoped he didn't notice how profusely she was sweating, even though it was a cold day. *We are in so much trouble if he asks for any specifics.* She hadn't the faintest idea what the Holy Grail was. The only reason she'd even thought of it in the first place was because of the Monty Python movie.

"That is indeed a quest worth pursuing," the soldier said. Behind him, his compatriots nodded.

Lancelot piously bowed his head. "We do it not for personal glory or honor, but seek only to serve the Lord with our swords."

With Lancelot's false devotion, the soldiers released their weapons and took up their horse's reins. "Your piety is admirable," the spokes-soldier said. "We wish you Godspeed on your journey."

Britt blinked. *They believe us? And they're letting us go without further interrogation?*

"Thank you," Lancelot said with enviable smoothness. "We hope God sees fit to show us the right path."

Britt bowed her head and followed Lancelot when he nudged

his gelding forward. Together, they continued down the road at a peaceful pace. It took a great deal of self-control to keep from turning around and gawking back at the soldiers. Based on the snorts of their horses and the jingling of their bridles, the soldiers watched them for some time before urging their horses back into the woods.

"I can't believe that worked," Britt muttered once they were gone.

Lancelot shifted slightly so he could peer behind them. "It was well done, for now we have an excuse to wander about the area."

"At least we know they must be close by. Which reminds me, was it really necessary to use your real name? They might have let us go, but now they know knights from the Round Table are in the area. Merlin is going to be ticked."

"I would have used an alias if I could have, but I am unfortunately all too recognizable," Lancelot said.

"Are you kidding me?" Britt asked. "Nobody in this time has cameras, or pictures, or Facebook."

Lancelot gave her a puzzled frown, but Britt continued her tirade. "You could've said you were literally anyone in Britain, and they would've had to believe you."

"If I wore unmarked armor and rode an unmarked horse, perhaps," Lancelot said. "Unfortunately, before I joined your court, I rode frequently through all of Britain. As a result, my charger and its barding are rather recognizable, as is my coat of arms. While we might have been able to fool them this time, if they saw us again in the future, they would perhaps learn the truth. That would not end well."

Britt was not entirely convinced. She thought it was just as likely that Lancelot was merely an idiot and hadn't thought to use a different name. But his expression was unusually serious as he narrowed his eyes and stared ahead.

"I recommend we continue to ride down the road, and once

we reach an acceptable distance, circle back and move into the woods," he said.

Britt stretched her arms in front of her, then reached down to hug Roen. "Fine by me." She cast one final glance over her shoulder at the eerily empty road behind them.

5
THE QUEST FOR THE HOLY GRAIL

Britt jumped down the last few rungs of the hay loft ladder just as Merlin finished scratching a rough map into the packed dirt of the stable floor.

After regrouping once everyone had finished their spying assignment, Gawain and Percival reported they had found a kind farmer who would let them stay in his stable overnight. Although spring had almost come, nights were still cold and windy, making camping a miserable experience.

So Britt, Merlin, and her knights gladly set up camp in the stable. Their bedrolls and packs were stowed in the much warmer hayloft, and their horses contentedly chewed on hay in the few spare stalls the farmer had.

"Based on our observations, it seems the Romans are moving northeast," Merlin said. He frowned as he drew arrows in the dirt that represented the Roman soldiers they had run into.

Britt paused to pat Roen on the neck. "I think it's worth mentioning all the groups are small companies, not huge armies."

"Indeed," Merlin said. "It's unfortunate. Bigger armies are easier to spy on, track, and predict in terms of movement patterns."

Kay twitched his mustache. "It seems they are spreading across the land like a disease."

Merlin glanced up from his drawing to the taciturn knight. "Yes. They are all moving separately and as individual units rather than following one path to a specific location."

Gawain tossed his horse another flake of hay. "It's an unusual strategy, particularly as the troops are all foot soldiers."

"True. I've heard of small companies of knights moving like this, but when we went up against the other kings after I was crowned, the armies always stayed collected," Britt said.

Mordred tapped his fingers on his sword belt. "If we could intercept orders for several of the companies, I believe it would shed light on the mystery of their actions."

"Of course it would," Percival said. "But how would we accomplish such a task? Unless, Merlin, could you do it with magic?"

"You mean scrying for them, or some such nonsense?" Merlin shook his head. "'Tis impossible. Though it is a commonly used spell in stories, even the faerie folk cannot manage such a thing."

"I was not thinking of magic, but subterfuge," Mordred said. "King Arthur's adventure with Duke Maleagant has got me wondering. Perhaps a female would find it easier to infiltrate the camp."

"I'm certain it would be easier. At a minimum, she would be viewed with less suspicion." Merlin frowned down at his map and patted out one of the arrows, then redrew it. "But it matters not, for we cannot afford to risk Britt. And unless Gawain's bossy aunt pops out of the underbrush, which I find unlikely, we have no other possible agents."

"I wouldn't mind," Britt said. "I have enough experience. I'm pretty sure I can pull it off without a hitch." (The biggest danger would be that the Romans wouldn't *want* to let her leave, given that she was a female. But she was not going to remind any of them that that was a possibility.)

"Out of the question." Kay reached to rest his hand on the hilt of his sword, but it was unbuckled and stored in the hayloft with the rest of their equipment, so he settled for scowling instead.

"I wasn't necessarily picturing sending a real female to the Romans," Mordred said.

Merlin wiped his dusty fingers off on his dark cloak. "Explain."

"Could we not do the reverse of what Britt does?" Mordred asked.

Gawain leaned against a stall door. "You mean disguise ourselves as females."

"Correct."

Lancelot vaulted down from the hayloft with the ease of a cat. "That is a horrifying idea, Sir Mordred. We are men! We fight boldly, and our strength lies in our masculinity and charm. To dress as a *woman*?"

The horror was so apparent in his voice that Britt suspected he would've shivered if he had not felt it to be a cowardly gesture. Still, she was pretty ticked at him for his words alone, so she was preparing to rip into him when Gawain beat her to the punch.

"Some of the strongest people I know are women," he said.

Percival nodded, most likely thinking of his mother.

"You might remember, Sir Lancelot, that Britt has never lost a sword match to you," Kay said, earning a brilliant smile from Britt.

"Why, thank you Kay!" She said.

Kay ducked his head in acknowledgment.

"That does not count," Lancelot argued, "for no one has bested our king in a sword match."

"It does not matter, Sir Lancelot, for I was not thinking of you wearing such a disguise." Mordred smiled slightly and clasped the dramatic knight on the shoulder.

Lancelot nodded in satisfaction, until Mordred added, "I'm

afraid to say I don't think you would make a very convincing woman. Subterfuge does not seem to be one of your many skills."

The handsome knight's face froze.

Britt grinned; she couldn't help herself. "Cheer up, Lancelot," she said with a devious smile. "You are only human. There has to be *something* you can't be competent at."

The challenge riled him up, as Britt had intended. "I am the best knight in Camelot," he said, speaking carefully and pronouncing his words clearly. "If there is a dangerous quest or task to undertake, I will always be the best one to do it."

Mordred, playing Lancelot just as effortlessly as Britt had, raised his eyebrows and tilted his head back. "I don't know…"

Lancelot turned back to the ladder that led to the hayloft. "I shall prove it. Did we not bring a pack containing a spare dress or two, in case it was necessary for Britt to keep up a female disguise?"

Mordred joined him at the ladder. "Indeed. It is in the satchel by my packs."

Lancelot shimmied up the ladder and disappeared from view.

"What is our next goal?" Gawain asked as he turned his attention to Merlin. "I imagine you have a plan?"

Straw rustled as one of the horses shifted in its stall. "I believe we should split up," Merlin said. "One group should travel south to find where the Romans are coming from. The other shall return to Camelot to inform our allies and begin preparing for battle. Kay, I believe you should lead the group that goes to Camelot."

Kay nodded.

Lancelot had returned from the loft, carrying a blue dress. He flapped it once to straighten it out, then held it in front of him. "I believe the color will bring out the blue-green of my eyes," he said. (His face said the thought did not please him, but he was so bent on proving Mordred wrong he made himself admit it out loud.)

Mordred held the dress against Lancelot's face. "It is a fetching combination."

Britt held in her laughter, but it took all of her self-control to school her features as she kept her attention on Merlin's map. "The group that travels south should maybe use the search for the Holy Grail as their cover story. It worked pretty well when Lancelot and I used it."

"It is an inspired idea, one I would not have thought of," Merlin said. "The Romans are quite religious and would naturally respect such a quest."

"Really?" Britt asked.

"Indeed. Since the times of Constantine, they have mostly been ruled by Christian emperors," Merlin said.

Britt ran a hand through her slightly tangled hair. "I guess I missed that in my European history class."

"Citing the Holy Grail would also explain why you travel as a group," Kay said.

Britt snapped her fingers and pointed. "I had thought of that. Most of our knights go out solo, but for a quest that epic, at least a handful of knights would be together."

"How will the two groups be divided out, Merlin? Who else will return to Camelot besides Sir Kay?" Gawain asked.

In the background, Mordred and Lancelot continued their female impersonator conversation.

"See? Certainly I could perform such a feat as spying as a female." Though Lancelot's tone was triumphant, one of his coal black eyebrows twitched as he studied the gown.

"I don't know.... I don't believe that dress would fit you very flatteringly in the shoulders," Mordred said. "I would say there are other knights from Camelot who would play the role with more finesse. Wouldn't you agree, Sir Percival?"

Percival joined Mordred in scrutinizing Lancelot and the dress. "Perhaps Sir Safir or Sir Lanval would be a better match," he said after some moments.

"I beg your pardon," Lancelot said flatly.

Britt coughed to cover up her laugh.

"Obviously, the king will return with me," Kay said.

Britt ripped her attention from the outraged Lancelot. "Actually, I was thinking I should go south with the spying group."

Merlin rubbed his chin, considering the idea, but Kay emphatically chopped his hand through the air. "Absolutely not."

Mordred, leaving Percival to explain to Lancelot why he felt the other knights would be a better choice, rejoined the circle around Merlin's scratched out map. "May I request to be put in the group that returns to Camelot?"

"Why?" Merlin asked.

"I wish to help alert our allies," Mordred said.

Merlin narrowed his eyes as he stared down the younger knight. "Sending out messages is why we have messenger pigeons and courier riders.... Unless you believe, due to your parentage, our allies will take it more seriously if you present the information?"

Mordred smiled enigmatically.

"If Kay and Mordred both return, I should stay behind," Britt said with a winning smile.

"Really?" Merlin drawled. "Are you truly that eager for quality time with Sir Lancelot?"

Britt was sorely tempted to stick her tongue out at the wizard, but she didn't think it would further her cause.

Kay mulishly folded his arms across his chest. He looked ready to launch into one of his lectures, which would run an astounding four or five sentences in a row, when the kind farmer who was hosting them trundled into the barn, his two sons trailing behind him with wide eyes.

"Forgive my intrusions, sirs, but I have your dinner!" the farmer said.

Kay and Gawain moved to help, taking the heavy, cast iron stew pot from his hands and the wooden bowls from his sons.

"Mordred," Lancelot called. "How easy do you think it would be to fight in the dress? Sir Percival believes it would be quite difficult. I believe it wouldn't be any more difficult than combat in a robe."

Mordred turned on his heels to rejoin the eccentric conversation. "I, too, should think it would be more difficult. But the real question is where would you hide your weapons?"

All three knights scrutinized the dress, stretching it out between them.

Britt shifted her gaze from the knights crowded around the gown, to Kay who was thanking the farmer, and then rested on Gawain, who was smiling and speaking to the peasant boys. *They are not what I pictured when I thought of Knights of the Round Table back in America. They're far better than that.* Britt smiled, her eyes crinkling with affection.

"Tell me, lass. Why are you so eager to stay?" Merlin asked.

Britt rocked back on her heels as she thought. "I've said it before, but my worst nightmare is to become a passive king. I want to see and judge this threat with my own eyes, lest I forget what I'm asking my men to do."

A quirk of a smile pulled on the corners of Merlin's lips. "That would never happen. You are too kind and too brave."

Britt could feel her cheeks flush, but she was grateful for the moment. Since Merlin had been running interference with Vivien, they hadn't had a real heart-to-heart conversation. It was gratifying to be reminded that Merlin really knew her.

"Thanks, Merlin." She hesitated. "I've missed you."

"As have I." Merlin reached for her hand, his fingers barely grazing her palm.

"Ahem."

Britt and Merlin froze, then looked into the stony face of Kay, who was glaring at Merlin. (If he placed his hands on his hips and tapped his foot, he would be the perfect disapproving mother.)

"My Lord? I have your stew." Gawain held up a wooden bowl after he put several ladles of stew into it.

Britt cleared her throat. "Thank you, Gawain." She ducked around Kay to approach Gawain.

"It is settled," Merlin announced. "Kay and Mordred will return to Camelot. The rest of us will track down the origins of the Romans."

Britt almost whooped in glee. "Awesome! Thanks, Merlin!"

"It is a good plan," Mordred echoed. "We should ride through Baron Marhaus' lands. We can spend a night in the village and then move on to Camelot."

"This is foolish, Merlin," Kay argued. "It is too dangerous."

"I don't believe the threat will be too large, provided we are careful," Percival added. He shifted uncomfortably when Kay glared at him.

"Though I know you would like nothing more than to shut Britt up in a tower, keeping her locked in Camelot all the time is unreasonable," Merlin said. "Percival is right. The group we have is strong and experienced. As long as we are careful, the dangers should be minimal, and rather than choke her until she rebelliously gallivants off on her own quest, I would much rather allow her to journey when I can watch her."

Britt triumphantly grabbed her bowl of stew from Gawain's hands. She was going! She would get to see the Roman troops for herself! She was so giddy, even Lancelot's usual boasts did not ruin her good mood.

"Worry not, Sir Kay! I will guard our king and see that she is safe at all times!" he declared. "I am, after all, her champion!"

"I would suggest you stop trumpeting that around, Sir Lancelot," Merlin said dryly. "Particularly when a cast-iron stew pot is within Britt's reach."

"I'll be careful, Kay," Britt promised.

Kay sighed. "I just don't want to see you hurt."

Britt grinned. "Don't worry. You brought me Excalibur yourself. As long as I have it and the scabbard, there's nothing to fear!"

THE WIND RUFFLED Britt's hair as she gazed at the horizon. It was their second day of traveling south and spying on the Roman forces. They had long ago left the skeletal, leafless forests, and now forged their way across plains and pasture lands hemmed in by sweeping hills. Boulders dotted the countryside, as if giants had played bowling there, and Britt could see the green of spring invading the brown grass and bushes.

"The plot to bring Roman soldiers into Britain by putting them in uniforms and colors belonging to King Ryence was an inspired idea, or so I thought," Merlin grumbled. "However, only an idiot wouldn't realize that the sheer number of soldiers we've seen dressed in King Ryence's uniform outstrips the number of people in his lands."

"Thus far the soldiers are still moving in small clusters," Gawain said. He rode next to Britt, his horse occasionally nickering to Roen. "Unless one were to travel south, as we are, and take inventory of all the soldiers, I believe it is understandable that those who witness only a group or two would accept it."

"It's reassuring, at least, that they're all following a similar pattern." Britt adjusted her reins when Roen pranced a pace or two. "If they suddenly change their tactics, I'd be far more worried."

"Your words are true," Merlin said. "But the sheer number of soldiers is alarming. I did not think the Roman Emperor would send so many of his troops this far north."

"Fear not, for we shall beat back the Roman invasion with ease," Lancelot promised. "I'm certain once my father and uncle receive word of these movements, they will be able to watch for Rome from across the sea."

"That will help only if Rome is traveling to Britain from French shores," Percival said.

"Mordred's idea of attempting to intercept orders is starting to look more and more beneficial," Britt said.

Merlin eyed her. "Don't be mistaken into thinking, Lass, that just because your overprotective brother is not here I will let you sashay into danger."

Britt would've scowled at him, but a blob of red caught her eye. Squinting, she raised her hand to block what little sunlight shone down and peered out at the hill spread in front of them.

"What do you see, My Lord?" Gawain asked.

Britt's armor creaked as she pointed at the blob. "Is that a knight?"

Merlin nudged his horse forward and also shielded his eyes. "He's no Roman soldier, that's for sure."

"I say, is he being attacked?" Percival asked.

The party was silent until they drew closer and were able to make out the fight between the red knight and five armed men.

The red knight twirled his sword, the blade flashing silver, as he parried the sword strike of one of his attackers. A man crept up behind him, but he lashed out, kicking the man in the kneecap and kneeing him in the face when he fell.

When the man with the sword lunged at him, he sidestepped him, grabbed him by the shoulders, and flipped him over his back. He stomped on his chest, forcing the air from the swordsman's lungs.

Whirling around, the red knight charged one of his attackers, who was fumbling to put a bolt in a crossbow. He clotheslined the man—extending his arm and slamming it across the bowman's throat—tossing him to the ground so hard he made the man gurgle.

He stiffly moved to face the remaining two attackers, his red armor gleaming dully. The two men rushed him together. The red knight plucked up a spear from one of the fallen warriors and swept it in front of him, pulling his attackers feet right out from underneath them.

Lancelot rubbed his clean-shaven chin. "He's a good warrior. Not as good as us, of course, but he comes close."

Britt rolled her eyes at Lancelot's hubris, but watched with interest as the red knight removed his helm and tossed it aside.

The knight waited until his attackers recovered, then approached them with his hands up in supplication.

Surprisingly, the attackers, appearing disgruntled and bruised, turned their backs to him and wandered towards their horses.

The red knight hurried after them, waving his arms.

The armed men ignored him and climbed onto their mounts.

Peeved, the knight grabbed one of the men and attempted to pull him off his horse. The man kicked him in the face, freeing himself, then turned his horse in a smart circle and set off with the rest of his comrades.

His shoulders hunched, the red knight reluctantly picked up his helm and trudged back to his waiting horse.

"That was an odd event to witness," Percival said. When he raised his eyebrow, he more closely resembled his noble father, King Pellinore.

Britt scratched her side and considered it. "I've seen weirder," she finally said.

"I believe I know the red knight," Sir Gawain said. "His name is Sir Pelleas. My Lord, I ask permission to approach him."

"It's fine. We're not on a schedule, right, Merlin?" Britt asked.

Merlin shrugged. "As long as we don't get caught up on some ridiculous rabbit trail of a side quest, it's fine."

"Come!" Lancelot proclaimed. "Let us offer our services to this poor, downtrodden knight."

"Let it be said that no one could ever believe that one of Lancelot's talents is listening well," Britt said dryly.

Percival grinned, then nudged his horse to follow Lancelot and Gawain, who galloped towards the red knight.

Britt watched her knights canter off with a mixture of amusement and affection, then followed them at a walk. "They really are maturing. Well, everyone except Lancelot."

"Your oath of the Round Table gave them a code of conduct to follow. It helps them more than I had predicted," Merlin said.

"The oath is just a guide. They could do whatever they want when I send them out on quests, and you know it. They excel because they choose to act as they should." She tilted her head as the three knights approached Sir Pelleas. "Though Lancelot's behavior does bother me."

"He has not done anything suspicious for some time," Merlin said.

"It's not his behavior towards *me* that bothers me," she said.

Merlin gave her an appraising look as his horse shook its head. "You are better with your men, your knights in particular, than I ever thought possible."

Though his praise warmed her heart, Britt deflected it. "You're giving me too much credit."

"No, it is rather that I don't give you enough credit. You understand your men, and you work with them. Your vision for Camelot is idealistic—overly so—but the camaraderie you have with your knights is unmatched throughout history."

Britt ripped her gaze from the red knight, trusting Roen to keep walking, and met Merlin's gaze. Her heart thumped in her throat at the unfathomable expression in his eyes. She swallowed hard and tried to think of something to say.

Naturally, Lancelot had to ruin it. "Merlin, Sir Galahad!" he called, remembering to use Britt's alias. "You must come listen to Sir Pelleas's tale of woe!"

Merlin winked at Britt, then switched his attention to the red knight. "Sir Pelleas, I do not believe I have had the pleasure of making your acquaintance, though I've heard much about you. I am Merlin, chief counselor to King Arthur, High King of Britain.

This is Sir Galahad, one of the best knights of the Round Table, and for certain the purest."

"Greetings, Sir Pelleas," Britt said. She pulled Roen to a halt just short of Percival's horse.

Sir Pelleas bowed his head. "It is my honor to meet you all."

"Please, tell us your story," Merlin said. Based on the kindness in his voice, Britt guessed that Sir Pelleas must've been a knight of relative renown.

Sir Pelleas sighed and covered his eyes with an arm. "It is a story that will one day kill me. For I love with great passion the beautiful Lady Ettard."

Merlin's blue eyes narrowed with cunning. "Lady Ettard…the heiress who owns the lands upon which we stand?"

"Yes. I love her with the burning passion of a wildfire," Sir Pelleas declared. "Her eyes sparkle with such beauty the sun nor moon can compare. Her laughter is sweeter than the trill of a songbird, and there is no piece of music that can compare to the sweetness of her voice."

Britt was beginning to wish she had asked for the "too long, didn't listen" version of the story. Just as Sir Pelleas begin to praise the fineness of Lady Ettard's hair, Britt saw a small frown crest Gawain's lips. She maneuvered her horse next to his. "Something wrong?"

"I don't recall Sir Pelleas being quite so…demonstrative," he said.

"Interesting," Merlin said, popping up behind them.

Britt tuned back in to Sir Pelleas's spiel. He still hadn't moved past Ettard's hair, so when he paused to take a breath, Britt was quick to interject, "I understand you are filled with great admiration for the beautiful Lady Ettard. But why should this cause you sadness? Love should bring joy and happiness."

"Alas," Sir Pelleas sighed, "she does not return my affection. Nay, she can barely stand the sight of me. She will not let me into her castle, nor will she allow me to speak to her, unless her men take me captive and bring me before her themselves."

"Unfortunately, it seems like Lady Ettard's men are growing weary of playing messenger," Sir Percival said, greatly shortening the conversation. "No longer will they take Sir Pelleas captive and into their lady's castle."

Britt shot the young knight a thankful look. "I see. I believe I understand your plight, Sir Pelleas."

"Is your heart not moved, Sir Galahad?" Lancelot asked. "Are you not filled with the desire to help this fellow man?"

"Not really," Britt said. She never had much patience for dramatic love affairs. It's why she had such little sympathy for Tristan and his love potion. Even when she had first fallen for Merlin, she would not let herself sink into a pit of despair when he rejected her.

"But you are the purest of us all. Can you give him no insight to the female heart?" Lancelot asked.

Britt was filled with the desire to kick Lancelot, but unfortunately, he was stationed across the little circle into which their group had gathered. "Females, in case you did not know, Lancelot, are all individualistic. I could give romantic advice, but that doesn't mean this particular lady would appreciate what I advise."

"Is there no way we can help him?" sweet Percival asked.

Britt swiveled to Merlin and raised her eyebrows.

Merlin shifted in his saddle. "We have unadorned armor we can lend him. We could travel to Lady Ettard's castle and smuggle him inside with our group."

"A brilliant idea!" Lancelot proclaimed.

"What happened to rabbit-trail-side-quests?" Britt asked.

"It is just as well. I have a contact in Lady Ettard's castle with whom I would like to speak. He can send off word of our findings to some of my other men," Merlin said.

"Indeed, it is a wise plan." Gawain gestured to the horizon. "It looks like rain will soon be upon us."

Out of nowhere, an angry black cloud had rolled in. It looked like it would catch up with them in an hour or two and open up a downpour over their heads.

"Very well," Britt said. "Let us see this Lady Ettard. Perhaps we can help you, Sir Pelleas."

"If I only gaze upon her, I will be filled with enough happiness to sustain me for the rest of my life," Sir Pelleas said. "But I would not refuse any help you may lend me to bring her eyes to alight favorably on me."

Britt stared at him. "Right. Well. Let's go. But first, Sir Pelleas, you had better change out of that eye-catching red armor."

6
LADY ETTARD AND SIR PELLEAS

As Britt and the knights approached Ettard's castle, the gray raincloud had opened up and began splattering them with fat raindrops.

Britt peered up at the cloud and almost snorted a raindrop. She sneezed and moved Roen closer to the castle so it blocked the worst of the weather.

The castle portcullis—a rusted metal grate—was dropped down into place. Two guards were stationed inside the gatehouse, and they peered outside as Britt and the knights crowded around the gate.

"We are Knights of the Round Table from Camelot. We ask that you would grant us shelter for the night," Gawain said.

One of the guards approached the portcullis and peered out at them. "Camelot.... That's King Arthur's castle, is it not?" His fellow guard joined him. "You are King Arthur's knights?"

An icy cold raindrop slid down the back of Britt's neck, making her teeth chatter with the cold. "Yep. That would be us." She carefully avoided looking at Sir Pelleas, who wore plain armor and was packed into the middle of their little group, lest someone recognize his horse.

The first guard looked them over as the pitter-patter of rain hitting their armor broke the silence. He nodded at the second soldier, who trotted off, then returned his gaze to them. "Lady Ettard would be glad to host Knights of the Round Table." He retreated around the corner of the gatehouse, and a few shouts—muffled by the falling rain—sounded up and down the walls before the portcullis creaked as it was slowly raised up.

Britt, Merlin, and the knights nudged their horses and entered the castle.

Lady Ettard's castle was small and comfortable. It contained only a large keep and gardens, no city like Camelot or—on a smaller scale—Camelgrance. As Britt peered around, she saw brightly colored banners hung from windows, carefully manicured ivy tendrils climbing up the walls, and well-maintained buildings. Quaint was the word she would use to describe it. The gardens, still dead from winter, were quite large and impressive given the size of the castle.

Britt slipped from Roen's back and landed on the ground with a grimace. She refrained from rubbing her posterior, as she dearly wanted to, and patted her horse's damp neck.

Three stable boys came to collect the mounts, taking the horses with little bows to both the knights and the horses.

Britt rested her hand on the hilt of Excalibur as she watched Roen be led to the stable.

"This way, if you please, sirs," the portcullis guard said.

He led them down a tidy stone pathway, all the way up to the front door of the keep.

Britt sighed with relief when they entered the keep, finally leaving the dreary drizzle of rain. She was starting to wish she had worn her helm, as her damp hair kept shedding cold raindrops down the collar of her armor.

"Knights of the Round Table, I welcome you to my humble castle."

Britt swung around to face the newcomer, a genteel lady who was perhaps a little younger than her.

The lady, assumedly Lady Ettard, was pretty with dark brown hair that was plaited in a complex braid and dropped down her back. She did not look cruel or snotty, as Britt had pictured. In fact, already smile lines began to play around the set of her mouth. However, she *was* unusually matchy-matchy with her blue-green dress that complemented her blue-green jeweled necklace.

Britt smiled and did her best not to squelch all over the castle's stone floor. "We thank you for your kindness and generosity..." She trailed off when Percival, closely followed by Gawain, knelt almost reverently before Ettard.

"My Lady," Percival said worshipfully. He opened his mouth to say more, but his shy nature around women got the best of him, and he blushed and looked away.

Gawain was not quite so calf-eyed, but still just as admiring. "I have heard of your kindness and beauty, Lady Ettard. The rumors did not give you enough credit."

Britt had to reach out and grab Sir Pelleas by the shoulder as he lurched towards the twitterpated knights. She pulled him back and slipped in front of him when Lady Ettard glanced in their direction.

The sudden onset of Percival and Gawain's affections made Britt slightly suspicious, as Ettard, though pretty, was not as beautiful as Guinevere. She turned to look at Merlin and Lancelot with dread.

Merlin was entirely unaffected. He was too busy scratching his side and giving the castle a calculating look, probably trying to weigh out Lady Ettard's net worth.

Lancelot's brow was unusually puckered, and his eyes were slightly narrowed, though a clear smile played at his lips. "Your lands are lucky to have such a splendid lady ruling them?" Usually he would've said the statement in an utterly smarmy tone, but instead it came out a question, and he tilted his head like an unsure cocker spaniel.

Ettard, it seemed, did not notice anything unusual about their party's reaction. She smiled serenely and folded her hands in front of her. "May I inquire which knights I am addressing?"

Percival leapt to his feet. "I am Sir Percival, oldest son of King Pellinore of Anglesey."

"My name is Sir Gawain, and I'm the oldest son of King Lot of Orkney." Gawain also stood, but he gave Ettard a bow to decorate his words.

Lancelot's fake smile was back in full force, for he lived for introductions. "I am Sir Lancelot, the best knight of Camelot, the Champion of the Queen, and the son of King Ban across the sea."

Britt rolled her eyes, but she forced a smile when Ettard looked expectantly to her. "I am Sir Galahad. This is Merlin—Chief Counselor of King Arthur himself, and Sir..." She had to put an arm in front of Sir Pelleas to keep him from lunging at Percival and Gawain as she scrambled internally for a fake name. "Sir John. Wayne. John Wayne. He's taken a vow of silence."

She cut herself off to scrabble with Sir Pelleas.

"I hope you find peace during your stay here," Ettard said. "My servants will show you to your quarters, but I assume you will dine with me this evening."

"The honor would be ours," Gawain said with another bow.

Ettard smiled, though Britt noticed her eyes looked tired rather than joyful, and her shoulders heaved a little in a barely imperceptible sigh. "Wonderful. I have long been an admirer of King Arthur and the Knights of Camelot. I will look forward to this evening with great anticipation." She gestured down the hallway, where a female servant waited patiently.

Britt grabbed Sir Pelleas by the arm and hauled him in the servant's direction. It was much harder than she thought, as Sir Pelleas was quite solid and practically a wall of muscle. But with a surly clang, he followed her. Merlin was not far behind them, but Gawain, Percival, and Lancelot could only be persuaded to leave Ettard with much bowing, smiles, and statements of regret.

The servant girl showed them their rooms, but as their bags and supplies had not yet arrived, Britt followed Merlin into his room and gestured for the knights to join them.

As soon as they were safely absconded in the room and the door closed, Sir Pelleas shucked his helmet and tossed it aside. "You blackguards!" He roared. He unsheathed his sword and strode towards Percival and Gawain.

Lancelot moved to intercept him, plucked his sword from his hand, and tossed it aside.

"You swore you would help me secure Ettard's affections. Instead, you stabbed me in the back and admire her with your own designs and intentions," Pelleas said.

"Sir Pelleas, we—" Gawain started.

Pelleas held up a hand to forestall him. "No, you revealed your true intentions in that hall. I will listen to no excuse."

Britt itched to strip her soggy underclothes and spattered armor, but she couldn't risk it with Pelleas in the room. She settled, instead, for sitting in a wooden chair. "Is charming Lady Ettard part of your plan to aid Sir Pelleas, Gawain, Percival, and Lancelot?"

"Lady Ettard is beautiful and good." Though he praised her, Sir Percival did not smile, and instead pushed his damp hair from his eyes.

"Truthfully, I don't know why I am so taken with her," Gawain said. He studied the greaves of his gauntlet with a frown.

Lancelot picturesquely arranged himself by the lit fireplace. "Something is afoot," he said.

Britt unhooked Excalibur from her belt and used what small patch of dry cloth her cloak had left to mop it dry. "What, you were surprised she didn't fall at your feet?"

"Not at all," Lancelot said. "My heart was actually moved when I saw her."

Britt's eyebrows almost leaped all the way up to her hairline. "That is incredibly strange."

"Galahad…" Merlin's voice held a trace of a warning.

"What? Lancelot has the loyalty of a tomcat. If he's moved, Ettard is either one knockout girl, or we've entered the Twilight Zone."

"Twilight zone?" Percival asked.

"Ettard is worthy of all praise," Pelleas insisted, though he shot Percival and Gawain a dark look. "I find it no surprise many should adore her, but I thought your word would hold you to true conduct."

Britt rubbed her nose, the pervasive smell of wet horse still invading the air. "What do you think, Merlin? You didn't seem at all affected."

Merlin shrugged. "I am not going to dally in this romantic affair. My priority is to make contact with my man. You yokels may do as you please."

Britt flicked raindrops from her armor. "I guess we will see more tonight, when we dine with Lady Ettard." She glanced at Gawain and Percival with some worry. "I'll admit, I didn't think the two of you were the type to fall in love at first sight."

"What about me?" Lancelot asked.

"What about you?"

"Do you not believe that I am loyal enough that I would not fall for such a romantic dalliance?" He gave Britt the clear smile that he used whenever he was trying to make her heart flutter.

Unfortunately for him, usually it filled Britt's heart with the desire to deck him. "You are exactly the type of person who would frequently fall in love at first sight," she said caustically.

"No matter the outcome, Sir Pelleas, you have my word that I will do my best to aid you," Sir Gawain said.

Pelleas glared at him with suspicion and folded his arms across his chest. "I'm afraid I don't believe you after witnessing your conduct in the hall. It appears I will have to stay close to

Ettard so as to make certain you do not act unchivalrously towards her."

"Sir Gawain would never!" Percival glared at him, and his fingers twitched for his sword.

"At least Gawain and Percival don't act like love rivals," Merlin said as he leaned against Britt's chair.

"Thank heaven for small miracles," Britt said. "Why is it that whenever we set out on a quest, really weird and bizarro things happen?"

Merlin shrugged. "This is England. Faerie folk and magic rub shoulders with nobles and peasants alike. The land itself is quite unpredictable."

"I guess." Britt was still dissatisfied, but at that moment, there was a shy tap on the door.

Gawain opened the door for a servant bearing Merlin's bags.

Britt straightened in her chair. "Have all of our bags been delivered?"

The servant bowed slightly. "Indeed, they are all in the hall."

Britt bolted. "Excellent! I am most eager to shed this armor before it rusts. Men, I will see you tonight. Don't kill each other while I'm gone."

~

THE FOLLOWING MORNING, Britt sat on a stone bench in the large gardens, gnawing on a loaf of sweetbread for breakfast.

The sun was playing peek-a-boo in the clouds, and the air was fragrant with the smell of growing plant life, but Britt was absolutely enthralled with her bread.

"Do you really find bread to be that tasty?" Merlin asked. He sat on his own bench, papers spread around him as he shuffled through the information his contact had given him.

"The bread of Camelot is so tough, it almost cuts your gums

and cheeks when you eat it," Britt said. "This stuff is light, airy, and has just a hint of sweetness. It's *lovely*."

Merlin slightly shook his head as he flipped a paper over.

She sighed. "This must be because a woman owns the castle. I swear, with all the knights holed up in Camelot, all they want to eat is meat, meat, and more meat. I'm so sick of venison and fowl —especially in stew. I'm almost desperate enough to eat a dandelion salad. But this bread!" Britt held the half of the loaf that remained aloft, as if it were a gift from Heaven.

"I'm glad to see there's something that can tempt your appetite," Merlin muttered.

"Yeah. I'd kill for ice cream or a Big Mac, but this bread is right up there." She took another bite out of it, almost humming when the subtly sweet taste—it had to be honey—hit her tastebuds. She looked out over the gardens and shook her head with affectionate frustration as Lady Ettard—with Percival, Gawain, and Lancelot trailing behind her—strolled a short distance away.

All three men were trying to resist in their own way. Gawain, in fact, was still doing his best to aid Sir Pelleas's cause.

"My Lady, I have heard you have previously entertained Sir Pelleas. He is a great man—though he cannot compare to your good nature." Gawain shook his head, as if trying to clear his words.

"I do know Sir Pelleas." Wrinkles spread across Ettard's forehead.

"He is most skilled in combat, is he not?" Gawain continued to try and press his argument, though he couldn't seem to help blurting out, "though you deserve a champion of the highest quality and caliber."

"Lady Ettard, you are so beautiful and graceful, you must have faerie blood in your veins," Lancelot said. "Tell me, were any of your ancestors enchanters or enchantresses?" Though he asked the question in a honeyed tone, Britt could see the glitter of cunning in his eyes.

Ettard laughed. "You overestimate my charisma, Sir Lancelot. I'm afraid both myself and my ancestors are all perfectly human."

Lancelot lifted his chin. "I see..."

Ahhh, so Lancelot thinks he's under a spell, does he?

"Will you not sing for us, Lady Ettard?" Percival asked. He fought whatever attraction he felt for Ettard by hanging the farthest back, and on more than one occasion, Britt had seen him bite his own knuckle to keep from speaking.

Britt scooted to the end of her bench so she could address Merlin in a quiet voice. "Do you really think this is okay? You don't see a need to intervene?"

Merlin flicked his blue eyes up as the wind ruffled his fine blonde hair. "You are wondering if this is an enchantment, like the one Morgause held over your knights?"

"The thought occurred to me," Britt admitted.

"If it is, it's not anything high-leveled or black." Merlin turned his gaze to appraise the lady and the knights. "No married man fawns over her, and it appears that the majority of her servants, advisors, and guards are also unaffected."

"So it's harmless?"

"Relatively so. Unless one is obsessive, like Sir John Wayne over there." He nodded to where Sir Pelleas skulked in the shadows, his hand resting on his sword.

Britt had no doubt that he was stewing over Lancelot, Gawain, and Percival's actions. She thoughtfully chewed some more on her sweetbread.

"Excuse me."

Britt turned curiously to face the speaker.

A subtly beautiful woman bowed at her. "Am I addressing King Arthur?"

Britt almost choked on her precious bread. "No, no. I'm afraid I'm only Sir Galahad."

"Then you are King Arthur." The woman was fair skinned, with long, shiny black hair that reminded Britt of a river at midnight, and the blue eyes of the clear lake. "I am Ragnelle, handmaiden to the Lady of the Lake. She instructed me to find you and ask for your assistance."

Britt breathed easier with the introduction. The Lady of the Lake, Nymue, was a close friend of Britt's and was also aware of Britt's alias as Sir Galahad. "Oh. That does change things. What's the problem?"

Ragnelle tilted her head. "I believe you will need assistance in fulfilling my Lady's request."

"Not surprised," Britt muttered. She brushed breadcrumbs from her lap and stood. "Sir Gawain!" She called. "You mind coming over here for a moment?"

Gawain bowed to Ettard and joined Britt. "Yes, Sir Galahad?"

"This is Ragnelle. She works for my old pal Nymue. She needs our help. As the Ladies' Knight, I thought you were best suited to lend me a hand." Britt gestured for Ragnelle to continue her story.

Ragnelle nodded serenely to Sir Gawain. "I was instructed to pass along a specific message that outlines the task. What follows are my lady's exact words." Ragnelle took a breath and spoke without any facial expression whatsoever. "Britt—you selfish loafer—I'm calling in one of the favors you owe me. Sources tell me you're currently at the castle belonging to Lady Ettard. This lady has something that belongs to one of my handmaidens—a necklace with a blue-green jewel. My handmaiden set it down on the lakeshore while entertaining Sir Pelleas as he passed through. She promptly forgot about it, and he took it. But rather than return it—*as he should have*—he gave it to Ettard. By the by, if you see Sir Pelleas, warn him to stay away from water."

The message was delivered with Nymue's exact inflection and wording, though Ragnelle was blank-faced as she recited it. "Normally I don't care about little trinkets like necklaces, but this particular piece is faerie marked. It makes any eligible young man fall in love with the lady who wears it. There are some exceptions

—if a man is already in love or is particularly unromantic, it won't work."

Ragnelle continued. "Get that necklace back and hand it off to my handmaiden, or so help me, I will leave the Lancelot Hate Club."

Britt's frown sharpened. "Now she's just playing dirty."

Gawain kept his face suspiciously placid with this reveal, but Merlin heaved his eyes to the heavens. "Behold, even the faeries know how you disdain Lancelot. It's a miracle his father has not sent us a nasty correspondence yet."

Britt ignored Merlin's complaint. "Is that the entire message, Ragnelle?"

"Indeed, it is, Sire." She curtsied with great elegance and glanced almost curiously at Gawain.

"I am relieved to hear there is a reason for my disreputable actions," Gawain said, relaxing his stance.

"It explains why Merlin isn't affected either," Britt added.

"Why?" Merlin stood abruptly, disturbing his papers.

Britt blinked in surprise. "Because you're excessively unromantic," she said slowly.

"Oh. Yes. Of course." Merlin adjusted his blue and silver tunic, then sat down again.

"Lancelot was probably only half affected because everyone knows he's mostly in love with himself." Britt traced Excalibur's hilt as she studied Lady Ettard and her worshippers. "You think she knows?"

"Wouldn't she have to?" Merlin's voice was crusted with open disdain. "I'm sure her sudden popularity made her pause to think, and she always wears the necklace in public."

"True.... Which also means she's unlikely to hand it over if we ask, and if we do ask, that will reveal our hand." Britt smiled when she noticed Ragnelle still standing at her side. "I'm sorry, Ragnelle. Did you need something more?"

"No," the water faerie said. "But I would like to offer my assistance, should you need it."

Gawain blessed her with one of his sweeter smiles. "That is very kind of you, lady, but it is our task to complete."

Ragnelle demurely lowered her eyes.

"If we're going to snatch it, we need to do it soon. Aren't we leaving shortly?" Britt asked.

Merlin shook his head. "I'd like to rely on Lady Ettard's good will for another night while I wait for responses. Moreover, we need to restock our supplies, and the lady seems willing enough to share."

"She's not an ally, is she?" Britt asked. "I don't remember you ever mentioning her."

"She swore allegiance to you when you were first crowned king," Merlin said.

"If we are to remain here another night, I believe our best chance will be this evening, after dinner," Gawain said. "If we can lure her out to the gardens, it will be dark and should be easier."

"That's a good idea." Britt brushed her bangs out of her eyes. "You'll have to be the one to do the luring, I think. She'll find it suspicious if I suddenly act all amorous when I haven't yet."

Gawain bowed slightly.

"Do you think you'll be able to do it? Act against her while still under the influence of the necklace, I mean," Britt said.

"I believe so. Though I find it hard to resist admiring her, my loyalty to you, My Lord, far outweighs mere attraction. I will not let you down."

Britt placed her hand on her shoulder and squeezed. "Thank you, Gawain."

"Sorry to break the touching moment," Merlin said wryly, "but is there anything else you can tell us about the necklace, Ragnelle?"

Ragnelle knitted her hands together as she considered the question. "Only that if a man is already in love with the woman before she puts on the necklace, it causes the love to become obsessive."

"And there would be the explanation for Sir Pelleas-the-stalker. Got it." Britt squared her shoulders and smiled at her companions. "Tonight, we steal!"

BRITT'S LEGS started to burn as she crouched behind a bush and waited for Gawain to lure Lady Ettard outside. A leaf tickled her cheek, and she batted it away.

Britt was almost gleeful that she was the one who got to snatch the necklace. Merlin had to stay out of the grab so he could fish Britt out of the dungeons if they were found out, and Lancelot and Percival were busy keeping Sir Pelleas occupied. (With the knight being as passionate as he was for Lady Ettard, he was likely to strike out when he realized they were taking the necklace he gave her.)

She didn't mind being the one to do the dirty work. She so rarely got to, it was actually a bit of a thrill.

It's a good thing Kay is not along, or he would have a heart attack.

Her calves started to quiver from the strain of doing a continuous squat, so Britt was extremely happy when she saw Gawain, arm-in-arm with Ettard, saunter into the garden.

"Thank you for accompanying me on the stroll, Lady Ettard," Gawain said. "A walk in the gardens is always pleasant, but it is even more pleasurable when I have you as a companion."

Britt felt slightly scandalized at Gawain's smooth words. He was not a player like Lancelot; he was far too sweet for that. But there was no denying he definitely had the makings of a ladies' man. The thought boggled Britt's mind, for when he first came to Camelot, he was still a teenager and had a bit of a parental complex.

She struggled to try and pinpoint exactly how many years ago that had been. By now, Gawain was probably about 20 years old. *Where has the time gone?*

As the pair drew closer to Britt, Lady Ettard gave Gawain a wavering smile that looked a little forced. "I am happy to oblige. What kind of hostess would I be otherwise?"

Ettard's conduct was a bit of a puzzle. Other girls who flung around love spells, like Vivien, usually reveled in the attention they received. But though Ettard received the attention gracefully enough, she also seemed perpetually tired.

Gawain stopped walking directly in front of Britt's bush. "I have a gift for you." He reached into the small pouch fastened to his sword belt and pulled out a simple gold chain decorated with a golden lily pad charm. Ragnelle had lent it to them for this event.

"You are too kind," Ettard said with a gracious smile. "I could not possibly accept. Would not a lady at Camelot be a better recipient?"

"I have gone on many quests and performed many deeds for the ladies of Camelot under the blessing of King Arthur. I proudly wear the title he gave me as the Ladies' Knight. And that is why I insist, you must take this necklace." His words were loaded with more meaning than Ettard knew.

"Very well, I thank you for your kindness."

Gawain held up the necklace and undid the clasp. "May I put it on you?"

"I would be honored." Ettard turned her back to Gawain, revealing her neck to the sputtering torch light in the gardens.

Gawain deftly draped the necklace into place, then worked quickly to undo the clasp of the enchanted necklace. "I beg your pardon!" Gawain exclaimed as the necklace slid from her neck. He deftly twitched it so it fell to the side.

Safely hidden behind her bush, Britt snatched it up and began her hasty retreat.

"My necklace," Ettard said in a tight voice.

"Let me grab a torch, so we may inspect the ground with more clarity," Gawain said before they fell out of Britt's hearing range.

Britt maneuvered around the twiggy skeletons of the last few hedges, then slipped inside the castle keep. Her heart thumped with extra adrenaline, but this was far more fun than skulking through Duke Maleagant's castle, somewhat afraid for her life.

She turned the necklace over in her hands, studying the blue-green jewels with curiosity. "I guess things haven't changed much. In both ancient Britain and modern-day America, everybody's foremost concern is love and battle."

She trotted up the well-lit hallway, picking up her pace when she heard guards leave Lady Ettard's feasting hall behind her. She darted around a corner, losing her sense of adventure when she heard guards approach her hallway from the opposite direction.

Sandwiched between two sets of guards, someone was bound to notice she was carrying the necklace that Lady Ettard perpetually wore.

Britt hastily searched for a hiding spot in her clothes. She had stupidly left her cloak behind—she thought she would catch attention if she insisted on wearing it to dinner. But as her tunic and stuffed doublet lacked pockets, there was a limited number of places she could hide the necklace.

No pockets! That has got to be one of the most simplistic things that I miss. Considering how logical these people are, you'd think they'd see the value of having pockets in your tunics, but no.

As the stomp of the soldiers' footfalls drew closer, Britt, egged on by sheer desperation, slung the necklace around her neck, hooked it so it wouldn't fall, then pulled up the collar of her doublet to hide it.

Breathing easier with the eye-catching jewels out of sight, Britt resumed her walk down the hallway, going so far as to nod at the oncoming guards when they met. She took pains to walk casually all the way back to Merlin's room.

She busted in without any hesitation, almost slamming the door shut. "Merlin, we have got to do something about the lack of pockets in this era." She sat down on one of the wooden chairs with a plop, sagging with relief. "Or purses! Pouches on the belt are great and all, but they kind of drag your tunic down. I should speak to a tailor about designing a purse when we get back to Camelot." She looked around and realized that Ragnelle, who was supposed to pick up the spelled necklace, was not present.

Merlin stood in front of his lit fireplace, holding a small scrap of paper that had probably been delivered by pigeon. Unnervingly, his eyes seemed just as brilliant as the fire as he stared at her, an odd combination of fascination and frustration flickering on his face. "Britt," he said, his voice a little huskier than usual. "You're wearing the necklace, aren't you?"

"Oh yeah." Britt fumbled to take the trinket off. "I was nearly discovered by guards, and I didn't have a pouch—or *pocket*—to hide it in."

"I see." The lightness had returned to Merlin's voice as she removed the necklace and slapped it on the chest at the foot of his bed. She leaned back in her chair and yawned, just as a gentle tap sounded on the door.

Britt reluctantly got to her feet and opened the door for Ragnelle. "I got it. It's over there on the chest." She nodded at the spelled jewelry.

"I thank you for retrieving it." Ragnelle reclaimed it, then glanced from Merlin to Britt. "Where is Sir Gawain?"

Britt tugged on her doublet, hitching it back into the right spot. "He's probably still entertaining Lady Ettard."

Merlin frowned. "Do you hear that?"

"Hear what?" Britt asked.

Merlin held his finger to his lips, and Britt could faintly hear the echo of a roar traveling up the hallway. It grew louder until the door to Merlin's bedroom was slammed open.

"You craven heathens!" Sir Pelleas declared as he stormed into the room. "Are you not Knights of Camelot, bound by the Oath of the Round Table? Yet you steal from ladies?"

Ragnelle, Britt was relieved to see, tucked the necklace up her wide, drooping sleeves before the knight noticed it.

"Calm yourself, Sir Pelleas," Merlin said.

"I will not!" Sir Pelleas said. "I accepted the help of your party because I thought you were honorable, just men. Thus far you have made eyes at my lady, robbed her, and taken advantage of her offer of shelter."

Britt considered arguing, but the furious knight was actually correct. "How did you hear her necklace had been stolen?"

"I was speaking with your treacherous Sir Lancelot and Sir Percival when I heard the guards' shout." Sir Pelleas breathed like a dragon.

Fantastic. That was just her luck. She was wondering how to settle his rampant emotions when an equally angry howl rippled down the hallway.

"Sir Pelleas!"

Merlin's quarters became quite crowded as Lady Ettard stormed in, Lancelot, Gawain, and Percival on her heels.

Interestingly, Lady Ettard showed more ire and rage than she had when Gawain "lost" her necklace. "Have I not tossed you from my halls dozens of times? Why do you play these games?" she hissed.

"They are not games!" Sir Pelleas bowed his head and laid his right hand over his heart. "The heavens as my witness, I swear my eternal love for you."

"Come off it!" Lady Ettard snapped. "I'm not wearing the necklace now. There's no need for you to fawn over me any longer."

Sir Pelleas furrowed his brows. "I beg your pardon?" He shook his head. "That is right! One of you must've stolen the necklace, jealous of the symbol of my affection on the beautiful Lady Ettard." He stabbed his finger at Gawain, Lancelot, and Percival.

Percival smiled and replied evenly, in the kingly aura he had inherited from his father, "Lady Ettard is truly a lovely noblewoman. But I can now say with certainty, Sir Pelleas, that you are the only knight in this room who seeks her favor."

Sir Pelleas frowned. "What? How can you say that after you spent all day mooning over her?" He started to draw his sword, an action Lancelot was only too eager to copy. "Defend yourselves, you disloyal knaves!"

Britt, realizing the argument was swiftly turning from a shouting match to a possible bloodbath, raised her voice. "*Enough*!"

Merlin easily adapted to her plan and gestured at the fire, which roared twice as high and burned bright blue. When everyone fell silent, he released it, and it returned to a happy orange color.

Britt smiled in thanks at the wizard, then turned her attention to the lovers' quarrel. "Sir Pelleas. You found the necklace you gave to Lady Ettard on the shore of a lake, did you not?"

Sir Pelleas nodded. "I did."

"Then you must know that this is the property of one of the handmaidens of the Lady of the Lake, the close friend and personal ally of King Arthur."

A great deal of the rage dropped away from Sir Pelleas's face, and he had the decency to look repentant.

Britt rested her hands on her sword belt. "Yes, we took the necklace—because it was never yours to give away in the first place."

"I regret my actions," he admitted. "But I should be the one to bear the punishment. Please do not take the necklace away from Lady Ettard." His shoulders drooped slightly with this request, but he looked entirely forlorn when Lady Ettard spoke.

"It does not matter. Indeed, I do not want it back," she said.

Even the set of Sir Pelleas's mustache looked mournful. "It

was the only thing I ever gave you that you seemed to genuinely like. I see, now, that even it has your disfavor."

Ettard shook her head. "I realized soon after I began to wear it that it was enchanted. I should have given it back then, but I was afraid..."

Gawain stepped forward. "Afraid, my lady?"

Ettard looked down and stared at her slender hands. "I feared Sir Pelleas's affection for me was only temporary. He is a great knight and deserves more than this small castle and myself. The necklace, I knew, would keep him in love with me.... But it was not the reassurance I sought. Knowing he loved me because of that dratted trinket was worse than the fear that his affections would fade. Desperate to keep his love but wracked with guilt, I threw him from my presence."

Ettard shifted, then met Sir Pelleas's gaze. "I apologize for my poor conduct. You did not deserve the onslaught I made you bear."

"My Lady," Sir Pelleas breathed. He knelt before her and slowly reached out to hold her hands in his. "There is nothing you could do, nothing you could say that would destroy my love for you. You may throw me from your castle—from your presence—a thousand times. But I will still return, and I will eternally love you."

Ettard's eyes filled with tears, and a few dropped down her cheek. She mutely nodded, her lips pressed together with the strength of her emotions.

Britt watched the spectacle, both happy for the outcome and jealous of Lady Ettard. (Who could possibly look that good while crying besides some kind of faerie lady?)

"I believe my mistress will be pleased with the outcome of this situation," Ragnelle said quietly.

"Great," Britt said just as softly. "When you see her, please tell her that at the next Lancelot Hate Club meeting, we're going to be knitting purses."

Ragnelle bowed her head slightly. “I shall do as you wish.”

“You have a rather interesting relationship with the Lady of the Lake…Sir Galahad.” Gawain joined them with a light smile.

“We’re practically soul sisters. She’s just as snarky as I am—your aunt Morgan is our third pea in the pod,” Britt whispered wryly.

“I thank you for your help in this endeavor, Sir Gawain.” Ragnelle curtsied to the young knight.

“It was my honor. I am glad I could be of assistance.” Gawain smiled at the handmaiden, then glanced back at the joyful Sir Pelleas and Lady Ettard, so he missed the pink blush that bloomed in Ragnelle’s cheeks.

Britt schooled her face so she didn’t grin, and she also refrained from ribbing the oblivious knight and his new admirer. “All’s well that ends well, I guess.”

“Indeed!” Lancelot pushed his way into their small circle and draped an arm over Britt’s shoulders. “The triumph of love is always a reason to celebrate. Come! Let us return to the feasting hall and toast this new-found love!”

Britt shrugged his arm off. “I could use a drink after all this excitement.”

“Wonderful! Sir Pelleas, lead the way with your dear lady!”

7
THE CHARACTER OF SIR LANCELOT

A dry branch crackled, and Britt froze. She exchanged looks of worry with Sir Gawain, who was crouched behind a bush not far from her. Carefully, she peered around the trunk of a huge tree and studied their targets.

The Roman soldiers either hadn't heard the crunch, or it didn't bother them, for they were still working in a well-organized formation, setting up their camp. A centurion yelled at one of his men, probably for using wet leaves as kindling for their fire that was making an inordinate amount of smoke and smelled awful. The rest scurried like ants, setting up tents and unloading provisions from carts.

Britt, using a slightly burned stick and a curl of birch bark, tallied the number of soldiers she saw, careful not to double count anyone.

Gawain finished before her, but waited until she gave him the hand signal to indicate she was done. Together they slithered through the underbrush, moving as quietly as possible. (They had shed their armor before setting out for this very reason.)

Though they quickly fell out of hearing range of the camp, Britt dared not utter a word lest they run into any scouts. So she kept her mouth shut even though she burned to talk to Gawain about Ragnelle during this rare moment they had alone.

Several days had passed since they left Lady Ettard's castle. The evening they had managed to bring lady Ettard and Sir Pelleas together, Ragnelle had remained with them for quite a while. (Until the celebration was over, actually.)

It was obvious to Britt that she mostly stuck around because she had a huge crush on Gawain, but the gallant knight either didn't notice it or wasn't interested. Britt suspected it was the former, but she also guessed he would be horrified if she told him her observations.

She breathed out heavily through her nose in a combination of frustration and amusement. *When Merlin had me crowned king, I never thought matchmaker would be part of my role.*

When they had walked so far they could no longer smell awful smoke from the enemy camp, Gawain finally spoke. "I don't know if it is bothersome or encouraging that all the Roman fortifications have similar numbers."

"Probably a bit of both," Britt said. "It means there's definitely a pattern, and I'm certain Merlin will be able to figure it out. But to be honest, I'd much rather have them disorganized and impulsive."

"Aye," Gawain said grimly.

They wound their way around a naturally occurring hedge, popping out where Merlin waited with their horses.

"We got them," Britt said. She and Gawain passed off their estimations. "Just like all the other groups, it seems they're heading north and then east."

"It's a curious thing that we haven't found any traveling east," Merlin said.

"Is it possible they made alliances with kings and rulers in the east?" Gawain asked.

Merlin frowned at their numbers. "Anything is possible, but Britt has some staunch supporters there. I would've thought we'd have heard something from them if they suspected their neighbors of treason."

"Is it possible they mean to split Britain down the center, so the east and west cannot rally together and attack as one?" Britt asked.

Merlin frowned. "That particularly sunny deliberation had not occurred to me. I thought it was more likely they meant to deal with you and Camelot first, as you are the greatest threat to their expansion. But now I have another worry to warm my bed at night."

"Sorry," Britt said.

Merlin shook his head. "Don't be. We should consider all possibilities, no matter how grim they may be. Besides, if that is indeed their plan, we may have already outmaneuvered them by sending Kay and Mordred back to Camelot to inform our allies of their movements." Merlin finished his explanation with the brilliant smile, one that Britt automatically returned.

Though Britt dreaded the thought of a war with the Roman Empire, she had to admit it was a thrill to be back with Merlin. To be able to talk to him without fear, to laugh and joke with him again...it made her realize just how much she missed him back in Camelot.

"We have your numbers!" Lancelot proclaimed as he and Percival approached the group from the opposite end of the clearing. "Because I so desired to get such precise numbers, My Lord, I daringly approached our assigned camp. Indeed, I nearly crawled my way straight to the center. Ask Percival if you do not believe me!"

Britt rolled her eyes. "No, I believe you. Only you would do something that stupid."

"Stupid?" Lancelot crowed. "It was dashing and brave!"

"It was foolhardy," Britt said. "What would you have said if they caught you? 'Excuse me sir, but I'm looking for the Holy Grail. Do you have it hidden in the middle of your camp?'"

Lancelot frowned. "I would never be caught."

"It was perhaps a little dangerous," Percival said in a calm manner. "But as a result, he has far more accurate estimations than I do." Both he and Lancelot handed over their birch bark computations to Merlin.

The wizard nodded in thanks. "Both groups you observed perfectly match the patterns we've seen in the other companies and squadrons. Adding up all the numbers makes them a huge force. I can't believe they have the cheek to prance around in King Ryence's colors and pretend it's a legitimate disguise."

"As far as we know, we are the only ones who have ventured this far south to spy on their movements." Gawain checked over his horse's tack and equipment. "A person in the north—or the south—would have no way of knowing there's a line of soldiers moving south to north in Ryence's colors. It becomes noteworthy only if you've been aware of the movements for a while."

"Sir Gawain speaks the truth," Lancelot said. "Only men of Camelot are smart and cunning enough to pursue such accuracy."

"What is it supposed to even mean?" Britt asked.

"I believe he means to say that Knights of Camelot are more inquisitive—and perhaps a little protective—and as a result would be more likely to be suspicious of random soldiers in King Ryence's colors marching through the country," Percival guessed.

Lancelot smiled brightly. "Exactly!"

Britt patted Percival on the shoulder as she passed by him, moving to untie Roen from the tree branch he was hitched to. Percival smiled shyly, but his brow was slightly furrowed in confusion at the pity in her gesture.

Since leaving Lady Ettard's castle, Percival and Lancelot had been matched frequently for spying duties. It surprised Britt, but Percival seem to get along well enough with Lancelot. (Probably because he had the sweetest temper in all of Camelot besides Sir Tor.)

Roen nuzzled and lipped Britt's cheek as she fussed with his reins. Abruptly, the gelding jerked his head up and swung around, his ears flattened. Branches crackled as something crashed through the underbrush nearby.

Alarmed, Britt unsheathed Excalibur. Gawain, Lancelot, and Percival all grabbed their swords as well.

Britt raised her sword, hoping the crashing was not a wild boar—boars could kill men and horses alike if you weren't careful. Her heart thudded painfully in her chest, and the source of the crashing finally careened into the clearing.

It was a knight, though he appeared half wild and hadn't cared for himself or his mount in days. His armor was dingy and smeared with mud; the horse's hooves were crusted with dry dirt, and the animal's barding was so dirty, the symbol on his rump (a female lioness), was barely visible.

Britt blinked. "Ywain?"

The knight flung his helm off and swung his horse around so he could blearily face her. It was Ywain, but his face was gaunt, his chin bristled with unkempt beard growth, and his hair was greasy. "My Lord…it's over. She won't take me back."

Britt slid Excalibur back into its scabbard and secured Roen to the tree branch again. "Who won't take you back?"

"Laudine." Ywain stared at the ground.

"Your wife?" Gawain asked.

Ywain did not acknowledge his cousin and kept staring.

Merlin eyed the young knight, and Britt could tell he was getting ready to whack Ywain in the head, so she quickly intervened. "Tell us everything, Ywain. It's okay, we will help you."

Britt approached him and placed her hand on top of his. Ywain finally raised his gaze and smiled sadly at Britt.

"It seems to me that—with this new addition to our party—we should probably pitch our camp for the night," Percival said.

"Here is no good," Merlin said. "We're far too close to the Romans for my comfort."

Lancelot flung himself on the back of his dapple gray horse.

"There is a fine little meadow just south of here. It's less than an hour's ride and is downwind of the Romans. They shouldn't see any hint of our activity."

Merlin raised an eyebrow at the fashionable knight. "How do you know of this meadow's existence?"

"I am ever so glad you asked." Lancelot gave Britt his most dazzling smile, his white teeth twinkling. "I discovered it last year! I fought a recreant knight there in honor of My Lord. I sent them to you; he was one of many I defeated to illustrate my regret over angering my dear king."

"I'm sure," Britt said dryly. She squeezed Ywain's hand. "Do you mind a short ride with us?"

Ywain sighed deeply; it was almost a moan tugged from the depths of his soul. "A short or long ride, it matters not. All is lost to me without Laudine's love."

Britt winced and gratefully took Roen when Percival led the gelding up to her. "I'm sure it's not as bad as it seems, Ywain."

He shook his head. "No, it is far worse. And I have only myself to blame."

BRITT WAITED to question Ywain until they reached the meadow and cared for their mounts.

"Sit, Ywain. Explain to me what happened—and I want the whole story." Britt steered Ywain over to the campfire and sat him down on the ground.

She joined him, cleaning the brow band of Roen's bridle to give her hands something to do.

Gawain gently brushed Ywain's horse, grooming the ignored mount and caring for its hooves. Percival scooped up the horse's barding and was attempting to clean it. Even Merlin had the decency to pretend he wasn't listening, and instead puttered around with the notes they had all taken. Only Lancelot was foppish enough to waltz over to the fire and sit down across from Ywain and Britt.

Britt glared at him and scrubbed the brow band harder.

It didn't matter though, for Ywain didn't appear to notice Lancelot's presence. He stared into the campfire, which was not strictly necessary as darkness had not fallen, though the sky was gloomy enough to make it a welcome thing.

"Originally, I set out with those who chased after you once you were kidnapped," Ywain began. "I thought to stop by and see how Laudine was doing, believing I could easily catch up with the rest of the group as they approached Duke Maleagant's lands. I rode into Laudine's castle, my spirits high and eager to see her. But she turned me away." Ywain heaved a rattling death sigh.

"What do you mean when you say she turned you away?" Britt asked.

Ywain rubbed his thumbs over the grooves of his sword's scabbard. "She refused to speak to me, or even see me. She said, through her handmaidens, I was gone too long. And if I so easily forgot her, she did not need me. She said I was to consider myself free, and that she was no longer my lady."

Britt set aside the brow band and began brushing fur from Roen's saddle blanket. "And she barred you from returning?"

Ywain nodded. "I have lost her love, and with it much of the light of my life has gone out."

"She didn't say she stopped loving you." Britt paused and spat when she accidentally got a horse hair stuck to her lips. "She just sent you away."

"But if she will not see me, she must not love me! How else could she do such a cruel thing to me?"

"As she has cast you off, Sir Ywain, I see only one recourse," Lancelot piped up.

Britt suspiciously eyed the knight, certain she wouldn't like whatever came out of his mouth next. "Oh? Please, illuminate us."

"All you must do is find a new lady to serve. There are plenty out there," Lancelot said.

Britt wondered if she could suffocate him with Roen's blanket. "Are women so easily replaceable to you?"

Lancelot shrugged. "I'm aware in our oaths as Knights of the Round Table, we are to love only one lady. But Ywain doesn't have much of a choice, does he? His lady has forsaken him and cast him off without a second thought. He's a free man and should be allowed to find love elsewhere."

Britt was silent, but only because her rage was still building. "He's married. That's not something you can just walk away from and toss aside like a used handkerchief."

"But she has expressed her wishes. Should he not respect them?" Lancelot asked.

"It does not matter. I could never love another as I love Laudine," Ywain said. "Though she has hardened her heart against me, I will always love her."

Some of the tension in Britt's shoulders eased. She'd spent significant time in Camelot trying to drive respect for females into her knights. She had to remember that Playboy Lancelot, or the Debaucher as the Lady of the Lake called him, did not reflect the honor and chivalry the rest of her knights exhibited.

Ywain struggled to rise like a feverish man. "Indeed, I still love her deeply, as I always have! I never stopped thinking of her, never stopped believing her to be the joy of my heart. Yet she doubts my affection.... I must not have shown it well enough, or perhaps I did not do enough to earn her love."

Britt grabbed him by the shoulder and forced him to sit back down. "Hold up, hold up. Do you mean to tell me you really don't know why she's angry with you?"

Ywain met her gaze with lost eyes and a hopeless expression. "My Lord, I don't know what to make of the situation at all except to understand that the woman I love wishes to never see me again."

His expression and words grabbed Britt by the heart. Ywain was a more dramatic and emotion-driven knight. Because of that, she had, in the privacy of her heart, questioned the intelligence of his sudden marriage to Lady Laudine.

To be honest, she didn't know if his affection for the lady would hold out. But seeing the love in his eyes, she felt ashamed. He was one of her most loyal and faithful vassals. Surely, if he said he loved Laudine, he meant it from the deepest part of his heart.

Britt had been sad to see him leave Camelot for Lady Laudine's lands, particularly because she did not exactly like Laudine. (Laudine was perhaps a little older than Britt, was a bit of a bossy boots, and was possessive of Ywain—though she was gracious and kind.) But, for Ywain's sake, she would put her feelings for Laudine aside.

"Here's the thing, Ywain. I guarantee she's ticked at you for spending all winter in Camelot," Britt said.

Ywain tilted his head. "But why? The magical fountain that causes turbulent weather is mostly frozen during the winter. It can cause no harm and poses no threat to Laudine's lands. The fountain was always her greatest concern whenever I mentioned my desire to see the walls of Camelot again."

"I'm sure she was happy to send you off for a short visit to Camelot," Britt started. *That's not very likely based on the little conversation I had with her when we met, but I'm not here to start fights.* "But you were gone for most of the season. That's many weeks, including Christmas and New Year's."

Ywain nodded. "Yes, and...?"

Britt stared at him. "You don't see a problem with that?"

"No, of course not. I would leave your halls for weeks at a time as well, My Lord."

"Yeah, except I'm not your wife," Britt pointed out.

Ywain tucked his head. "No, you certainly aren't."

Britt set Roen's blanket aside. "And you still don't see the connection. Very well, let me think....I got it! So in the spring, summer, and fall, you're stuck guarding the spring—and yes, it is a spring, not a fountain—right?"

Ywain nodded.

"Okay, so while you're stuck guarding that spring, let's say Laudine decides to visit Camelot. You'd be fine with that, yes?"

"It would bring me great joy to have Laudine come visit you in Camelot," Ywain said.

"Right. Turns out Laudine and I have so much fun together that she stays with me for all of summer, and even part of fall, and never sends any news back to you. What would you think of that?"

"I would miss her very much. And I would begin to worry that you have lured her into that female companionship club you have with Morgan le Fay and the Lady of the Lake."

Britt, caught off guard by his astute observation about the Lancelot Hate Club, coughed to cover her surprise. "Yes, well... that's pretty much what you've done to her. You're her husband, not a knight who only serves her and performs great deeds in her name. Above all else, she treasures your presence—not the quest you do for her, not whatever treasures you win for her, but you as a person."

"You mean to say the relationship I have with Laudine as my wife is different than, say, the relationship between a knight and the lady he chooses to honor."

"Yes." Britt was more than a little horrified that he had ever thought it would be the same thing. *Poor boy has no clue how females think. Maybe I should begin holding workshops for the rest of the knights.*

Instead of rallying, as Britt thought he would, Ywain seemed to collapse in on himself. "Then it really is my fault. I have hurt Laudine so deeply that she cannot possibly forgive me. I have ignored her for weeks. How unforgivable of me!"

Gawain had finished cleaning up Ywain's horse, so he

approached his fellow knight and placed a hand on his shoulder. "You cannot lose hope, cousin. For your actions to hurt her, she must still love you just as you love her."

Ywain rested his forehead in his hands. "Laudine is a lady of justice and respect. She would not have turned me away if she did not mean her words. Indeed, I am not worthy of her."

"That is a dangerous way of thinking, my friend." Sir Percival joined the knights by the fire. "One you must not follow. My mother commonly exiles my father from our lands, but they still love each other, and she will always be his ladylove. Perhaps you only need to give her time to think."

"But I have hurt the woman I love! How can I be a knight? How can I claim to want to serve her when I have so grievously wounded her?"

Britt looked around for Merlin, hoping he might have some wizardly wisdom to add. Based on the way he rolled his eyes and the slight curl of his upper lip, he was actually finding more sympathy with Laudine than Ywain's dramatic display.

"Take heart," Lancelot coached.

Ywain put his desperation aside long enough to slightly narrow his eyes at Lancelot. "I will not seek out a new ladylove."

Lancelot waved the comment away. "I figured as much—you are a man after our king's heart, after all. What I meant to say is you won her once, surely you can win her again!"

Surprised he actually had something of worth to say, Britt blinked at Lancelot.

But it didn't matter, Sir Ywain did not take the encouragement well. "I suppose though she does not wish to see me, I could still roam her lands and fight recreant knights on her behalf. I would wear black armor, like the blackness of my soul in the withered spring of love in my heart. I could be like death, for that is all that it is left for me now that Laudine has scorned me."

Merlin wriggled his fingers at Britt, motioning for her to join him.

Britt cast another glance at Ywain, then stood, cracked her back, and ambled towards the wizard. "Yeah?"

"I'd suggest you do something to make him stop his absurdity," Merlin said.

"He's genuinely hurt and concerned."

"He's only making himself more miserable. You and I both know this is a silly argument between a married couple, not something that is going to 'turn his soul black.'"

"What do you want me to do?"

"I, personally, would favor hitting him upside the head. But as I recall, you used words to coax him out of his foul temper when you first met him. Since then, you've used a combination of lectures and appeals to his knightly nature."

"But you hit it exactly. This is an argument between him and Laudine. I don't want to get involved."

"The only reason you don't want to get involved is because you don't like Laudine all that much to begin with. If Ywain was making calf eyes over one of your friends, say, Morgan le Fay, you would be all over this argument like a rooster on bugs."

Britt frowned, but he was right. The identity of Ywain's wife was making her a little reluctant.

"Though you aren't married, you know as well as I do that he is perfectly capable of winning back his wife. Tell him so."

Concerned, Britt glanced back at the down-spirited knight. "Are you sure you just don't want me to do this because you're sick of hearing him in his despair?"

"Of course I am! But that doesn't change the fact that you also owe him. He is your knight, and you are his king and friend. I can't believe you truly *want* him to continue on in this manner."

Britt drew her shoulders back. "You're right. I'll see what I can do."

Merlin reached out and brushed her hand, almost making her leap in surprise. "May the heavens be with you—or they'll certainly soon be with the young Ywain, for I don't care to hear him carrying-on for the remainder of our mission."

Britt snorted. For all of Merlin's bluster, she knew he did genuinely care about her men, so she strolled back to Ywain with a spring in her step. She stood between him and the fire and listened as Gawain, Percival, and Lancelot continued to do their best to cheer him up.

"Couldn't you give her gifts?" Lancelot asked.

"Or proof of quests and adventures you've undertaken in her name?" Percival added.

Ywain shook his head. "The only thing I wish to give her is my heart, but she has already rejected it. I'm sure she feels she can never trust me again."

"Ywain, that's enough," Britt said.

Ywain blinked and looked up at her. "You wish for me to deny my grief?"

"No, not at all. Expressing and showing your emotions is healthy. In fact, I'm proud of you that you are able to so clearly state what is in your heart. The problem is this: you figured out the problem, but rather than fixing it, you intend to sit here and stew."

Ywain stood, a hint of anger in his expression. "What else would you have me do? What else is there?"

"Haven't you been listening to anything your fellow knights have told you? Go out there and win her back! She is your wife, and you are her husband. I can't *believe* you are so easily giving up on her! Try talking to her, and ask for forgiveness. That's one of the most important parts—*apologize* for staying in Camelot so long without giving a thought to how she feels!"

Britt could see he was thinking over her words, but he wasn't committed quite yet. "Ywain," she said in the much softer voice.

He raised his eyes so he could meet her gaze.

"Isn't she worth the fight?" She asked in a gentle tone.

"She's worth more than I could ever offer her."

Britt smiled. "Then show her that."

The light started to return to his eyes, and he nodded, then bowed. "Thank you, My Lord. My friends." He looked at everyone present in the camp. "I will do as you have suggested. I will win her back! I must set out first thing to begin this new quest!"

Gawain held up his hand to forestall his cousin. "Before then, you owe your horse a rest. Stay with us tonight. Drink, eat, and ready yourself for the battle you are about to enter."

Ywain nodded, but his movements were quick and brimmed with excitement. "Thank you all for your help and support."

"I will always be here for you, Ywain. You are a companion of the Round Table and a companion of my heart," Britt said. "I want you to be happy. That's all I'll ever want for your sake."

Ywain looked like he had a hard time swallowing, and his eyes glittered with emotion. "And I will always wish the same for you, My Lo—Britt."

~

BRITT DASHED FORWARD in a series of lunges and twists, fighting an invisible foe. Her unusual night activities didn't seem to bother the forest life, for the chubby birds that were resting for the night did not startle from their tree as she danced past them.

Several days had passed since the party had parted ways with Ywain. Just a few more days of travel, and Merlin would have them turn around and take a more direct route back to Camelot. Hopefully, Kay and Mordred would've gotten enough messages out to the allies that they were beginning to move towards Camelot as well. In any case, by the time they returned, Duke Maleagant and King Bagdemagus would probably be waiting for them.

Britt paced back and forth, flexing her muscles as she prepped for another round of swordplay exercises. She glanced at the crackling fire, making sure she hadn't woken any of the other knights. Lancelot, Percival, and Gawain were all rolled up in their bedrolls, tucked around the fire. They had made their camp at the back of a rather large rock formation, which provided shelter from the wind that blew across the sweeping plains and up the squat hills.

Merlin was the only one who slept slightly apart. He dozed, propped up against a tree. The horses were tethered just beyond him, secured in a little copse of trees.

Britt glanced longingly at her bedroll, but although they were traveling and spying, her insomnia still plagued her. Instead, she paused to adjust her grip on Excalibur and fix her stance, then raised her sword again.

She spun, swinging her sword with perfect precision. She heard a rustle by the fire but ignored it and instead continued practicing. Only when she was hot and sweaty in spite of the chilly night did she pause and take great heaving gulps of air.

"I'm beginning to understand why you are unmatched at the sword," Lancelot said.

Britt had been almost certain the rustler was Gawain, so she glanced at the handsome knight with some surprise. She was quiet for a moment, but the silence quickly grew awkward. So she shrugged. "I do practice more with it than the average knight."

Lancelot's smile was unusually wry. "That you do." He watched her as she drew her shoulders back and stepped into an offensive stance.

She half expected him to ask to join her, so she was more surprised when he folded his arms across his chest and leaned against one of the trees. Only half his face was visible in the flickering firelight of the campfire. The other half was cloaked in shadows. "My Lord," he began, "I find myself much desiring a heartfelt talk with you."

Britt doubted Lancelot could be "heartfelt" about anything. "What do you want to talk about?"

"I wish to know why I have never heard you call me the companion of your heart, or swear so solemnly that you wish for my happiness, as you did to Ywain."

She stabbed Excalibur forward with extra feeling. "Give it a rest, Lancelot."

"I'd rather not. I am seriously seeking answers," he insisted.

"Maybe, but examining the different levels of affection I have for my knights is only going to end in disaster. Being a Knight of the Round Table is not a popularity contest for whom I love most. You never would've thought something so *stupid* before you found out I was a woman, and though my gender might have been different than what you thought, the way I organize my knights has not changed at all. So put a sock in it."

Feeling jaunty, Britt tossed Excalibur in the air, then caught it by its hilt and twirled it with great satisfaction.

"But I genuinely do not understand why you keep me at arm's distance," Lancelot said. "I am the best knight in Camelot; I am *your* champion."

"You're the *Queen's* Champion. In case you've forgotten, I still go by *King* Arthur; that means you're not my personal champion. But even if you were, it wouldn't matter." Britt grunted as she whirled Excalibur in a complex pattern of parries and blows. She paused to regain her breath. "I pick my friends based on their character, not their abilities."

"That makes your refusal of my friendship even more puzzling," Lancelot argued. His expression appeared to be open and honest, but Britt was certain he was putting on an act for her benefit. "For I am one of the most virtuous knights of Camelot. I complete my quests with great swiftness, and I have sent the most recreant knights back to Camelot to swear their loyalty to you."

Britt shook her head. "Beating men reveals nothing about

your character. You might say you're virtuous, but in reality, there is a disconnect between your words and your actions."

Lancelot sputtered. "I beg your pardon!"

Merlin fidgeted by his bush.

Britt glanced at him, worried they had awoken him, but though the wizard shifted, he did not open his eyes.

Britt slid Excalibur back into its scabbard. "You say exactly what everyone wants to hear, giving every appearance of being a great knight, but your actions betray you. If you are as virtuous as you claim, you would not have told Ywain to abandon Laudine."

Lancelot narrowed his eyes. "You don't even like Laudine."

"It doesn't matter whether or not I like her. Ywain is a Knight of Camelot and should act with honor and loyalty. Dropping his wife because she simply expressed her pain and frustration is not the way a virtuous knight behaves. The fact that you advised that does not reflect very well on you."

"You are my king, but what care do you have for the movement of my heart?" Lancelot asked.

"You're right; I don't care whom you love. What I care about is that you are loyal to the woman you choose to love." Britt couldn't keep some of the pent-up frustration and anger out of her voice. She stomped over to Roen and draped an arm across his neck to calm herself. "After all, if you can't even stay loyal to the woman you profess to hang your heart on, how on earth can I expect you to stay loyal to the causes we fight for?"

Lancelot's expression was no longer open and free, but hardened even in the flickering firelight. "Very well, but that is just one example."

Roen sleepily nuzzled Britt's torso as she continued. "You want to hear more? Fine. Then there's the fact that you won't help anyone unless you personally gain from it. You move if it's for a quest or something that will bring honor to your name. But a simple task—like caring for a fellow knight's horse when he is unable to, or helping a servant girl who has more than she can carry—you would never do."

Lancelot clenched his jaw. "I am a prince."

"And I am king, but I know that the role of a king—the role of any leader—is to serve those who follow them. That's something that Gawain, Ywain, Percival, Kay, and Mordred all understand. That's why I call them the companions of my heart. And until you drop your pompous fixation with yourself so I can truly depend upon you, you and I will *never* be friends." Britt nearly spat the last few sentences, which she had been holding in her heart for a long time.

When she first met Lancelot, she hated him because of what the legends said about him. As time went on he became annoying in his own right. But over the last few seasons Britt had come to befriend Guinevere, whom previously she had disliked nearly as much as him. It was then that Britt realized that Guinevere had proven her worth; Lancelot, on the other hand, had proven to be quite like his legendary self.

She had no doubt that Lancelot was ruthless enough to seduce his best friend's wife. And that was something she would never tolerate.

The venting had done her some good, but it had only served to incense Lancelot, as she thought it would. *But he was the one who insisted we talk about this! Seriously, why is it that the only male who frequently talks about feelings is the one I can't stand?*

Lancelot clenched the hilt of his sword. "Very well. I now see the imaginative picture of me you have painted in your mind. But I hope you will allow me to point out the hypocrisy of your words."

Britt frowned. "What?"

Lancelot stabbed a finger in Merlin's direction. "The man you so clearly love is just as ruthless and cunning as I. You talk about serving those beneath you? When has he ever done that? Merlin is perfectly willing to sacrifice anyone to see his goals accomplished."

Britt's mind screamed. *How did he know?* No one besides Merlin himself—and his mentor, Blaise—knew of her affection for him. Not one knight had picked up on it before! Caught off guard, she blurted out, "That's not true!"

"Isn't it? Do you deny that he has made you go against your own will and befriend those you would rather cast out? The fact that he used you, a woman who was clearly not from Britain, to be king only proves my point. He will disrupt anyone's life if he sees a gain in it!"

There was a sliver of truth to Lancelot's tirade, which is what made it particularly dangerous. Though Merlin had told Britt he was sorry he brought her back to medieval Britain, she knew he would do it again.

"He may be cunning, as you are," Britt acknowledged, "but his heart is as far away from yours as day is from night. He does not put airs on himself, nor does he scheme in order to further his name. If he has any fault in his motivation, it is that he sees too much of the big picture and is too concerned with the well-being of Britain that the lives of those in front of him occasionally are overlooked."

Lancelot's chin rose. "You make excuses for him only because you love him."

Britt clenched her hands into fists. "It's not an excuse, but a fact. When you come to love someone enough that you would willingly lay down your life for them at no personal gain, then you will understand why I love Merlin."

He shook his head. "I've heard enough. You are either a hypocrite, or daft. You hold it against me that I am not one of your mindless do-good followers, but at least I see the world as it truly is!" Lancelot stomped back to the campfire, where he snatched up his pack and belongings. "I may not aid everyone under the sun, but at least I do not *judge* them with your stiff-necked condescension!"

Britt watched worriedly as he tacked up his horse and secured his bags on its back. He mounted the dapple gray and turned it savagely in a tight circle. "One day you will look back and regret this night," he vowed.

Britt pressed her lips together as she gazed up at him. "I doubt it."

Lancelot glared at her, then kicked his horse. Regardless that it was the middle of the night, he rode off, quickly disappearing into the darkness though his horse's hoof beats did not fall out of hearing range for some time.

Britt drooped and rubbed her eyes. "That could've gone better." She turned, and her heart dropped into her toes when Merlin's blue eyes met her gaze.

"I don't believe it could have been a smoother conversation, even if you had been prepared for it." Merlin shrugged off his blankets and stood with a groan. Absentmindedly, he patted his horse on the neck.

Britt scuffed her boot in the grass. "Are you going to yell at me?"

"Why would I?"

"Because I just ticked Lancelot off, and he is the son of one of our important allies?"

Merlin released a bark of laughter. "With Rome storming Britain, King Ban and King Bors will come regardless of how you treat their children. Too much rides on our battle against Rome for them to stay out of it. And I'm certain that by the time the war is over, Lancelot will be back in Camelot."

"Yeah, he has too many admirers there." Britt pinched the bridge of her nose. She could feel a blush building on her cheeks. Merlin had heard the majority of their conversation, or at least he seemed to have. If that was so, he certainly also heard her defense of him, and Lancelot's accusation that she was in love with Merlin.

She and Merlin were on uneasy ground. Since the start of this mission, they had returned to their straightforward friendship, but there were still some rather perplexing depths to their relationship. First and foremost was the fact that Merlin knew Britt loved him, and that he had thoroughly kissed her before pretending to fall for Vivien's spell.

Still, if he wasn't going to broach the topic, she certainly wasn't going to! "I wish I had guarded my temper better," she said, anxious to fill the silence.

Merlin shrugged. "I saw confrontation building between you two for some time now. Truth be told, it is probably just as well that Lancelot realizes how clearly you see him. He's a good knight, but if you angered him at the wrong time, he would become an equally great liability."

"So you agree with my estimation of him, then." Britt smiled widely. Her dislike of Lancelot in the beginning of her reign had been a point of contention between her and Merlin.

Merlin scratched his neck. "I wasn't too worried until he discovered that you were female. His actions grew—what was that word you use—'shadier' after that." He ambled up to Britt and lifted her chin with his fingers so she met his gaze. "Try not to worry about it. It's more important that we finish scouting and return to Camelot. Ireland and Scotland are far bigger concerns than Lancelot at this moment."

Britt wanted to nod, but the enamored part of her brain loathed the idea of taking her chin from Merlin's grasp.

They stared at each other for several long moments. Merlin furrowed his blonde eyebrows. "Britt…"

Back at the campfire, Percival stirred. He sat up and sleepily looked around. "Where's Lancelot?"

Britt leaped back from Merlin. "We had a talk. He left."

Percival blinked blearily. "I beg your pardon?"

Britt joined him at the fire and thumped him on the shoulder, her heart still beating erratically. "I'll explain in the morning. Go back to bed."

Percival nodded and was asleep before he finished lying down.

Britt turned back to Merlin, but the wizard was already rearranged in his blankets, his eyes closed.

Britt rubbed the back of her neck, unsheathed Excalibur, and strode back to her practice area. Knowing she had no chance of finding sleep now, she threw herself into practice, unaware that Merlin's eyes followed the striking picture she made as she whirled Excalibur around her.

~

LANCELOT'S HORSE tossed its head, jingling its bridle when he angrily snapped the reins. The horse snorted and pranced a few steps, then calmed as they continued down the forest path.

Lancelot, however, was not so easily pacified.

How dare she!

Lancelot knew Britt held him in distain, but he suspected it was because she disapproved of his popularity with the females. When he pressured her to admit it, he never imagined the wrath she would pour out on him.

"I am not dishonorable!" Lancelot ground his teeth together. "She's just self-righteous and overly emotional. I do countless good for Camelot, for her!"

He ducked a branch that boasted buds in the first sign of spring foliage. He was so furious, he rode without thinking. He didn't care where he was going, nor did he care what happened to *King Arthur* and the party of spies.

"She wants all of her knights to act out of goodness and kindness only? What an unrealistic, daydreaming fool she is."

He knew from the anger burning in his gut that he was mad

not because she insulted him, but because she was right...and she was one of the few people he actually wanted to befriend. Instead, she had thrown his faults in his face, all too clearly able to see through his smiles and falsified good cheer. She had completely and utterly rejected him, and that was even more intolerable than being ignored.

Rage boiled in Lancelot's veins. "She doesn't think I'm good enough, does she? *Fine.* It is time I show her exactly what I'm capable of. But how should I tackle that self-righteousness of hers?"

Angry as he was, Lancelot still knew she was a good ruler. Her presence had brought more peace to Britain in the last few years than it had experienced in decades. He had no desire to see that change, for he enjoyed his recreational life as a knight. Even he wouldn't risk peace and prosperity for a bit of revenge. Camelot would have to be left alone. But after the insults she had laid on him? Britt Arthurs—the woman, not the king—needed to be brought to her knees.

But how...

Lancelot absentmindedly turned his gelding down a fork in the road. He paused, then turned around in the saddle to glance back at the fork, cursing colorfully when he realized he had automatically begun the journey back to Camelot—the dedicated territory of the person he most wanted to hurt at the moment.

But where else could he go? Camelot, for better or worse, was his home. He enjoyed his reputation, the adoration, and the respect. He wouldn't leave it just because of *her*.

Which brought him back to the topic of revenge. How could he teach her the lesson she so badly needed?

"I say, Sir Lancelot! Fancy meeting you here!" Lady Vivien, riding a dainty chestnut mare, simpered as she approached Lancelot from the opposite direction.

Lancelot cleared his stormy expression, easily sliding on a

brilliant smile. "Lady Vivien! You are as beautiful as ever. But why are you so far from the safety of Camelot?"

"I fear Camelot has lost much of its charm with its brave knights, king, and chief advisor gone. With the company in such dire straits, I had no choice but to search for you all myself!" Vivien smiled beautifully, but Lancelot was not deceived.

The pretty girl was undoubtedly a Roman spy. He knew when she first arrived at court and assumed Merlin knew as well. (He must've, based on the way he threw himself between Vivien and Britt.) Undoubtedly, she was chasing after them because she was worried the obvious love spells she'd placed on Merlin were no longer working, or because she wished to sniff out new information to pass on to her superiors.

Though Lancelot still raged at Britt, traitor he was not. "King Arthur and his brave knights, as well as clever Merlin, still ride south. They are seeking after the Holy Grail, which our king saw in a vision. I was spoken to by God himself, and I felt moved to return to Camelot as my part of the quest has been completed."

"The Holy Grail? I see.... That is indeed a quest worthy of undertaking." Vivien gathered up her reins with a smile. "I would wish you safe travels, but I believe it is unnecessary, for you are a knight with unmatched strength."

Lancelot bowed his head. "You are too kind, Lady Vivien."

"Not at all!" Vivien said with a laugh she probably meant to be charming, but it sounded more like a screeching bird. "Though I would dearly love to tarry with you, I feel I must move on. I do miss Merlin so, and I am fearfully worried for brave Arthur. What would happen to Britain, should he be injured?"

What a twit. It is beyond me how anyone can mistake her as a mere girl. She reminds me of a spider that eats her own kind. "I would not worry excessively after the king. He is greatly skilled at the sword." *Not to mention she has a magic scabbard.*

Lancelot paused and considered the thought. *Britt Arthurs has a magic scabbard.... Yes, I know exactly how our dear little king can be brought down the step or two she deserves.*

Vivien did not notice his thoughtful expression. "Yes, it is quite silly of me, for Merlin is also powerful and can surely keep the entire party safe—though there are magic users about who seem stronger than him." She smiled smugly. "But my affection for him, and my admiration for the king, makes me do silly things. If you'll excuse me, Sir Lancelot."

"It speaks highly of your character, Lady Vivien. Though before you go, please allow me to assure you—dear King Arthur is not in any danger," Lancelot said with a smile—one that held a hint of malice.

Vivien pushed her eyebrows up her forehead. "Oh?"

"Indeed," Lancelot said to the Roman spy. "You see, the scabbard of Excalibur keeps him from bleeding..."

8
POOR LOVE AFFAIRS

Britt and the party rode south for only one more day after her argument with Lancelot before Merlin declared it was high time they return to Camelot.

"Are you really sure we should stop our survey?" Britt asked Merlin. They rode side-by-side as Gawain and Percival led the way, comparing jousting techniques.

"Yes," Merlin said. "To begin with, we have enough information to make basic inferences that will greatly affect our planning —such as the likely scale of the conflict. But, most importantly, our priority is making certain *you* make a swift return. Our allies will begin pouring into Camelot if Kay has done his job right. You must be there so the plans can commence."

"Doesn't that mean it's just as important to have you there as well?" Britt asked. "You are the tactician, after all."

Merlin shrugged—which was more of a heaving motion as he was still bundled up in a wool cloak. "If I miss a meeting or two, it will be no great matter."

Shocked, Britt turned and gaped at the usually meddlesome wizard. "*What* did you say?"

"You are perfectly capable of conducting a meeting between

dignitaries—you've had plenty of practice thanks to the Round Table."

"But you trust *me* to run the show? Alone?"

"With Sir Bodwain, Sir Ulfius, and Sir Ector at your side, yes," Merlin said. "You've proven yourself to be a great leader, Britt. I'm certain you'll be fine."

Still in shock, Britt stared at Roen's mane. "I don't know what to say…though I wonder what I could bring up that you usually forbid me from mentioning. Perhaps I could tell King Ban what a prat his son is."

Merlin narrowed his eyes at her. "Let it be added that if you abuse my confidence in you, I will place Sir Lancelot in the squad of knights that will serve as your guard during the battles to come."

She winced. "That's playing dirty!"

"It would be exactly as you deserve," Merlin said.

Britt chuckled. They rode in companionable silence for a few moments before she ventured, "Do you think he'll willingly ride with me?"

Merlin glanced at her. "Lancelot is many things, but close to his bones is a desire for recognition. There's no better place to make a name for himself than at Camelot, and no better way to further his reputation than by serving as your best knight. It might take him some time to cool off, but I'm certain he'll show up before we ride against Rome."

"Arthur?" Gawain called.

Britt shifted her attention to her supposed nephew, surprised by the use of her alias. "Yes?"

"A lady approaches." Gawain gestured to a woman mounted on a horse, lingering at the edge of the forest towards which they rode. "I believe it may be Lady Vivien."

The news was a slug to Britt's gut. She glanced at Merlin, who furrowed his eyebrows as worry lines spread across his forehead. He covered his eyes and squinted. "Yes. It is her." Immediately, but with great casualness, Merlin directed his horse away from Britt and Roen.

"Merlin! Your Highness! Greetings!" Vivien waved and giggled loudly when Merlin nudged his horse into a canter.

Britt watched their reunion with a forced expression of indifference. "Perfect," she sighed. "Just perfect."

"Lady Vivien!" Merlin said in a delighted tone. "You are as lovely as a vision. How I have missed you!"

"And I, you. I simply couldn't bear to be parted from you any longer," Vivien lied. (She probably figured out they were up to something and rode after them in hopes of uncovering more info to feed her Roman contacts.)

"While I rejoice in your affection, I must say it grieves my heart that you rode this far without an escort," Merlin said.

Vivien flapped a hand. "There's nothing in this area that could harm *me*." She looked past Merlin and waved to Britt, Percival, and Gawain. "I heard from Sir Lancelot that you were searching for the Holy Grail. Did you find it?"

Alarmed, Britt exchanged glances with Gawain. "When did you meet Lancelot?"

"Yesterday. It was he who told me you were traveling south, though it appears you began the journey back to Camelot?" Vivien asked.

Roen, catching on to Britt's unease, snorted. Britt patted his neck and pulled him to a stop when they joined Merlin and Vivien. "Indeed."

"And the Holy Grail?" Vivien persisted.

Britt was torn between worry that Lancelot had said something to Vivien and trying to come up with a believable excuse.

She was relieved when Percival smoothly stepped in. "We could not claim it. I don't believe any mortal man could claim it, for it is a holy relic, but we did see it rise back up to heaven in a vision. It was a glorious thing, and perhaps the most important quest I have departed on since I became a knight." Percival gazed so piously up at the heavens, for a second Britt almost looked up as well—he was that believable.

"To even see the Holy Grail, to witness the splendor and glory, is a great thing," Merlin said. "I believe we can consider the quest of the Holy Grail finished."

"It was an inspiring thing," Britt agreed. "But, I am eager to make haste towards Camelot."

Vivien tilted her head and widened her eyes. "Why?"

Britt internally reamed herself out.

"Because I…miss Guinevere. Yes, I much desire to see her!" Britt held a hand over her heart for impact.

Vivien smiled, though clearly it was only skin deep. "How admirable it is to see two people so deeply in love. But perhaps you are not that deeply in love, for she is not your queen."

Gawain frowned. "King Arthur is an honorable man, and before Guinevere joined him in Camelot, he made a vow that he would not marry until he became King over all of Britain. He will see that promise through, and then the entire country will rejoice with him."

Britt certainly hoped that would not be the case, but she was impressed that Gawain had remembered her excuse/promise to buy herself some time so no one would begin demanding she marry and produce an heir. "Your faithful memory is both impressive and touching, nephew," Britt said. "But, I would like to continue on our journey. You will join us, Lady Vivien?"

Vivien smiled widely at Merlin. "Of course!"

"As if I would allow you from my sight after we've been parted for so long," Merlin said. (Britt was at least slightly mollified to hear the obviously forced affection in his voice. Vivien had to be incredibly self-confident to believe it was her spell that made Merlin act so. That, or she had no notion of sarcasm.)

Wordlessly, Britt nudged Roen forward, into the shadows of the forest. The rest of the party followed her, moving around as they tried to find a new organizational pattern that would fit their unwanted guest.

Merlin moved to ride at the front, and Vivien of course trailed after him. As they passed Britt, Britt noticed Vivien's gaze lingering on Excalibur. It struck her as slightly odd. Though it was known that Excalibur was a magical sword given to her by Nymue, no one seemed to show much appreciation for it besides herself.

Uneasily, she remembered Vivien's encounter with Lancelot. "Lady Vivien, you mentioned meeting my best knight, Sir Lancelot. Tell me, how has he been since leaving our company?" She nodded to Gawain as he joined her, riding side-by-side with her as Percival took up the rear.

"He seemed well enough!" Lady Vivien said. "As handsome as always."

"I hope you did not find him *too* handsome," Merlin said.

Vivien giggled. "You jealous thing!"

"And how are his spirits?" Gawain asked.

"Fine, I assume. I only saw him briefly, for he seemed intent on riding forward when I so desired to find Merlin." Vivien paused to smile at Merlin. "He mentioned your search for the Holy Grail, but said little else besides that."

Britt bit the inside of her cheek. Had Lancelot held his peace because he did not know Vivien was a spy? Or had his temper already cooled?

Either way, she did not relish the idea of their inevitable reunion. But for now, she had greater things to busy herself with, like Rome.

~

After a few days of riding—and putting up with the sight of Vivien and Merlin—they reached the Forest of Arroy.

"We're in the home stretch now." Britt covered a yawn with

her hand. "Do you think we'll reach Camelot in another day?" she asked her companions.

"Two is more probable, I should think," Percival said. As twilight settled in the woods, it softened his features. "The forest is impressively large—and that's only if we aren't led around by faerie folk."

"Not a chance," Britt said. "I've never been bothered by—"

"King Arthur. I challenge you!"

Britt almost cracked her neck, she swung around so quickly.

Standing in the middle of the road that meandered through the forest of Arroy was a knight. He held a huge war axe, his armor was an artful combination of black and silver, and the longer Britt looked at him, the more she was positive that he was not human. (The biggest hint were the little sparks of light that hovered around him like fireflies.)

The strangled gasp Merlin gave affirmed Britt's guess.

"I'm afraid you're mistaken, Sir Knight," Britt was quick to say. "King Arthur does not ride with us. We are but his humble servants."

The knight levied the axe in Britt's direction. "You are no mere knight, but King Arthur himself. I challenge you to a fight."

Nope! No way is that gonna happen. Magical scabbard or not, Britt knew better than to fight a magic knight.

Gawain moved his horse so it stepped closer to Roen. "We should turn around, now."

"Amen." Merlin muttered.

"But it's a challenge," Vivien said. "Shouldn't Arthur, king or not, agree to fight? It is his personal honor at stake!"

"Personal honor is not worth fighting a faerie knight," Gawain said in a lowered tone.

"You refused to fight me?" The faerie knight growled.

"Yeah, pretty much," Britt said. She was following Gawain's advice, and intended to retreat, but the faerie knight slammed his war axe into the ground, making the earth rumble.

"Your refusal will bring you dishonor and shame," the knight said.

Vivien, perched daintily on her saddle, nodded vigorously. "He's right, My Lord."

"Don't care," Britt said. She fought Roen to get him turned around, but the warhorse kept pawing at the ground and snorting at the knight.

"If you do not wish to fight me, then you can display your intellect and answer my riddle," the faerie knight said. "If you answer correctly, I shall let you pass. But if you answer incorrectly..." The knight picked up his axe and whirled it, slicing straight through a sapling tree.

"I don't mind a bit of a detour," Percival said brightly. "The forest of Arroy is a lovely place." Both he and Gawain had their horses turned around.

(Britt was glad it was they who traveled with her, and not Lancelot or Ywain. Both of those warmongers would've insisted on fighting the faerie knight.) But, Britt's curiosity got the better of her.

"May I ask you what your riddle is before committing?" She asked.

"Indeed. My riddle is this: what does every woman in the world want most?" the faerie knight said.

Britt blinked. "Seriously?"

The knight, his face obscured by his black and silver helm, nodded. "It is a mystery scholars and scientists have never been able to confirm."

Britt frowned, considering the riddle, as Merlin hissed under his breath—upset but unable to outright go against Vivien.

An old woman dressed in frayed clothes popped out of the forest next to Merlin and Vivien with a cackle, making their horses spook. "I know the answer to the riddle, My Lord." The old lady gripped the edges of her skirt and curtsied to Britt. "I will gladly tell you the answer, if Sir Gawain will agree to marry me!"

Vivien faked a swoon of horror, and Gawain narrowed his eyes at the old hag while Britt shook her head at the entire mess.

"Sometimes such weird and bizarre things happen here in medieval England, I question my sanity," Britt said.

"Take the offer, My Lord," Gawain said.

"Gawain, no! Arthur, it's a simple matter of turning around and going back. There's no need for Gawain to sacrifice himself in this way," Percival said.

"I still believe Arthur should face the knight in combat," Vivien said, recovering herself. "Arthur cannot be beaten as long as he is in combat."

"I'm afraid you have overestimated our delightful king," Merlin said. Though his voice was pitched to sound carefree, Britt could hear the clear struggle in his voice as he held back to keep from screaming at Vivien. "Though Arthur is quite talented with the sword, I don't believe anyone could stand up to what is clearly a fae knight and his magic blade."

Gawain leaned alarmingly out of his saddle so he could closely address Britt. "Take the old woman's bargain, Britt," he whispered. "We can't afford to delay; we must return to Camelot and prepare for Rome."

The hag cackled. "I promise I will make a fine wife for you, Sir Gawain!"

Judging that the magic knight wasn't about to pounce on her, Britt tuned out the chaos her party was raising.

Thinking over the knight's question, she considered the females she knew best from this era. Guinevere, Nymue, Morgan, and Morgause. *Is there one thing they all desire? Thinking over their behavior, they're entirely different people and would want entirely different things. But faerie folk are tricky, so there must be something...*

Guinevere had done everything in her power to get out of her father's clutches and secure freedom for herself. Morgause had taken great risks to try and secure her own personal goals, and Morgan worked hand-in-hand with her sister while Nymue made decrees with the efficiency of a queen. *What* could they possibly all want?

"Gawain, you're the Ladies' Knight and the eldest son of a king. You can't marry *that*," Percival said.

"If my marriage will spare the king, I shall do it gladly," Gawain said.

Vivien sighed in appreciation. "So honorable!"

"What say you, King Arthur?" The hag tapped her claw-like fingers together. "Will you take my reasonably priced bargain?"

"My patience is draining, King Arthur," the faerie knight said.

"*Arthur*," Merlin hissed.

"I got it!" Britt said. She lifted her eyes and gazed straight at the knight. "The answer to the riddle is women most want their own way."

Silence ruled over the road and forest for several long moments.

"I beg your pardon?" the hag asked finally.

Britt scratched an itch on her scalp. "Women want to do whatever they want, um, phrasing it so you would understand it...women want to follow their own will."

"You're right," the knight said, sounding flabbergasted and shocked.

"He's right," the old woman repeated, clearly just as shocked.

Britt glanced back and forth between the pair, their reactions unexpected. *Are they a racketeering team? Do they work together to hold up knights in the middle of the forest? But if that were the case, demanding for the lady to become Gawain's wife is a stupid demand. Not to mention if Nymue found out about their little operation, she'd stamp them down flat.*

"Well done, Arthur!" Merlin trumpeted. "Using your head! What a wonderful answer! Though, might I add, you were quite foolish to blurt out the answer when we could've easily avoided this whole mess by turning around?" There was a hint of a bite to Merlin's tone, and Britt knew she was going to get an endless lecture if he managed to corner her in Camelot without Vivien.

Gawain and Percival smiled peacefully, less upset with the risk Britt took due to their overconfidence in her abilities. "As usual, you show great insight, My Lord," Gawain said.

Britt barely noticed his warm smile, she was so preoccupied with the way the old lady stared up at Gawain like he hung the moon.

"Your wisdom is far greater than your years," the faerie knight awkwardly said as he began shuffling to the side. "You have won the right to move forward. If, now, you'll just excuse me..."

Britt held up a hand to forestall him. "Wait just a moment. I wish to speak to the lady, privately." She slid from Roen's back, and as she approached the hag, the old woman anxiously knit her fingers together and bit her lip in a youthful expression.

Britt placed her hand in the middle of the woman's back and drew the crone farther down the road. When she was certain they could speak without being overheard, she paused and stepped back. She gave the hag a careful inspection, wondering if her vague gut feeling was correct.

Gawain had a lot of admirers, almost as many as Lancelot. But none, as far as she knew, had magic. Except… "Ragnelle? Is that you?"

The old lady blushed like a neon sign. "How could you tell?" she asked, her voice nearly a squeak.

"It was just a hunch." Britt rubbed her eyes. She hadn't thought it was going to be Nymue's handmaiden, but knew it was a faint possibility. Really, she had hoped the handmaiden would have known better. "I'm assuming Nymue did not put you up to this, and this is instead your own little scheme you hatched to get Gawain's attention?"

"My Lady was not at all involved!" Ragnelle said. Her voice was no longer scratchy, but tranquil like a lake. "The faerie knight is a friend of mine who agreed to aid me. Please, do not be angry with him or with my Lady, King Arthur! We never would've harmed you!"

"I believe you, but I have to say I'm quite disappointed with you. Did you not learn anything from Lady Ettard and Sir Pelleas' ridiculous love affair?" Britt asked.

Ragnelle blushed and stared down at her holey leather shoes. "But when I attempted to approach him at Lady Ettard's castle, he was attentive but uninterested."

"Trying once does not count as a serious attempt," Britt said. "Nymue is always visiting Camelot; you could come with her and try talking to Gawain again. Or you could visit us alone! The possibilities are endless—you didn't have to set up a roadside robbery."

"I apologize. My actions were extremely shameful," Ragnelle said mournfully.

Britt groaned and tried to avoid looking at her. (She always was a sucker for a sad person. That was how Guinevere had conned her into inviting her coming to Camelot.) She rubbed at the bags under her eyes. "My gosh. Does everybody from this time have screwed up ideas about how they should begin a dating relationship? This place needs 'eHarmony: the Camelot edition.' Like, yesterday."

"Are you going to tell Sir Gawain of my dishonorable actions?" Ragnelle asked timidly.

Britt tapped her foot on the dusty road. "No. Do you know why? Because that would bring you to his attention, and your punishment for this little stunt is going to be that you have to create a normal relationship with him in an emotionally healthy, responsible way. That means no magic necklaces, no magic potions, no roadside robberies."

Ragnelle stared at her with wide eyes that were completely out of place on her old woman disguise. "You're not going to banish me—or forbid me from seeing him?"

"No. To begin with, Gawain is responsible for his own love life. But if I'm being honest, you've shown more pluck than a lot of the girls who sigh after him have." Britt rubbed the back of her neck and studied Gawain thoughtfully.

He was eyeing the faerie knight, who still lingered at the edge of the woods, and spoke quietly with Percival, who held Roen's reins. Though Merlin was speaking with Vivien, who—based on the speed at which she fluttered her eyelashes—was probably flirting with him, the wizard managed to give Britt a glare or two, clearly disliking her being outside of grabbing distance.

Making up her mind, Britt returned her attention to the handmaiden. "I feel like I should probably give you a good example of a way to *normally* approach Gawain, as most love stories seem to be lacking common sense. So I'm going to help you—but just this once!"

Britt waited for Ragnelle to nod happily before she continued. "We're still too far away from Camelot, so we'll have to camp out tonight. Find a good spot for a campsite just a short ways up the road, then pop out of the woods—as *yourself*—and tell us you have prepared a place for us to rest. That gives you an excuse to talk to us for a while this night, and it will give Gawain a favorable impression of you."

Ragnelle looked crestfallen. "That is a much better idea than mine."

"Yeah. But the fact that you realize it that quickly is a good sign for you." Britt smiled at her. "We'll see you soon."

She turned to go, but Ragnelle momentarily forestalled her. "Oh, I wanted to let you know, My Lord: I passed your message onto Lady Nymue. She said she did not know what a purse was, but she trusted that as it was your idea, it must serve a lethal purpose that would allow you to suffocate Sir Lancelot."

Britt almost choked on the gurgle of laughter that threatened to spill from her lips. "Thanks for telling her, Ragnelle. We'll see you shortly."

Ragnelle curtsied with her usual amount of grace, then faded into the forest like a shadow, the faerie knight moments behind her.

Britt shook her head and turned back to her companions. "Everything's fine! We should have a safe ride from here on."

Percival squinted up at the small patches of sky that could be seen between the leaves budding on the trees. "We won't be able to travel much longer."

"Splendid!" Britt said with a winning smile. "We'll just have to be on the lookout for an appropriate campsite then."

~

In the early hours of the morning, just before dawn began to brighten the eastern horizon, Britt dozed fitfully in her blankets.

As Britt had suggested, Ragnelle found a perfect campsite for them the previous night and spent the evening with them before Merlin and the knights retired. Britt had stayed up several more hours, plagued by her insomnia, but she was exhausted enough that sometime after midnight, she was able to collapse in her bedroll and sleep.

Still, she'd never been a particularly sound sleeper, so when she heard something rustle nearby, she blearily woke up and pushed her hair out of her face.

The overripe taste of sleep still in her mouth, Britt pushed herself up on her elbows. A woman dressed in a cloak carefully hefted a sword, struggling to find the best way to hold it as she quietly stole up to a saddled and bridled horse. Britt's mind sharpened with sudden clarity when she realized the woman was Vivien, and she was taking Excalibur.

Britt deftly rolled out of her blankets and popped to her feet, stretching all of her muscles so she was able to grasp Excalibur's hilt with one outstretched arm. She yanked back, pulling the magic sword free from its enchanted scabbard.

Vivien whirled around, her eyes narrowed with hot rage.

Britt adjusted her stance so she put her weight on the balls of her feet, raised Excalibur as if to run Vivien through, and sucked in a breath to wake her companions.

Vivien held up a hand and clenched it, cutting Britt's air supply off mid-breath.

Britt's lungs burned, and her throat spasmed as she tried to get air. She would've dropped Excalibur, but she was terrified the traitor would run off with it. She sank to her knees—the bit of air she had in her lungs unable to keep her standing. She couldn't make a sound, but just as the world started to grow hazy, she saw Merlin sit upright in his bedroll.

She lost her sight, but she heard him roar with the ferocity and volume of a dragon. There was another howl, but this one sounded like the mindless utterances of a roaring fire, and Britt felt heat pool around the campsite.

Her throat and lungs abruptly popped open, and she gasped, thankfully gulping in air. She blinked, trying to clear her tear-blurred eyes. Her vision focused enough that she could make out Vivien, throwing herself onto her horse and galloping away into the darkness of the night.

Britt finally dared to let go of Excalibur and rub her throat. "She has the scabbard," she croaked. She glanced up at Merlin, and froze.

The wizard wore a look of such rage, it shut down his normally pleasant features and made his face dark and closed. His blue eyes glittered almost black, and his jaw was clenched.

With Britt's words, lightning streaked across the sky, following the path Vivien had taken. Several bolts struck trees in the forest with an unusual blue tint to their sparks.

"Gawain. Percival. Wake up." Though Merlin did not raise his voice, the darkness in his tone made both the knights roll out of their bedrolls, swords raised.

"What is it?" Gawain asked.

Percival dumbly stared at the ground, where black scorch marks bore witness to the fire Merlin had created when Britt was blacking out.

Merlin threw his saddle on his horse, briskly tightening the girth. "Vivien made her move and took Excalibur's scabbard. I'm going to get it back. Take Britt back to Camelot. Get her there safely, and keep an eye out for any Roman ambushes."

Rain began to fall, but it was not a gentle sprinkle, or even a wet downpour. Instead, the raindrops hit with such force they stung, like bits of hail. Britt coughed as she peered up at the sky. When she first met Merlin's mentor, Blaise, he had jokingly told her how Merlin had, as a young child, flattened Stone Hedge. He said Merlin had better control now, but as blue lightning snaked across the sky, Britt highly doubted it was the wizard's calculated plan, but more likely his anger manifesting because he could not —or perhaps would not—withhold it.

Merlin threw himself on top of his leggy horse and turned in the direction Vivien had ridden.

"Be careful," Britt called, her voice still hoarse.

Merlin glanced down at her, pushing enough of his rage aside that he could offer her a tightlipped smile, though his furrowed eyebrows made the expression look painful. He urged his horse forward, disappearing into the darkness even faster than Vivien had.

Thunder rumbled, and Britt shivered in her newly soaked clothes.

Percival and Gawain had begun disassembling the campsite the moment Merlin told them to return to Camelot. Percival doused the fire, and Gawain packed up the saddlebags, divvying out the equipment Merlin had left behind between the pile meant for his horse and Percival's.

Britt retreated so she was under the overhang of a large oak tree. "It's not even dawn yet. Don't you two want to try sleeping a little more?"

Percival offered Britt a smile, though she could see his worry in the slant of his eyes. "I don't much fancy trying to sleep through this." He glanced up at the sky as lightning illuminated it, and thunder rumbled so loudly it shook the ground.

"If we stretch it—and if we make good time—we may be able to reach Camelot tonight," Gawain said. He tied his saddle pack shut. "With this experience, I would much rather see you safely behind Camelot's walls than gain a few extra hours of sleep."

Britt nodded, and began to pack her own belongings. She used the dress Mordred had given her before separating with Kay to wrap her sword. (It would be stupid of her to ride with the blade uncovered.)

The loss of the scabbard made her wince, for the enchanted thing had saved her more than once, but she was primarily relieved that she had managed to snag Excalibur. Though technically the scabbard was more valuable, Britt had never come across a sword that was more suited for her than Excalibur. (Indeed, she had never *dreamed* of a sword that fit her as well as it did.)

So while she would be extremely grateful if Merlin were able to reclaim the scabbard, her primary concern was that the wizard would make it through the encounter in one piece.

There was no doubt Merlin was excessively powerful, but there was also no doubt Vivien practiced black magic, with which she would find it far easier to end Merlin than he her.

Lightning struck less than a mile away, shaking the ground and sending blue sparks into the sky. Britt shivered as she laid Roen's saddle blanket on his back. *Perhaps I'm worrying too much. He is ticked.*

Gawain grimly shook his head.

"What's wrong?" Britt called out to him. "Are you that worried for Merlin?"

The knight shook his head. "No. It is more what Vivien's activities mean that has me uneasy."

Britt heaved her saddle on to Roen's back. "What do you mean by that?"

Gawain flicked rain off his face. "It is guaranteed Rome has no spies closer to us than her, so if she made her move, it must've been because the war is upon us."

9

A UNITED BRITAIN

Britt, Gawain, and Percival did not make their goal of reaching Camelot that night. The horses' fatigue combined with the thunderstorm that squatted over the forest forced them to camp out one more night. However, when dawn arrived, it brought with it a sunny, bright day, and by midmorning Britt knew they would be home in time for lunch.

"I'm a little surprised Merlin has not caught up with us yet." Britt stared up at the trees, enjoying the sight of the fresh green leaves and the song of the birds. Spring had come.

"He will not easily give up recovering your scabbard," Gawain predicted.

"Yeah, but I thought it would be an easy win for him against Vivien," Britt said.

Percival lingered at the back of their little line. "As the lady in question is a practitioner of black magic, it'll make the fight against her that much more difficult."

Britt winced. "True."

Gawain held up his hand, wordlessly requesting for silence.

Off in the distance, Britt could hear the sound of someone

whistling cheerfully, and the muffled clop of horse hooves falling on the dirt road.

"Someone from Camelot, perhaps?" Percival asked. "We are close enough now."

"If that's another faerie knight, I'm going to chew Nymue out," Britt grumbled.

Gawain's hands stole to the hilt of his sword, but he need not worry. The whistler rounded a bend in the road, slowly ambling into view.

It was Sir Tor, wearing his armor and mounted on his charger, with his squire riding a white donkey.

Percival smiled. "Sir Tor!"

The knight, who was built a lot like a defensive lineman from a football team, smiled broadly. "King Arthur, Sir Percival, Sir Gawain! Welcome home!"

"Are you out questing already? We haven't had an official ceremony for the Round Table yet," Britt said.

Tor shook his head. "No, I'm not on a quest. I, and several other knights, were sent out to search for you."

Britt grimaced. "Kay sent you, didn't he? That man! We haven't been gone *that* long."

"Sir Kay did indeed send me, though not because he felt you were tarrying," Tor said earnestly.

"Is it the war with Rome?" Gawain asked.

"There are new developments with that, but that was not why I was sent," Tor acknowledged.

"Sir," Tor's squire, a squat dwarf who was probably one of the best in Camelot (though he had a fierce tongue), frowned up at his master. "Just spit out the reason instead of answering so badly!"

Tor's smile turned sheepish. "Ahh, I am being vague. Very well! I was sent to find you because the kings of Ireland and Scotland have come, and they wish to be named your allies."

Britt screeched. "*What?!*"

CAMELOT WAS in a barely controlled uproar when Britt and her party clattered into the keep courtyard.

Both the castle keep where Britt and her knights lived, as well as the city, which lay outside the inner gate, was a swarm of activity. Horses paraded past, dressed up in their best tack; oxen pulled wooden carts that rumbled and groaned, heavily laden with supplies and weapons.

The meadow surrounding Camelot was a sea of tents and soldiers. Couriers on the swiftest mounts zoomed back and forth between the castle and the armies outside, carrying messages and orders.

"It seems Kay took his charge of preparing for war seriously," Britt said as she boosted herself from Roen's back and landed on the ground.

A stable boy was at her side in an instant, taking Roen before Britt could even pat the gelding on the neck.

"It seems he did," Gawain agreed.

"Oh, this isn't all Sir Kay's work," Tor said.

Before Britt could further question the cheerful knight, Sir Bodwain, Sir Bedivere, and Sir Kay charged out of the keep.

"Welcome home, sire," Bodwain said. The swarthy man was stroking his beard, one of his nervous tics, but paused long enough to give Britt a deep and respectful bow.

"I am filled with joy to see you here safe and sound, My Lord," Bedivere said. A frown briefly settled on his lips. "Although it seems it was good luck that you were taken as it allowed you to forge an alliance with King Bagdemagus, I cannot help but think the method of your departure is still an embarrassment to us."

Britt laughed. "You mean he snatched me right out from underneath your noses? Yeah, my pride took a hit from that. I assume Kay told you about King Bagdemagus?"

Bedivere nodded. "He did, but I found King Bagdemagus's account to be much more detailed."

"Ah," Britt said. "Wait, what?"

Eagle eye Kay interrupted before Bedivere could explain himself. "Merlin does not ride with you." His gaze dropped to Excalibur, which was still wrapped with the dress minus sword belt and scabbard. "... Where is your scabbard?"

Britt scratched the back of her neck and wondered how she could break the news without enraging Kay. "It's kind of a long story."

"It will have to wait until after we meet with the kings of Scotland and Ireland." Bodwain said. "They're waiting for you in your throne room."

Britt started for the impressive doors to the castle keep without further prompting. "Tor mentioned some kings had arrived and expressed a desire to become allies."

"King Bagdemagus and Duke Maleagant have arrived as well," Kay said.

Britt grinned at her foster brother as they swept inside and started up the hallway. "And you didn't kick Duke Maleagant out immediately? I'm impressed, Kay. I thought you might hold a grudge against him."

Kay shrugged. "King Bagdemagus is honorable enough. It is a shame Duke Maleagant does not seem to take much after him."

Bedivere laughed outright. "What Sir Kay is not saying is that Duke Maleagant complained of the inaction for the past week, so two days ago Kay challenged him to joust and hit him so hard, he knocked him unconscious."

Britt whistled. "Wish I had been here to see that!" She and her men turned a corner in the hallway, making their way towards her throne room.

"Thankfully, King Bagdemagus did not seem to take Duke Maleagant's...lesson poorly," Bodwain said dryly.

"King Bagdemagus knows Duke Maleagant is a bit of a jerk.

He probably approved of Kay's actions, so I don't need to worry about it affecting a possible alliance." Britt smiled at the knights and servants who bowed to her as she passed them, welcoming her home.

"King Bagdemagus is not only interested in an alliance," Bedivere said, his eyes bright with excitement. "He, along with the kings of Ireland and Scotland, wish to swear oaths of fealty to you!"

Britt stopped walking. "*What?*"

Kay twitched his mustache, the dead giveaway that said exactly how pleased he was. "They wish to take oaths and become vassals."

"Indeed," Bodwain rumbled proudly. "With their oaths, you will have successfully united all of Britain—with the exception of King Ryence."

Britt almost ran the remaining distance to her throne room. "But why? What on earth would possess them to swear fealty to *me*?"

The soldiers standing at the doors hustled, pushing them open so Britt could get a good look at the inside of her throne room.

Her wooden throne was still positioned on the dais, and skylights let in shafts of warm sunshine. What was unusual, however, was the ring of foreign dignitaries who stood near the dais of her throne.

King Bagdemagus was the only one of the bunch she recognized, but they couldn't have made their decision based on his testimony alone. Heck, when she left his lands, he was just looking for an alliance!

The group rearranged slightly when they noticed Britt standing in the doorway. They spread out so they stood in a straight line, revealing Mordred.

Mordred stood with a slightly older version of himself—a man who wore a golden circlet and had Mordred's dark hair and puppy-dog eyes. They had to be related. Brothers or cousins, possibly.

Mordred smiled charmingly, flashing his dimples. "My Lord, King Arthur!" He left the line of kings and approached Britt. "Please, allow me to introduce you to my older brother. I have much longed for you to meet him."

Britt looked back and forth from Mordred to his brother. "Would your brother happen to be an Irish King?" She asked, sounding deceptively calm.

Mordred laughed. "He is indeed."

Britt raised her eyebrows slightly. "No wonder you worked so hard to keep Merlin from finding out your parentage. Well done. I never even detected a hint of an accent in your words."

"I spent much of my youth in Britain," Mordred said. "It was why I was chosen for my role."

"Role?"

Mordred bowed his head slightly as his smile turned wry. "I'm afraid I have not been entirely honest with you, My Lord. Let me be clear: my oaths of fealty to you were absolutely true, for I have sworn my life to you, and I will serve you first before anyone else. But originally, my brother asked me to travel to Britain and look into the rumors of King Arthur, High King of Britain. I rode through the countryside for quite a while, and my interest in you was so piqued I had to visit Camelot for myself."

Britt was quiet, both because she was shocked and because she was trying to process what the young knight was telling her. "And?"

Mordred met her gaze head-on. "I learned that you, King Arthur, are honorable and just. You care about your knights and your people. You are not afraid to break from tradition if it will make your kingdom stronger, but you will not trample anyone as a monarch—quite the opposite. You teach those in positions of power that it is their duty, and their honor, to care for those beneath them. Though I was born in Ireland, you, Arthur, are my

King. I believe, no, I know you can defeat Rome. You are the only one who can."

Britt hesitated, touched by Mordred's kind words. "Mordred..."

"When we parted ways in King Bagdemagus's lands, I knew I needed to return home and inform my brother of King Ryence's traitorous movements. He listened, and he has rallied his allies and his armies. We arrived just yesterday, but my brother and the other kings are in agreement. You are Arthur, High King of Britain." Mordred smiled and rested a hand on her shoulder, squeezing it slightly.

Britt blinked back the sting of unexpected tears and smiled at him. "I don't know what to say. Thank you."

Mordred shook his head. "You owe no one here thanks, My Lord. All of this is because of the kind of ruler you are."

Britt nodded once and breathed deeply, rallying her courage. She smiled her genuine smile, which she was still unaware made her entire being brilliant, and started towards the kings. "Welcome to Camelot. I am Arthur, King of Britain. I'm afraid I bear grim news about King Ryence and the movement of the Roman armies..."

WHEN AMBASSADORS from Rome arrived in Camelot several days later, Merlin hadn't yet returned. So, with no small amount of anxiety, Britt marched to her throne room, preparing to meet the enemy without her chief advisor.

"You will be fine, My Lord," Sir Ulfius said calmly when she reached the throne room doors. He stopped her long enough so he could polish out a smudge on her gold armor. It, and the beautiful and heavy crown perched on her head, were far too ornate for her to wear and do anything useful in. But Merlin had told her when he gave her the dragon-emblazed armor that its main purpose would be intimidation.

Britt still didn't understand exactly what he meant. Though she was tall, even with her armor, she was still leaner than the average knight. But with the wizard missing, she needed every advantage she could get.

"Remain calm and in control," Sir Bodwain advised. "Whenever you wear a calm but unbothered attitude in a situation where most would be screaming, it is quite disconcerting."

Britt pushed her crown up so it didn't fall exactly on her eyebrows. "Thanks. Stop me if I say something stupid."

The two older knights gave her looks of disapproval. "That will be entirely unnecessary," Ulfius said sternly.

Britt grinned at the pair, then nodded to the guards who opened the doors for her. She strode into the throne room, purposely ignoring the three Roman ambassadors—more for her own well-being than as a power play.

As she climbed the stairs of the dais, a guard announced, "King Arthur Pendragon, son of King Uther, High King over all of Britain!"

Britt seated herself on her throne, half blinded by her own armor when the sunlight struck her. She could barely see anything due to the golden reflection she generated, but she was vaguely aware of the ambassadors approaching the dais.

"King Arthur," one of the ambassadors began. "We are ambassadors from Rome, sent by Emperor Lucius Tiberius. Too long Britain has forgotten that it is under the rule of Rome. As such, Emperor Lucius demands tribute and homage, or he shall bring war to these lands."

Britt waited several long moments, but they said nothing else. "That is all you have to say?" She asked, hardly believing her luck.

The ambassador bowed his head. "It is a promise, Sire. One you should take seriously. If you do not, there will indeed be war."

She barely refrained from saying "I know," and instead flicked her fingers, indicating she understood them. "Of course, but that is truly *all* you have to tell me?"

The ambassador frowned and pushed his shoulders back, but eventually admitted, "Yes."

Britt wanted to laugh and snarl at the same time.

Usually any sort of meeting involving other rulers took *ages*, particularly because politics seemed to demand that everything which could be stated simply had to be explained with an excessive amount of metaphors and sly remarks. The fact that this was not the case would normally indicate that she had extremely good luck. But, unfortunately, this was the one time she was counting on a long-winded discussion, just in case Merlin could return to Camelot in the hours she assumed it would take them to poetically threaten her.

It had never occurred to her that they would succinctly state their demands.

The ambassadors exchanged looks, and one of them out-right jumped when Britt abruptly stood.

"Very well," she said. "You've brought before me a serious matter I would like to consider and discuss with my knights and my vassal-kings. I will return with a response for the Emperor."

Britt swept down the stairs, the picture of nobility with her eyes slightly narrowed in thought and her hand on the hilt of Excalibur. (In reality, she was squinting and had her hand on Excalibur in case she needed to use it as a cane thanks to her excessively shiny armor.)

She strode out of the throne room, removing her crown the second the soldiers closed the door behind her. "I like them," she announced.

Sir Ulfius gaped at her. "I beg your pardon?"

"The only reason they were so brief in their address to you is because they already have soldiers swarming Britain," Sir Bodwain said.

"Of course." Britt started down the hallway, making her way for the hall that held the Round Table. "You two will keep an eye on them?" She called back to the two older knights.

"It is our honor," Sir Bodwain said.

Britt grinned and waved at them, then jogged along.

The servants, always privy to the castle's activities, gave Britt cheers of encouragement as she jogged along, clanking loudly in her armor.

A gangly teenage boy loped up to her, bearing a tray of food.

Britt glanced at him. "What's this?" She asked as he kept pace with her.

"Your lunch," he said.

"Lunch was two hours ago," Britt protested.

"Yes, and you didn't eat then either." The young teenager eyed Britt with a mixture of suspicion and bossiness.

Britt finally placed the kid as the young pageboy who had, in her early days as ruler, been all too interested in making sure she ate. *When did he grow up?*

Feeling old, Britt laughed and slowed to a walk. "Very well, you win. Here, I'll take the tray."

The boy sidestepped her. "Do you swear to eat it?"

"Sure, as long as it's not blood sausage or something."

The boy looked like he didn't believe her, but he allowed her to take the tray and march on without his supervision.

Britt juggled the wooden tray and her gold crown, but she looked up just in time to see Sir Lancelot stepping out of an intersecting hallway.

The handsome knight showed no signs of the anger that had caused him to leave the forest previously. His smile was charming, as usual; his blue eyes twinkled, and—as the ladies of Camelot would say—his golden brow *glistened.*

"You are an unusual king, Arthur," Lancelot said. "You are the only one, I believe, who answers to his servants in regards to his dietary needs."

"It's because they care." She glared out of habit. Secretly, she tried not to gawk at him and instead attempted to gauge his mood by the smoothness of his steps.

She heard he had arrived in Camelot the previous night, but she had honestly done her best to avoid him, particularly since hearing about the ambassadors. She had enough trouble on her plate the way it was, and she didn't need the handsome knight stirring up any additional drama.

Lancelot glanced at her side. "I see you have a new scabbard for Excalibur."

Britt's hackles rose, but she kept walking. "Vivien stole the old one."

"So I was told when I returned last night," Lancelot said.

Britt yanked her gaze to him so fast she almost dropped her crown. Normally when something like that happened, Lancelot would carry on loudly and dramatically. Stating he had already heard in such a lighthearted tone was unusual for him. *Did he have something to do with it? Or is it just that he is still angry with me?*

Britt took in a breath and opened her mouth, thinking to question him further, but they reached the door of the hall too soon, and the eager knights and kings had a lookout posted.

Sir Griflet shouted through the open doors, "He's here," then turned his attention to Britt. "Tell us, what did those spineless slugs have to say?"

"Surprisingly, not much." Britt smiled at the crowd of knights and kings gathered around the Round Table as she breezed inside, making her way to her seat. She set her tray and crown down with a clank, then plopped down in her chair. "They said Emperor Lucius demands tribute and homage, or he'll bring war to us."

"How dare they!"

"As if we didn't know his plans!"

"I'll die before I send that pompous pincushion a tribute!"

Though the subject was a grim one, Britt let herself smile,

vastly amused by the outrage the knights and lords voiced. She poked at her food, then chose to begin eating her baked potato.

King Anguish, Mordred's brother, rested his elbows on the table and knitted his hands together. "The answer, obviously, is no."

"Hear, hear," King Pellinore said. "I can pledge at least 20,000 men for your disposal, King Arthur."

"It's just Arthur," Britt quietly reminded her fellow king—who was also the only king who knew her true gender.

"I can pledge 20,000 as well. I already have that many on their way," King Anguish said.

"Orkney can offer 10,000 *mounted* soldiers," King Lot, Gawain's father, said with haughty forbearance. Though he and Britt still weren't on friendly terms—and she suspected he didn't get along with his children any more now than he had before they all came to live at her Court—Britt knew there was no way he would let Orkney, and himself, look weak or pitiful. Even if it was for Britt's sake.

King Urien, who had been studying Ywain's empty chair, snapped to attention. "Naturally, I can offer 10,000 mounted soldiers as well."

At Urien's utterance more kings and lords spoke up, vowing to bring soldiers and provisions of their own.

Britt listened, smiling serenely and nodding approval whenever someone looked to her. She was relieved to see Kay was scribbling away in his logbook, hopefully taking notes for Merlin.

By the time the last of the knights and lords made their pledges, King Bagdemagus rubbed his square chin. "So it seems to me that we have over 200,000 men available for this war. Based on the numbers provided by King Arthur, Rome will still have us outnumbered."

"But we will be fighting on our own soil, and our soldiers

won't have traveled far, whereas the Roman soldiers have been traveling north to reach us for months," King Pellinore said.

Sir Griflet tapped his fingers on the scratched surface of the Round Table. "It's too bad they had not arrived sooner, for if we fought them in winter, we could've frozen them out."

"Emperor Lucius might be stupid enough to ask for a tribute, but even he knows that fighting in winter is not a winning strategy," Sir Bedivere said.

"So it's agreed," Gawain said. "We shall go to war against Rome."

The room was filled with murmurs of agreement.

"I don't think we had much choice in the matter," Britt spoke up for the first time.

"In that case, there's no reason to let the Roman ambassadors hang about," Agravain, Gawain's younger brother, said. "You ought to have them thrown out on their rumps, Sire."

Britt grinned at him. "I assure you there's nothing I would like to do more, but I'm sure Merlin would prefer a *delicate* way of telling them they are being thrown out on said rumps."

King Lot drummed his fingers on the table. "You still listen to that sideshow hack?"

Britt's grin turned wry. "Why King Lot, you're beginning to sound like your wife now. And yes. Merlin is still one of the wisest men alive; I would be an idiot not to listen to him. Unfortunately, he's out of Camelot at the moment."

"You'll think of something," Sir Kay gruffly said.

"Indeed!" Sir Ector boomed. "You are the King of Britain! You handle yourself with more charisma and charm than Merlin could dream of!"

Though Britt was touched, she was somewhat unconvinced by Sir Ector's argument. (As her foster-father, Sir Ector was widely known to be overindulgent with her.)

"That does raise a question, though." Bedivere rubbed the hilt of a dagger tucked into his sword belt. "Do you think some of the Faerie folk might fight on our side?"

"I can travel to the forest of Arroy and ask the Lady of the Lake myself," Lancelot declared.

"That's unnecessary," Britt was quick to say as she continued to pick at her baked potato. "I'm sure the Lady of the Lake will aid us however she can." *Especially when I explain to her that she was spared a visit from the Debaucher.*

The discussion continued on this train of thought, and Britt fell quiet as she leaned back in her chair. Mordred, seated close to her, leaned in and spoke.

"You are not the High King of Britain because Merlin is your advisor, My Lord," he said. "I'm certain you can handle the ambassadors."

Britt, lacking any other "manly" way to show her thanks, smacked Mordred between the shoulder blades. "Hopefully. Goodness knows I've no reason to fear them with such amazing allies."

Agravain must've been watching Britt for any sign of telling off the ambassadors, for he jumped to his feet. "I volunteer, nay, I *request* to be one of the knights allowed to toss the ambassadors out."

"I feel up to a bit of ambassador tossing right now as well, if you wouldn't mind, My Lord," Sir Lionel, Lancelot's cousin, said with a wolfish grin.

She laughed outright. "Though your offers are tempting, I must refuse. As much as I would like it, I don't think anybody would call throwing ambassadors out head-over-heels an honorable gesture." Britt stood and addressed the room when it quieted. "I shall tell the ambassadors we refuse their demands, and we are prepared for war. Please, continue to strategize. I thank you for your generous offers of help, but as they are your men, and you are my precious allies, I would like to limit the number of deaths to the smallest possible amount. We must be as cunning as possible and use every moment we can to plan against the impending invasion. Thank you."

There was a collective inhale as Britt strode out of the hall, biting into a shriveled apple as she settled her crown back on her head.

Mordred and Gawain followed her out.

Britt gnawed on her apple as she made her way back up the familiar maze of hallways. "I don't know whether to be honored or worried whenever one of my speeches causes silence."

"It's because you have a unique way of looking at things," Mordred said.

"And you are not afraid to be openly affectionate or admit your admiration for others," Gawain added.

She snorted. "You mean your father doesn't call his allies precious, Gawain?"

"I suspect his heart would stop beating if he were to attempt to say such a thing," Gawain said.

Britt would've responded, but she felt eyes on her and spotted the budding nutritionist sulking in an inlet of the hallway, eyeing her. "I ate the potato," she said, sounding overly defensive. "I'm working on my apple!"

The young teenager planted his fists on his hips. "I am fully authorized by Sir Kay to refuse to serve you wine tonight, Your Highness, if you do not eat enough."

"A bossy little thing aren't you, considering you were barely the size of my dog when you first started serving me. Where is Cavall anyways?"

"I believe my little brothers have him," Gawain said.

"Does Kay know?" Britt asked. "He's always after me about taking Cavall everywhere with me."

"It was Kay's idea to send them off with Cavall," Mordred said. "I believe he said the 'fight would not be worth the win.'"

"In other words, lending them Cavall was the easiest way to

keep them from insisting on being present for the meeting," Gawain said.

"I see it now. Well then, bossy kitchen boy, find Gaheris, Gareth, and Cavall, and have them brought to me. Then I will sit down and eat after the Roman ambassadors are officially kicked out."

"Yes, My Lord," the pageboy said.

He peeled off from their little group at the next intersection, and Britt, Gawain, and Mordred continued on to the throne room.

Sir Ulfius stood outside the doors, his thumbs hooked on his sword belt. "You finished the discussion already?"

"Technically, we finish the discussion about a minute after I entered the hall. It's not like any of this is fresh news." Britt finished her apple and awkwardly held the core, not sure what to do with it. "The decision was unanimous...and obvious."

Sir Ulfius took the core and passed it off to a manservant. "I expected as much, but I thought everyone would keep you there for a great while. More correctly," he smiled wryly, "I thought you would try to get everyone to keep you there in another attempt to stall for Merlin."

"That's a great idea. I'm actually a little ashamed I hadn't thought of that myself," Britt said.

"It's too late to go back now, My Lord," Mordred said sweetly.

"Bossiness. All around me, bossiness!" Britt muttered. She winked at the knight, rolled back her shoulders, and nodded to the waiting guards.

Again, they opened the doors, and again Britt marched up to her throne, still half blinded by the golden reflection of her armor. It was a little different, for this time, Sir Bodwain stood near the ambassadors—he had been talking to them before she came in. "Thank you for your patience," she said. "I am happy to say I have a reply for you to take to Emperor Lucius."

The ambassador who appeared to be serving as the designated speaker, bowed. "What might we tell the mighty Emperor on your behalf?"

"That no one from Britain will give him tribute or homage, and if he is so eager for war, we will be happy to accommodate him." Britt smiled, but it was not a welcoming grin or a sly smirk, but the confident and grim expression of someone who knew the trials ahead, yet fully expected to win.

The ambassadors moved to stand closer together. "We shall tell him your message."

"Excellent. In that case, I wish you safe travels. My constable will see that you are given new provisions and will escort you out of Camelot."

The ambassadors exchanged glances. "You aren't going to kill one or two of us to set an example?" one blurted out. (Based on the way his companions smacked him, they were angry with him for giving her ideas.)

"Of course not." For the second time that day she glided down the dais steps. "You are ambassadors that were sent to me in good faith. To mistreat you would not only be dishonorable, but a show of pettiness and instability." She nodded at the ambassadors, finally able to see their faces now that she was out of direct sunlight.

There was a veritable stampede in the hallway, and Britt drifted away from the ambassadors. "Safe travels," she wished them again as the guards hurriedly opened the doors for her.

When she set foot in the hallway she whistled. "Cavall!"

Her mastiff padded up the hallway, two boys—who were almost teenagers—running behind him.

"Arthur!" The boys shouted. Instead of bodily throwing themselves at her as they used to, they bowed deeply to her, holding their practice swords to keep from smacking themselves on the legs.

"Gaheris, Gareth, when did the two of you grow so tall?" It seemed to Britt like it was just yesterday she would get a crick in her neck staring down at them—they were that short. "Has Kay lectured you about eating us out of Camelot?"

The boys laughed, and when Sir Bodwain joined them in the hallway, the soldiers closed the doors behind him.

The Roman ambassadors stared at the doors for several long moments.

"Arthur…He's not the usual king, is he?" One of the ambassadors said.

"I should think not." A second said. "He's the first man to successfully unite all of Britain."

"I don't know that the Emperor understands who he's up against," the first ambassador said.

The ambassador who did all the talking rubbed his chin. "Then we must do our best to warn him."

10
PREPARATIONS

When Britt finally had a break in the many meetings she and the other kings held, she and Cavall took to the walls of Camelot. Up on the walls, the air seemed cleaner and her problems smaller as she could alternate staring out at the patchwork quilt of farmland that spread behind Camelot and the idyllic thatched roof cottages that made up the inner-city of the castle.

Britt stifled a yawn and laid her hand on Cavall's back.

"Do you think you'll be able to sleep tonight without walking the walls, Milord?" One of her guards asked.

"Don't be silly," her Scottish nanny/guard boomed. "As long as Merlin is still gone, Milord will walk these walls."

"Sometimes I wish you all had not adjusted so easily to the reveal of my gender," Britt said tartly.

Her guards abruptly straightened and moved into a ready stance. Moments later, Guinevere climbed the last step to the wall with a smile.

"Hello, Arthur. Are you…busy?" she asked.

"No, not at all," Britt said. "I'm just staring out at the land like a sappy minstrel. Did you need something?"

Guinevere glanced at the guards, but they stared straight ahead and seemed to take no notice of her as she approached Britt and joined her leaning against a crenel—the indentation of the wall's sawtooth pattern. "I'm glad you were unharmed when you were taken by Duke Maleagant," she began.

"I like Maleagant about as much as I care for dung beetles, but I have to say I was pleasantly surprised that he appears to treat women with more care than I would've thought," Britt admitted as she squatted down to rub Cavall's chest.

Guinevere smiled, but it seemed to Britt that she did so more because it was expected of her, rather than because she actually found Britt's observation amusing. "Something is on your mind," Britt said.

Guinevere, her reddish gold hair loose, nervously ran her fingers through her locks. "I wanted to thank you."

Britt propped her arm up on the crenel. "For what?"

"For believing me and listening when I said I felt uneasy outside of Camelot—for investigating it, when you could've brushed it off as a silly worry." Guinevere speared Britt straight to the heart with her level gaze. "No one has ever done anything like that for me before. No one has ever believed me and taken my thoughts seriously."

The comment made Britt feel like a fake. "Yes, about that...I have to apologize, Guinevere, for I haven't always given you the respect you deserve."

Guinevere shook her head. "That is not true. You've always given me the esteem due my station. I have frequently enjoyed positions of honor during feasts and tournaments."

"I'm not talking about honoring you as a princess, but honoring you as a person." Britt shifted, still feeling ashamed. "You are so brave, Guinevere."

Guinevere surprised Britt by laughing outright. "Brave? Me? It's kind of you to say so, but I don't know what part of me you could possibly be referring to."

"It's the things you do," Britt said. "You dared to dream outside what life handed you. You dared to want more than a life as a bargaining chip. That alone is incredibly courageous during this century when everyone expects you to behave like a sheep. But your bravery doesn't stop there. I know you set your life on the line by pretending to be my lady when Vivien arrived in Camelot. You set yourself between a user of dark magic and myself. That kind of valor is as rare as it is powerful."

Britt sighed and tapped her fingers on the stone wall. "And it took me so long to see it in you. I'm sorry, Guinevere. Thank you for your patience, and thank you for standing by me when I didn't deserve you."

Guinevere's lips trembled as she smiled, and her eyes were glazed with tears. "Might this mean, then, that we are friends?"

Her hopeful manner warmed Britt's heart, and she internally vowed she would try her best not to make prejudiced, snap decisions about someone as she had with Guinevere. "We're more than friends. We are true companions."

Guinevere giggled and threw herself at Britt, embracing her in spite of Britt's armor-covered chest. "I am so glad! Oh! I also wanted to share the court gossip with you! It seems Blancheflor has officially rejected Sir Griflet, and the ladies have grown concerned for Sir Lancelot—for he's been acting so oddly lately!"

Guinevere's chatter was interrupted by guards calling up the length of the walls. "Merlin has returned!"

Britt scrambled to attention. "Merlin's back?"

A guard who had been running the length of the walls skidded to a stop by her. "Milord." He breathed heavily before he bent over in a bobbing bow. "'Tis true. Merlin has returned! He rides his steed through the streets of Camelot and should be at the inner courtyard in a few minutes."

The guard ran on to pass along the word, and Britt turned joyfully towards the inner courtyard. Merlin was finally back!

Watching hopefully, she said, "I'm sorry, Guinevere. What were you saying?"

Guinevere laughed. "Go."

"Go what?"

"Go greet him! I imagine he'll storm the gates soon anyway. Even I know he'll hardly be able to contain his glee when he sees all the kings who have taken their vows to you." Guinevere giggled again, though she serenely knitted her hands together.

Britt lunged for the stairs, but paused before going down. "Guinevere..."

"Yes?"

"Thanks. For believing in me when I didn't deserve it."

Before Guinevere could respond, the inner gates opened, admitting Merlin on his scraggly horse. Britt, unable to contain her anticipation, zipped down the stairs with Cavall on her heels as fast as she could while retaining some air of decorum.

She made it to the stable just as Sir Ector, Sir Ulfius, and Sir Bodwain ambled out of the keep.

"Merlin!" Sir Bodwain shouted. "What news have you for us?"

Merlin's usually fastidiously kept clothes were splattered with mud. He dismounted and shook his head. "Though I chased Vivien all the way to the main enemy camp, I was unable to secure the scabbard. I'm sorry, Britt." His expression was bleak, and dark circles ringed his eyes as he gazed at her.

Britt offered him a reassuring smile as Cavall sniffed her boots. "We'll get it back."

Merlin shook his head. "We can't. Vivien destroyed it."

"What?" Sir Ector roared.

"She was either afraid I would catch her, or she feared that Britt's rapport with Excalibur would call the scabbard back to her side, for she destroyed it as soon as we hit Roman territory and I was not able to openly ride after her." Merlin rubbed his face. "I was able to get quite a bit of information as a result of my trip, but I would have much preferred to reclaim the scabbard."

"The scabbard may have kept me from bleeding, but it wouldn't have saved me if I was grievously wounded," Britt said. "It is a little disheartening not to have it, but I'm much more relieved that you have returned. There's so much to tell you!"

"Indeed," Sir Bodwain rumbled. "To start with, Sir Mordred is the younger brother of King Anguish of Ireland, and talked all the Irish and Scottish kings into swearing an oath of loyalty to Arthur!"

"Sir Mordred?" Merlin said. "That little rat! I spent months researching his possible pedigree, but I never thought to look into Ireland!"

"It is maddening," Sir Ulfius agreed. "But have you not realized it? Britain now stands united! We have done it, Merlin!"

Sir Bodwain and Sir Ulfius laughed and slapped each other on the back. Sir Ector wore a huge smile and patted Britt on the head like the proud parent he was.

Merlin was smiling, but he didn't look nearly as triumphant as Britt thought he would when he realized he had achieved his dream. Instead, there was almost a worried wrinkle to the furrow of his brow. "It is indeed a reason to celebrate—particularly after we see this precocious Emperor Lucius out of Britain," he said.

"There's also King Ryence to deal with," Bodwain said.

"We shall see to him during the battle with Rome!" Ector barked. "This shall be the last time he stands against my Bri—Arthur."

"Yes, yes. Of course," Sir Ulfius said soothingly.

Britt laughed at the display, and was surprised when Merlin leaned into her side and whispered. "We need to talk."

She blinked at the abrupt request. "Of course. Maybe tonight?"

Merlin shook his head. "No. Now."

BRITT FOLLOWED Merlin into his study. Though Sir Ulfius intruded long enough to deliver a tray of food and drink for Merlin, the knight then left the two of them alone.

Britt scrutinized Merlin, taking in his furrowed brow. "Don't worry about the scabbard, Merlin," she said. "It was a neat insurance policy, but it's not like it could really save me if something went wrong. I mean, owning it didn't guarantee I'd die of old age or something—"

"You are not going to die of old age." Merlin sat in a wooden chair and stared at the food tray.

She paused. "Statistically, you're right. But I have to ask is it really necessary to tell me that so flatly? I mean, I know there's a pretty good chance I could catch a cold and die, but still!"

"You misunderstand me. It's impossible for you to die of old age," Merlin paused. "...Because magic has made you immortal." He hurriedly grabbed a goblet of wine and tipped it back, as if he had just delivered Britt a death sentence.

Britt tapped her chin as she replayed his words. "What?" she asked finally when she could make neither heads nor tails of it.

"The faerie spell I cast on you that brought you back through time is a powerful one. Truthfully, it's a spell no human should rightfully use. If I'd gotten help from a faerie enchanter, perhaps it could've been avoided, but then again, since you are so far from the future, perhaps not. In fact, there are also chances of other side effects in bringing you back so far." He said it in a rush, like he'd been holding it back for some time.

"Merlin," Britt interrupted, "what are you trying to tell me?"

Merlin stared at his goblet. "The spell that brought you here is what made you immortal. You're not going to age; you're not going to grow old."

Britt wanted to accuse him of pulling her leg, but his grim look was impossible to misconstrue. Feeling faint, Britt plopped down in a chair before her legs could give out. "You're joking. You have to be!"

He finally looked away from his stupid cup and met her gaze. "I wish I were, but you are now like one of the faerie. Ageless."

Britt's spine kicked in, and she snapped upright. "No. That's impossible. I will buy it that faerie don't age, but if it were possible to make a person immortal, everyone and their brother would be using this spell. No, Merlin, you're wrong."

"I suspect the faerie know about the side effect of using that spell," Merlin said. "And I believe I am the first person in history to use it, and very likely the last. Scientifically speaking, it's useless. It's impossible to cast on oneself, for you cannot call yourself back through time; neither are you likely to call an... employer...back through time, for I suspect the difference has to be centuries. I hate to say it, but you are likely an anomaly."

Britt sagged against her chair again. "There is no proof..."

He shook his head. "You've been here several years, Britt, and you haven't changed a bit. Your young knights have grown; they've bulked up and matured. Gaheris and Gareth no longer resemble baby squirrels, but bean poles. The fact that you are so surprised by these changes guarantees that the spell has done to you as I have said. Your grasp on time is tenuous at best because it no longer affects you the way it affects the rest of the world."

Merlin's observations resonated with Britt. For the past few seasons she'd been continuously surprised by the changes in Camelot and her knights. She assumed it was just because she was selfish and didn't want to let anyone go, but if she no longer stood in the flow of time, it would make sense. That was why she had a hard time reckoning her mature knights with the gangly teenagers they had been when she first met them.

With that realization, Britt felt like the floor had fallen out from underneath her. She was ageless? Immortal?

In high school, she had learned history was chock-full of explorers searching for the fountain of youth or something similar. But now that Britt realized she had been granted what most would consider a blessing, she could see it was little more than a curse.

She would remain young and watch everyone she loved die. Again, and again, and again. No matter how many friends she made, she would be destined to be alone, forever. She would make it even back to her time…and be forced to lose her family all over again as they died from old age.

The skeletal hand of panic began to close around Britt's heart. She was going to lose everything.

"No!" Britt shook her head and ruthlessly cut through the terror. "Perhaps you are right, Merlin. It will be impossible for me to die of old age, but that doesn't mean I'm going to be immortal. In fact, I can confidently say I will die. There's too much chaos in this world for me to survive it unscathed. If I'm not stabbed in the heart, I might die by drowning, or in a war. Perhaps someday Lancelot will finally give in to his darker side and slip me a bit of poison, or maybe I'll catch pneumonia. The bottom line is I may have stopped aging, but that doesn't make me immortal. It just means I'll get to go out looking and feeling young, whether that's a week from now or a century from now."

Merlin stared at her. "Only you could take something incredibly negative, like dying, and put a positive spin on it."

Britt grinned. "It's better to laugh, in cases like this, or I could lose my mind. Besides, you might accuse me of feeling idealistic about my kingdom, but when it comes to myself and my own well-being, I am a realist. The chance that I even make it to the century that I'm from is slim to none. So I'm not going to bother worrying about it when I've got a much bigger threat—which wears a toga and demands tribute—marching on my ally's lands."

Merlin leaned back in his chair, the tension gone from his shoulders. "I suppose I should've expected no less from you. But it doesn't change the fact, Britt, that I really have made a mess of your life. First by bringing you here, and now by this." He gestured, helpless to put her newfound immortality into words.

"There's no denying you blew my life to smithereens," Britt said wryly. She stood, too filled with nervous energy to stay seated. "But you've given me the most amazing gifts as well. You've let me become someone who helps shape the world, and you gave me free rein when it would've been easy to insist on doing everything your way. Thank you for bringing me back in time. Thank you for insisting I be your fake Arthur. I have friends and family here now who are so precious to me, and though I miss my old time, I do love it here."

He stood and slowly approached her as if she were a wild animal. The strange light she had witnessed in his eyes back in Ettard's castle was rekindled. "Britt..." He placed his hand under her chin, and the door opened.

"Merlin!" Sir Bedivere cheerfully chirped. "We've come to collect you to meet all the kings. They're quite anxious to hear your intelligence regarding the Roman base camp!"

Kay did not linger in the doorway as Sir Bedivere did, but instead squirmed his way between Merlin and Britt. "It is good we came when we did," he said as he narrowed his eyes at Merlin.

Merlin groaned, and though Britt really wished her foster brother had not chosen that moment to interrupt them, she cleared her throat and stepped away.

"Come, Merlin," Kay ordered.

Merlin glared at him. "You're doing this on purpose."

"Obviously."

"I always knew there was a reason we didn't get along. Fine. Let us go meet our new allies. I will simply find Britt later tonight, when you're *sleeping*!"

"I may be sleeping, but all her guards will remain with her," Kay said as he and Merlin stepped outside the room.

"I ought to turn you into a newt."

"As if you had enough magic to do such a feat."

Merlin squawked as they strode down the hallway. "You take that back!"

Their interchange warmed Britt's heart, not just because she was absurdly fond of both of them, but because of the way Merlin was carrying on.... Perhaps she had not misinterpreted their shared kiss. Maybe there really was more than just plain camaraderie now. (Especially with Vivien gone—good riddance!)

Britt bit her lip to keep from laughing and shouting. She let joy flood her all the way to her toes for a few moments before taking her emotions firmly in hand.

I am a king, she reminded herself. *I have to think of my country first, not squeal like a schoolgirl and wonder what Merlin was going to say.* The question still nagged at her for a while, but Britt forcibly cleared her mind. Rome had to come first. After that...well, with Merlin's revelation, it seems she had a long time to figure out what was next.

She leaned against the door frame and offered Bedivere a smile. "Am I needed at all in those meetings?"

"As you are the High King, I should think so," Bedivere said.

Britt sighed. "I thought being king meant I got to do more of whatever I wanted and not so many meetings."

"It could be worse," Sir Bedivere said. "After this war, they might try to name you the Roman Emperor as well."

Britt shivered in horror. "I hope not. The last thing we need is for Merlin to get it into his head that we should unite all of Europe, too."

Bedivere laughed, and Britt joined him in the hallway, shutting Merlin's study door behind her. She followed her marshal, pausing in surprise as they came to an intersection in the hallway and almost rammed into Lancelot.

The coal-haired knight bowed his head in deference to Britt. She nodded back at him and was surprised when he said nothing and continued on his route. Britt and Bedivere walked on, though Britt's thoughts were considerably grimmer now.

Sooner or later, I will have to talk to Lancelot about our argument. His silence is making me nervous.

WHEN THE TIME finally came for Britt and all her allies to depart, Sir Ulfius, Sir Bodwain, and Guinevere—who were to remain behind in Camelot—escorted her to the stables to bid her farewell.

Bodwain scratched his graying beard. "Maybe I ought to come along after all."

Britt laughed and handed off the satchel she carried to a stable boy, who loaded it onto her white mare, Llamrei. "I'm sorry to veto the idea, Sir Bodwain, but Merlin made it very clear he wants you and Sir Ulfius to run Camelot in our absence."

"That may be so," Bodwain argued, "but Sir Ector gets to go with you!"

"Sir Ector is mostly coming so I can keep an eye on him and make sure he does not go sticking his nose into danger," Britt said.

Sir Ulfius smiled. "I wish you safe travels and victory in battles, My Lord."

"As do I," Guinevere said with a hasty curtsy. "The ladies of Camelot and I await your victorious return!"

Britt smiled. "With the three of you here, I know I have nothing to worry about. Thank you, and we will do our best!" She nodded to the two older knights and briefly embraced Guinevere.

The knights bowed, and Guinevere offered her a smile that was tight with worry.

Britt winked and then vaulted onto Llamrei's back. "We'll be back before you know it, and then we'll all get to hear about Lancelot's many exploits for the next year. Take care!"

The trio waved as Britt directed Llamrei to the inner court gate that would open up into the city.

Merlin joined her there. "Ready, King Arthur?" He asked, his smile extra bright.

"Ready!"

A set of soldiers pulled the wooden doors open, which groaned on their great hinges. When the doors parted, Llamrei snorted and shied at the crowds that lined the streets, cheering and shouting.

"Hail, King Arthur!"

"Long live the King!"

"There goes the red dragon!"

"High King of Britain!"

Once Britt had Llamrei back under control, she laughed, touched by the loud support. She nudged her white mare forward, making her way down the empty and carefully swept cobblestone pathway that meandered through the city.

Men, women, and children lined the sides of the road all the way to the gatehouse. Some waved white flags with red dragons on them, and others stamped their feet and clapped their hands.

Britt waved and smiled while her heart brimmed with warmth.

It wasn't until they cleared the gatehouse that she could finally hear herself think again over the shouts.

Merlin zipped past her, leading the way through the maze of mounted knights and soldiers who were camped out around Camelot.

"That was an unexpected rush," Britt said.

Merlin stood in his stirrups, peering out over the crowd. "It is not that unexpected. Your people support you in times of peace and war. They know that a Roman overlord would be a bad thing, whereas you have brought nothing but prosperity."

"Couldn't you have just said 'They like you. Congratulations.'?" Britt complained.

"I apologize. They like you. Congratulations," Merlin said.

She rolled her eyes. "It's too late for that now!"

"Hail, King Arthur!

Britt swiveled Llamrei around, a beaming smile invading her

face when she saw her foster father, Sir Ector, and King Pellinore guiding their horses in her direction. "Good morning!"

"I wish you a good morning as well," Pellinore said.

"I was under the impression the armies were ready to leave, and we were holding them up," Sir Ector said. "I'm beginning to think that was nothing more than Kay, trying to get everybody out of Camelot lest he have to feed us one more lunch."

Merlin leaned back in his saddle. "He is a very devoted, very concerned seneschal."

"Indeed!" Pellinore said. "Though I suspect we do not have his keen mind for accounting to thank for the delay. When dealing with such large forces—and from so many different lands—something as simple as leaving turns into a rather grand procession."

"Spoken like a true king," Britt said.

Pellinore eyed her. "Are we renewing our passive argument to use kingly titles, again?"

"No!"

Ector laughed, making his belly jiggle. "No sense standing on ceremony when we're all such good friends."

"Exactly," Britt said emphatically. She glanced at Pellinore to make sure he was listening, but the king had his head cocked.

"Do you hear that?" He asked.

"Hear what?" Merlin asked. "There are thousands of knights and soldiers here; if we didn't hear anything, I would be concerned."

"The baying of many hounds," Pellinore said. "I hear it..."

Ector frowned. "Hounds? I don't believe we're taking any canines with us. Kay thought it was a good idea to even leave Britt's Cavall behind."

"It's not really dogs, just the sound of them," Pellinore said.

"I must say, Pellinore, I don't understand what you're talking about," Britt said.

A gleam appeared in Pellinore's eyes. "'Tis the questing beast!"

Ector frowned, "The what?"

Britt, having remembered that Pellinore used the questing beast as an excuse to frequently leave his lands on wild goose chases and crazy quests, tried to nip the idea in the bud. "Pellinore, no. We are leaving for war; you can't run after it now!"

"It is so close; it must be just past the tree line," Pellinore said. "Come, we may check up on it and be back before you decide how to organize us to leave."

"I am intrigued. I shall come with you!" Ector declared.

Together, the two older knights turned their horses towards the trees and spurred them on.

"Pellinore! Father!" Britt grumbled under her breath as she pointed Llamrei in their direction and gave chase. "Like wrangling cats!"

"They are grown men," Merlin pointed out as he followed after her. "They are capable of taking care of themselves."

"I don't doubt that," Britt said as they wove around a cart crammed with supplies. "What I do doubt is that they actually get back here before we start marching!"

They caught up with the older knights just as the forest began to invade the meadow. It was there that Britt had to admit Pellinore wasn't pulling her leg, for she did hear a strange noise that sounded like a combination of a roaring tiger and a snorting horse.

Pellinore took the lead, navigating his horse through the shrubbery and ducking low-hanging branches. They were far enough into the woods that the trees muffled the noise the troops made, and they could no longer see the edge of the forest when Pellinore held his hand up to stop them. Once he had their attention, he pointed to a small pond positioned in a break in the trees.

Drinking from the pond was a reptile-like creature that had the lean frame and muscle structure of a big cat, a wedge-shaped head like a snake, and bat wings folded on its back.

Britt almost started hyperventilating. For although she accepted with relative ease the idea of faeries, love spells, and magic, she'd never entertained the idea that dragons actually were real. "That's a dragon," she hissed.

Merlin nodded as if this were a commonly witnessed thing. "Yes."

"Calling it the questing beast makes it sound far more interesting than just plainly stating it's a dragon," Sir Ector stated.

Pellinore nodded wisely. "'Tis true. That is why I have dubbed it such."

"It's an honest-to-goodness dragon. It's just the size of a large dog. But it's a *dragon*!" Britt said, still doubting her eyes.

Merlin raised an eyebrow at her. "Why do you keep saying that?"

"I don't know, maybe because it's a *dragon*!"

"Are you going to slay it?" Ector asked Pellinore. "You've chased after it for so long..."

Pellinore smiled ruefully. "Yes, I have enjoyed chasing it many times."

Merlin, looking speculatively back and forth between the king and the dragon, asked, "You've caught it multiple times and let it go, haven't you?"

"It's a thing of beauty," Pellinore said. "And it represents freedom."

"It is also a good excuse to skip out on your duties at Anglesey, isn't it?"

"Adelind is more forgiving if she knows I chased after the beast than if I spent my time riding around picking fights with other knights," Pellinore admitted.

"If you're not going to kill it, then I suggest you scare it off," Merlin advised. "For it to be this close to so many knights and soldiers, someone else is bound to find it."

"You speak the truth," Pellinore acknowledged. He clucked his horse and burst through the bushes. "Be gone with you, questing beast! I shall chase after you another day!"

The dragon growled at Pellinore, but instead of attacking him, as Britt had feared, it turned around, whipping its tail in his direction, and slunk off into the underbrush.

"That was rather anticlimactic," she said.

"It's a rather docile creature, considering that it is a dragon," Pellinore said. "As best as I can tell, it mostly eats small game—rabbits and such."

"You know the creature that well and have been pulling the wool over our eyes this whole time that you have been so arduously chasing after it. Bravo, Pellinore. Lancelot should take acting classes from you," Britt said.

Pellinore laughed. "When you are my age, My Lord, you learn to protect those things in life that you treasure. Riding through the countryside, chasing after that little dragon...." He smiled with fondness in his eyes. "Before you were crowned, times like that were far too infrequent."

Britt turned Llamrei back in the direction of Camelot and the waiting armies. "I think you mean, before you were my ally, times like that weren't very frequent."

"Nay, things have changed—for the better—since you became king, Britt," Pellinore said.

"Hear, hear," Ector said as he nudged his horse and followed after Britt.

"Maybe, but it isn't just because of me," Britt said. "It was because of all the work Merlin did before I came here, and it's because I have experienced knights and lords who helped me—like you two." Britt smiled at Pellinore and Ector.

Ector blushed bright red and smiled brilliantly. Pellinore bowed his head, accepting her words.

"Thank you, by the way, for all your help," she continued. "Your experience and advice have been invaluable, and your mere presence has been a great example for my younger knights." She glanced at Merlin to see if he was going to remark about using pretty words, but he appeared thoughtful as he listened.

"It was my honor to become your ally, Britt, and it is now my honor to call you my king," Pellinore said.

"We're with you until the end, Britt," Ector said. "That's what family does."

Britt smiled sadly at the thought that she might be forced to watch these two great men grow old and die. *Enough. I can think that over later.*

They left the forest, rejoining the forces in the meadow.

"I feel someone scowling at me. Kay must've realized you left," Ector said.

"We better go find him," Britt said. "Or he'll have half the army looking for us."

"The woes of being a well-loved king," Pellinore teased.

"You would know!" Britt shot.

Ector roared with laughter as Britt glanced behind her and smiled at Merlin. The wizard had a small smile on his lips, and he held Britt's gaze with an intense blue light in his eyes as he rode past her.

Yep. No sense worrying about the future yet. She reminded herself. *Particularly when there's a battle just around the corner.*

~

LANCELOT WAS FUSSING with the reins of his palomino charger when his cousin, Lionel, lacking any sort of delicacy, bludgeoned him over the head with words.

"I've noticed you and our dear little king seem to be avoiding each other," he drawled. "Did something happen when you were spying on the enemy?"

"No, nothing at all. I've merely decided she's not worth my time nor my efforts," Lancelot said bitterly. Against his will, he sought Britt Arthurs out in the great army procession.

It was their second day of traveling, and she still rode at the front with Merlin, Gawain, Mordred, and Sir Ector.

"That's a right shame," Lionel said as he scratched his stubbly jaw. "She's quite a bit of fun. In fact, I think I like her."

"Perhaps your swinging emotions when it comes to our king have something to do with the fact that you're rather alike," Bors said, coming up behind him.

"What?" Lancelot snapped. "In what way am I like that self-righteous royal?"

Bors shrugged. "You are both highly skilled and deviously smart, not to mention proud enough to put a peacock to shame."

"Let me find a choir to sing amen to that," Lionel snorted. "But are you sure, Lancelot, you want to cut ties with her?"

"Why on earth would you think I'm not serious about that?" Lancelot asked.

Lionel squinted up at the sun that was playing peek-a-boo behind the clouds. "Mostly because she's the first one besides us you've shown your ugly side to."

Lancelot shut his mouth so fast his teeth made an audible click.

"Strategically all is not lost," Bors added. "Our king highly values truth, somewhat ironically so given what she hid from us for so long. If you are open and honest with her regarding your rotten personality, there is a chance she may consider you a close companion."

Lancelot glared at his cousin, both for the idea and the insult. "It does not matter. My mind is made up; I no longer care what the king makes of me. I only care that I am revered and admired by everyone else."

As if I would so easily forgive her!

Telling Vivien about Excalibur's scabbard had not greatly improved Lancelot's mood, as he had thought it would. Instead, Britt Arthurs' judgment against him nipped at his heels, bothering him whenever he smiled and chatted with ladies or laughed with any of the knights who admired him.

Lancelot was not so preoccupied with feeling sorry for himself that he missed the looks of disbelief his cousins exchanged. Irritated—with Britt that she still managed to rile him up even when they weren't talking, and with his cousins that they held so little faith in his hatred—Lancelot snapped, "Besides, our king is not the kind-hearted hero everyone makes her out to be. She's made up her mind about me, and she'll never treat me with the mercy and love she gives away to her dim-witted, undeserving knights."

"What if she did?" Bors asked.

"There's no use thinking about it when her very personality would go against that," Lancelot said. "Besides, it does not matter for, as I stated earlier, I intend not to involve myself with her anymore."

"We'll see about that," Lionel said with aggravating cheerfulness. "I say, though. I can't wait to get to the main camp. Battles and fighting Romans are very fine, but all this organization is maddening!"

"Father will be coming," Bors said, copying his brother and changing the topic. "I suspect he left mother back in Gaul, but it will be good to see him at least..."

Lancelot listened to his cousins with only half an ear. The rest of his attention was on the back of a certain girl king, watching as she rode along with her companions and laughed.

If she ever finds out what I told Vivien, I'm certain she'll scorn me for life. Then that will show her true colors...

11
MUSTERED FORCES

After several days of riding, Britt—accompanied by a force of knights—reached the central camp.

She trotted in, still riding Llamrei, with Griflet, Mordred, and Gawain. The other kings—including King Anguish of Ireland, King Lot of Orkney, and King Urien—rode with her company as well.

Mordred shielded his eyes from the midday sun and squinted, his slight spattering of freckles crinkling. "Is that King Bors of Gaul, and King Ban of Benwick?"

Britt turned Llamrei in the direction he faced and spotted the swarthy king and his well-dressed brother-in-law. "Yes, that is they! Merlin said they would meet us here, but I didn't think they would arrive before we did." She looked between the already-settled kings and those who had ridden with her, and connected the dots of Merlin's thinking.

She had assumed they were all riding together for the purpose of reaching camp and holding a meeting, but instead it seemed that they were all staying at the medieval equivalent of the "executive floor," for the camp sported much larger and more colorful tents made of high-quality and costly fabrics. She understood Merlin had done it for political maneuvering, but she couldn't help but wonder if it was a wise tactic to put all the allies and royalty together.

"Father!" Ywain, dressed in shiny armor emblazoned with a red lioness, strode through camp with a big smile. He marched straight up to his father, King Urien, embracing him in a bear hug when he dismounted.

When he smiled and laughed, Britt barely recognized King Urien. His entire countenance was transformed, and Britt could finally see the good humor in his eyes that seemed perpetually present in Ywain's eyes as well.

Their family reunion was not the only one.

Lancelot's cousins, Lionel and Bors, greeted their father, as well. Lionel and King Bors roared at each other across the camp and embraced like two bucks slamming into each other. Sir Bors the younger approached his father much more quietly and with a subdued smile, though he submitted happily enough to his father's rough embrace.

"You boys have grown! I imagine you've been on all sorts of adventures and quests! Some of them got back to Gaul—in particular I heard the one about the giant you two and Lancelot took out. Well done!" King Bors ruffled his sons' hair and chortled.

Lancelot, never to be outdone by a dramatic reunion, shouted, "Father! It has been too long!" He strode up to his father, King Ban, with a radiant smile.

King Ban clasped forehands with his son, then slapped him on the back. "It has, but I have heard you are called the best knight in Camelot. Well done, Lancelot!"

Britt could see the similarities between the father and son in their tall and lean builds, but it was especially obvious in the way they kept meticulous care of their appearance.

She smiled, happy to see the family reunions, but also a little sad as she missed her mother and sister with the pain of a long-borne ache.

"My Lord!" Ywain pulled himself from his father's embrace and marched towards Britt with great purpose, weaving around horses. Wherever he went, horses seem to spook, and it wasn't until they moved around Mordred's charger that Britt could see why.

At Ywain's side padded a small lioness. Britt was tempted to rub her eyes as she stared at the creature, wondering what on earth an honest-to-gosh lioness was doing in *England*.

Ywain didn't seem to notice Britt's shock or that she was reluctant to get off of Llamrei, who snorted at the big cat. He grinned as he reached up with a "helping hand" and pulled her straight off the saddle. "Thank you for your advice, My Lord!"

"I can guess by your countenance that you have spoken with Laudine again?" Britt asked, shifting her attention back and forth between Ywain and his cat.

"Indeed, I have! She has forgiven me, though I had to do a number of quests to get her attention. That's how I befriended this fine feline!" Ywain crouched down and petted the lion.

Britt was mildly fascinated and concerned when it started purring like a barn cat. "That is a very unusual traveling companion you have with you."

"I saved her, and ever since, she's followed me. Laudine loves her, so it works out well. But that's not what I wanted to tell you!" He abruptly stood, the set of his face serious as he met Britt's gaze. "You were right; I didn't understand what Laudine was feeling. I'll be more mindful of it in the future, but thank you, My Lord. You've helped me, and Laudine, in more ways than you know."

Britt shook her head. "I could've talked until I was blue in the face, but you are the one who chose to do something. If things are better, it is because you took an active role."

"But I'd still be moping across the countryside if you hadn't given me the lecture I needed. Laudine understands as well. She actually sent a number of troops who will be under my command during the battle."

Surprised by this development, Britt hesitated for a moment. "That is very kind of her, especially considering I know protection is a great concern of hers."

Ywain nodded. "It is, but she knows I have great loyalty to you, and Britain has flourished under your rule."

"Thank you for coming," Britt added. "I know it must've been hard to leave her so soon."

"I won't lie, I was sad to go. But what kind of shield would I be if I didn't come when you needed me most?" He grinned and shifted his gaze to Mordred and Griflet. "I trust your ride was uneventful?"

Though his horse still snorted at the lioness with bugged eyes, Mordred was calm. "It was."

"What in the name of all things holy possessed you to think that dragging a lioness to battle was a good idea?" Griflet asked. He peered down at the lioness from the safety of his horse's back with a dubious expression.

"Ah, she's as harmless as a kitten," Ywain claimed.

"I imagine she is one of the Romans' trained cats," Mordred supposed. He dismounted his horse and offered his hand to the lioness to smell. "I had not heard they ever use them in battle, but I know some of the old stories regarding Colosseum fights."

"I'm not convinced," Sir Griflet said as he watched Mordred pet the lioness, eliciting more purrs from it. "I doubt a battle cat knows how to purr like that."

Britt, feeling emboldened thanks to Mordred's actions, also started patting the lioness. "Perhaps she was a faerie pet. Don't they keep all strange sorts of animals?"

"Whatever she was, she's mine now!" Ywain said happily. He inclined his head, fighting to see over the sea of horses and mounted soldiers. "If you don't mind excusing me, my Lord, I would like to escort my father to the tent Laudine sent with me."

"Let me guess, does it have a lioness on it?" Griflet asked.

"Go ahead, you hardly need my permission," Britt laughed.

"I'll see you at dinner, then. Take care My Lord, Mordred, Griflet-the-fainthearted."

"You take that back!" Griflet shouted. He was too slow, for Ywain was already off striding through the horses. His lioness padded after him, causing chaos and spooking horses wherever she went.

Britt rubbed her head. "Has England always been this weird? Because I don't remember things being quite so strange when I first arrived."

"A tame lioness is a new one," Mordred acknowledged.

"It's probably just that your reign is now spreading so far, My Lord, that you're hearing tales from all over England and not just the forest of Arroy." Griflet dismounted and fondly patted his horse.

Britt smiled at Sir Tor, who beamed at her as he led three horses to a water trough. "Maybe…but it does make me wonder what changes, because it's certainly not like this in the…" She trailed off before she gave away more.

Though her knights were aware of her true gender and that she was not from Britain, they still did not know that she was, in fact, from the future.

But the thought still nagged her. Now, things like fairies, magic swords, and, apparently, dragons were commonplace. But in the twenty-first century, ignoring the occasional Nessie story, there was nothing magical in life.

"I need to water my charger. Would you like me to take Llamrei for you, My Lord?" Griflet asked.

"Thanks for the offer, but it's fine." She offered him a smile, but Griflet tucked his chin and pursed his lips.

"Llamrei needs water, and your time is better spent than serving as a stable hand for your horse," he insisted.

"I'm sure your time is better spent than playing stable hand for your horse as well," Britt pointed out.

He laughed. "Perhaps so, but I need to do something with my hands after riding so long." He plucked Llamrei's reins from Britt before she could protest and wandered off in the direction of the horse troughs. "Sir Tor! How goes it?" he shouted before slipping around a tent.

Britt watched him go, a thoughtful frown settling on her lips. "Guinevere told me Blancheflor rejected him. He seems to be taking it quite well."

Mordred chuckled and flashed his dimples. "I would suspect it's because he is not seeing it so much as defeat, as much as a temporary loss."

Britt pivoted so she could directly address Mordred. "He hasn't given up then?"

"No, indeed not! Why, before he left, he asked the lady Blancheflor to give him a handkerchief as a token for war."

"And?"

"He was rejected flat," Mordred said cheerfully.

Britt winced. "Poor guy. I guess the one bright spot is that Blancheflor doesn't seem to favor anyone else, so he still has a chance." She smiled and waved when Sir Lanval and Sir Safir bowed at her, then continued on their way towards a campfire.

"Truthfully, I think his chances of winning her over are higher now that she has at least acknowledged his presence enough to reject him," Mordred said.

"Perhaps..." She let her thoughts wander as her gaze settled on King Anguish and several of the other foreign kings. "I owe you my thanks, Mordred."

The handsome knight pulled his horse's reins over its head. "What for?"

"For convincing your brother and his allies to come." Britt smiled weakly. "Though I'm sorry to drag everyone into this mess, there's no denying that the more allies we have, the better off we will be."

Mordred rested his arm on his horse's neck. "I had heard it has been Merlin's mission to attack Ireland. Part of why I appreciate you, Arthur, is because you see war as a last resort, not the first thing to do. That is why I took my vows to you, and I will honor them to the best of my ability. You've changed Britain."

Britt shook her head. "People keep saying that, but I don't think they understand. It's not just me." She gazed out at the camp, her eyes tracing over the familiar faces of her knights and allies. "Camelot isn't great just because of the efforts of one person, but because of all the Knights of the Round Table, and all the men and women who serve there. Bandits are being defeated, and dishonorable knights are being routed not because of me, but because of the knights who go out and serve justice." She hesitated. "It's bigger than me now. If something were to happen to me, Camelot could survive as long as knights continued to serve there."

Mordred abruptly straightened. "Even so, it is to be hoped *that* is something we will never have to find out."

"True," Britt said with a forced laugh. *If Merlin's right and magic has stopped my aging, it might end up being the opposite. I might remain in Camelot, alone, without my knights.*

"Arthur, you rascal," King Bors trumpeted. He smacked Britt on the shoulder with enough force to send her sprawling. "You do have a way with women! Why, I would say you are even better with them than Lancelot is!"

Britt coughed, her lungs still rattling from the blow. "May I inquire as to what you are referring, King Bors?"

"Why, the ladies who are waiting in your tent for you, of course!" He winked at her. "Don't worry; we won't let word get back to your pretty little Guinevere. I should think even *she* would be jealous if she heard Morgan le Fay and the Lady of the Lake were lounging around in your personal tent."

"Morgan and Nymue are here?" Britt asked eagerly.

King Bors scratched his wild beard. "Yep. Arrived this morning!"

As Britt had seen neither of her friends since well before she had been kidnapped by Duke Maleagant, she brightened considerably. (That, and their timely arrival reminded Britt that she wouldn't be alone. For if she was immortal like the Faerie folk, she would have Nymue!)

"Thank you, King Bors! I will see you later!"

Britt made a beeline for the tents, looking for the biggest and grandest of them all—for she knew Merlin would never allow another king to have something better than hers.

She found it in the center of the camp: a red monstrosity decorated with black dragons and sword blades.

She eagerly threw open the tent flap and stepped inside, laughing when she saw Morgan and Nymue lounging on a mound of pillows and drinking from gold goblets. "You came!" she said.

"Of course we came," Nymue scoffed. "If we hadn't, you would never have let us hear the end of it."

Morgan stood, a gentle smile on her lips. "And the heavens know the Lancelot Hate Club must never be parted for too long." She gently embraced Britt in spite of the armor she wore. "It is good to see you, Britt."

Nymue patted the pillows next to her. "Sit. You've much to tell us, for Ragnelle mentioned she thought you and the Debaucher quarreled."

Britt sat down gratefully. "We did, but that's not my biggest news."

"Out with it," Morgan prompted.

As Britt settled into place—relieved she could finally discuss her newfound agelessness—she knew she was grinning like an idiot. Not because of the topic, but because her friends had come.

~

"When I followed Vivien to the main Roman camp, I was able to confirm that Emperor Lucius himself will be leading his troops," Merlin said. "This means there are several inferences we can make based on the tactics and strategies he has used in the past."

Britt only half listened to Merlin as he had already stated this in the morning meeting, and also because she was fighting a mild case of claustrophobia.

All day long she had been stuck in a stuffy tent with Merlin and dozens of men—mostly the kings and leaders of the troops. They were packed in so tightly, Britt couldn't even fidget without touching Kay or Ector, who sat on either side of her. (And she was in the front where it was *roomy*!)

But while everyone else was free to come and go during the long, exhaustive, *never-ending* battle preparation meetings, Merlin and Britt had been cooped up all day. (Britt because she was the High King; Merlin because he was the mastermind behind their strategy.) The constant comings and goings were the reason why Merlin was starting to repeat himself.

The leaders had to inspect their troops, and it wouldn't be wise to have everyone of importance crammed into one place at one time (never mind that there probably wasn't a tent big enough to house them all), so instead the tactical meeting was scheduled to last *all day.*

"Lucius always keeps his armies in one big group as he favors the classic head-on battle," Merlin said. "This means he will likely not split up his troops or attempt to flank our army. Normally, he overwhelms the enemy through sheer numbers. But while we are outnumbered, it's not the great discrepancy he usually fights at."

Britt exhaled. A muscle on her cheek twitched when she adjusted her feet and almost got herself entangled with Kay as a result.

Ector leaned over a smidge so he could whisper in her ear, "Why don't you take a break, Arthur? Surely you deserve one by now."

Britt shook her head. "It's my responsibility to be present for this kind of thing."

Now it was Kay's turn to incline his head. "Perhaps, but our forces will become concerned if you force yourself to remain here to the point of screaming."

"I am not that close to losing it," Britt scoffed. Someone shifted behind her, and she could feel their breath brush her hair.

Her eyebrow twitched.

"Go, Arthur. There's no sense in hearing the plans more than once when you are responsible for a single company of knights," Ector urged.

Britt pressed her lips together for a moment, internally debating the wisdom of their words. Her selfish side won, and she stood and slipped from the tent. She passed by Morgan, who squeezed her hand in encouragement before she glided to the seat Britt had abandoned.

Britt paused at the threshold of the tent and watched Morgan and Kay exchange smiles. Her heart warming at the sight, she pushed open the tent flap and stepped outside into the cool, fresh spring air.

She closed her eyes and breathed in and out several times, stretching her arms out and enjoying the open space. She rolled her neck, then looked around, her gaze settling on Lionel, Bors, and Lancelot, who were huddled nearby.

When they glanced at her, Britt offered them a smile and a nod, then deliberately turned her back to them, intending to slink away.

Unfortunately, she was thwarted by Lionel, who called out

after her. "My Lord! How goes the meeting?"

Britt awkwardly pivoted so she faced them again and scratched the back of her neck. "Well enough. Everyone's agreed on the tactics we've outlined thus far." She offered them another smile, her professional/political Arthur one, and began sidling away. "I trust your preparations have been going well?"

Bors smiled and approached Britt, breaching the few steps she put between them. "There's not much to prepare—we cleaned and cared for our weapons back in Camelot. I assumed father would need more of our help with his troops, but since he arrived earlier than we, the soldiers from Gaul are already settled and well organized."

Lionel threw his arm over Lancelot's shoulders and followed his brother, dragging Lancelot in his wake. Clearly, they weren't going to let her get away. "It is probably Uncle Ban's doing, as well. They always work better together. Isn't that right, Lancelot?"

"Naturally," Lancelot said. He wore a politely interested smile but with an unusually closed mouth.

Britt nodded in the awkward silence that ensued. "I see. That's good."

The brothers nodded and said nothing more, and Lancelot flicked Lionel's arm off him with a little more force than necessary.

Eager to escape the awkward situation, Britt began eyeing an exit route. "If you'll excuse—"

"Arthur!" Britt had never been so relieved to hear Nymue's prissy-sounding voice. "I'm bored. This camp reeks of unwashed men, and Morgan insists on not-so-subtly making eyes at your brother. Amuse me." The faerie lady waltzed down a narrow lane between two tents and latched on to Britt's arm. She spared the merest glance at Britt's conversational partners, then recoiled in horror. "You!" She declared.

Bors and Lionel bowed together. "Good day to you, Lady

Nymue," Bors said.

"How's your magic lake?" Lionel asked.

Nymue's face wrinkled with disdain. "Still recovering from your most recent visit. I'm amazed you didn't eat all the fish in the lake, only most of them."

Lionel laughed and rubbed his stomach. "I do recall you have good eatings at your sanctuary."

"And I recall you have the hunger of four packs of wolves combined."

"Well, there's an awful lot of me to feed," Lionel supposed.

Nymue rolled her eyes in disgust, but Bors laughed.

Britt relaxed slightly, heartened that the attention was now off her. She straightened in surprise when Lancelot broke under their loud conversation.

"You aren't going to apologize for your harsh judgment against me?" Lancelot asked. He almost drawled the question, and his voice was deceivingly relaxed.

Britt inspected him, searching for any sign of hidden anger. "No."

Lancelot laughed, drawing barely more than the briefest glance from Nymue, Lionel, and Bors, who were still arguing over appetites.

"I'm glad to see you stand by your word," Lancelot said. "If you had apologized, I likely would've lost all respect for you."

Britt shrugged. "You are the one who wanted to know what I thought of you, though I will admit I shouldn't have railed at you like I did."

Lancelot offered her a skin-deep smile. "No harm done," he said.

Britt didn't believe him for a moment.

"I am only sorry," he continued, "that I fall short of the lofty goal you wish us knights to pursue. I'm afraid even I am unable to reach the impossible feats of justice and honor you have in mind."

Britt frowned slightly. "What are you talking about? You absolutely are capable of being the sort of knight I praise."

He raised his eyebrows. "Oh really? When you so deeply criticized my true personality?"

"I don't care that you're catty, or that you don't really have the simpering personality you present my courts. What ticks me off is when you don't help those who truly need your help, merely because it won't benefit you. You're absolutely able to do that, you just choose not to."

"I beg your pardon, My Lord." Lancelot narrowed his eyes slightly as his expression turned cold. "But I have yet to meet a person who truly does something out of love, not personal gain. The knights you preen over may perform their great feats because they know it would make you happy, but it is because they directly benefit from your joy."

Britt shook her head and was about to correct him when Nymue stamped her foot.

"Fine," the faerie lady spat. "But do not dare to show your faces at my lake, or I will have you tossed out!" She turned to Britt, her chin high with disdain. "Come, Arthur." Briefly yanking Britt's arm as she passed, she sailed away.

Britt was not sorry to leave the three men, so she did nothing to attempt to stop her friend, merely nodded to the knights, then caught up with Nymue. "Thanks for that timely save," she said.

Nymue wrinkled her nose. "I wouldn't have rescued you if I knew to whom you had been speaking." She shivered in horror. "Truly, it is beyond me how you endure those three in your courts. Now, for more genteel topics. Though Morgan and I will not take part in the battle, we do plan to set up a station where we can dress wounds and injuries. One of my handmaidens, Ragnelle, is moon-eyed for your Sir Gawain, so she intends to help us as well."

"Oh, you're going to be medics?"

"I assume that is some futuristic, mumbo-jumbo term?"

"The irony of a faerie lady using the term mumbo-jumbo to describe futuristic events has not escaped me," Britt declared.

"You are odd."

"And you have the personality of a hag."

"You fish-wife!"

Britt laughed, and Nymue could keep up her act of disdain for only a couple moments more before she joined Britt with an unlikely giggle.

"Thank you for coming, Nymue," Britt said.

"You are my friend," Nymue said in a rare moment of sincerity. "In case you haven't noticed, I don't have many of those. So I will be with you as long as you need me."

The girls exchanged smiles and went on their way, enjoying the last bit of sunshine before the grim reality of the battle would ensue.

~

THE NIGHT BEFORE THE BATTLE, Britt sat just below the crest of a hill and looked out at the ocean of tents spread before her. Flickering campfires were plumes of light, illuminating the soldiers—who looked toy-sized from this distance—huddled around them and casting shadows on tents.

Britt was too far away from the camp to hear any of the murmured conversations shared between soldiers, but the occasional whinny from a horse or dog barking broke the silence.

The sight was strangely pretty, but at the same time haunting. As she watched the soldiers, she couldn't help but wonder who she would lose the following day. She prayed her knights would be spared, that she wouldn't lose anyone dear to her... But she knew whether or not she lost any of her personal friends, there would be men who wouldn't return home to their families because of her actions.

She tore her eyes away from the peaceful sight in front of her and pinched her eyes shut. Her heart ached.

A branch broke, and the guards surrounding her in a semicircle brandished their weapons in an instant.

"It's just me."

Britt forced herself to look up and offer Merlin a shaky smile as he marched past her guards and sat next to her.

The guards frowned at him and took shuffling steps closer to him and Britt.

Merlin frowned up at them. "Yes?"

"'Tis nothing at all, sir," the guard captain said, even as he drew closer.

"Then will you so kindly back off?"

"Sir Kay told us to take special care with Milord when you visit her," the guard captain said smoothly.

Merlin scowled. "I'm not going to accost her."

"Of course not," the captain agreed, "but we have our orders."

"Guys," Britt said. "It's fine. Thank you, but it'll be all right."

The guards looked unconvinced and gazed suspiciously at Merlin.

"You heard her," Merlin said. "Shoo!"

The guards slowly ambled away, stopping when they were out of hearing range.

"Your foster-brother is awfully meddlesome," Merlin observed.

Britt tried to chuckle, but the sound got caught in her throat, so she made more of a gurgling croak.

Merlin glanced at her but said nothing as he settled into place, joining her in looking out at the camp. "You can't let yourself carry too much of this burden, Britt," he said abruptly. "Yes, some will perish in tomorrow's battle. But you must remember that if these brave men wouldn't fight, their families would pay the price. Don't cheapen their sacrifice and take responsibility for the enemy's actions."

He scratched his chin and continued. "I know I once told you to make certain that every drop of bloodshed in battles is worth it, and you've done that. You have the biggest army Britain has ever mustered *because* you've proven that things can be better. These men march to your banner—and perhaps to their death—because they believe in the Britain you've created, and they want to protect it."

Britt's eyes stung with unshed tears. "How do you do that?"

"Do what?"

"How do you know what I'm thinking when I haven't said a word?" She studied him, hoping for some kind of revelation, but Merlin merely shrugged his shoulders.

"We haven't had a chance to speak privately since I told you of your status as ageless. Have you had time to adjust yet?"

Britt leaned back, bracing herself by placing her palms on the grassy ground. "I'm much more concerned about tomorrow's battle."

Merlin grunted.

"Besides, I meant what I said. No matter what you say, I will die one day, regardless of my immortal status. But I did think about it, and I realized I won't be alone. I'll still have Nymue and the rest of the faerie folk. Granted, besides Nymue, I'm not really friendly with anyone else, but it looks like I'll have time to fix that...."

"It really doesn't bother you?" Merlin asked.

"Well, it does a little. But most people would rejoice about it. I'm a little surprised you seem so worried I would take it badly."

"You are not like most people," Merlin said. "Relationships and friendships mean a great deal to you. You value them deep in your heart, and you don't easily let a person slip from you. Immortality is probably the worst thing that can happen to you, as you will be forced to see those you love die."

"You're right. It will be hard, but I will always welcome people into my heart."

"And that will lock you in an endless cycle of loving and

watching them leave you."

Britt's palms itched from the grass. "Maybe." She brushed her hands off on her thighs and leaned forward, hugging her legs to her chest. "But the joy of knowing and loving is worth the heartache of losing. It will hurt to say goodbye, but I will never regret loving my knights. I can't picture not knowing Ector, Kay, Gawain…or you, Merlin." She smiled at him, but Merlin would not meet her gaze.

Feeling rejected, Britt awkwardly cleared her throat. She plucked a wad of grass in the ensuing, oppressive silence. *I guess that was too much for him. I better think of something to lighten the mood.*

"The reason I can guess what you're thinking is because I love you," Merlin blurted out.

Britt dropped her chunk of grass in surprise and stared, open mouthed, at the wizard.

He still wasn't looking at her; he was staring down at the camp as if it was the most fascinating thing in the world. "I realized long ago you are far more important to me than uniting Britain. I knew it shortly after we had that wretched argument about your feelings for me. I could've gladly poked Lancelot's eyes out when he started sniffing around you after discovering you are a woman—and that's only after I would've killed him for stabbing you. And even though I knew how I felt about you, I couldn't just…I knew I didn't…" He huffed angrily.

Britt, still in a state of shock and delight at his obvious embarrassment, refrained from helping him.

With a frustrated sigh, he rubbed his forehead. "I should've better prepared for this. I should have taken notes or read a book or something. It is merely…I couldn't say anything," he spat out. "I ruined your life! I've caused you so much pain just by bringing you here. And my thoughtlessness will cause you so much pain in the future now that you're ageless." He finally met her gaze, and Britt was startled by the anguish in his eyes.

"I don't even know how to show you that I love you because the second I met you, you changed everything," he whispered.

Britt, finally taking pity, leaned over and rested her head on his shoulder. "I know. It's the same for me."

Merlin exhaled, a rattling noise that sounded as if it began in his heart.

"It's all right, Merlin," she continued. "It's like I said earlier. It's worth all the heartache, no matter the outcome." She sat upright, then held out her hand. "I have loved you regardless, and I'm still thankful that you brought me here."

Slowly, as if he were a tad frightened, Merlin extended his own hand and entwined his fingers with hers.

Britt smiled down at their hands, then yipped when Merlin yanked her into an unexpected embrace.

"I should say something here," he muttered into her neck. "But I can't think of anything that can accurately express my feelings without making me sound like one of those dramatic minstrels who skulk around your halls."

Britt laughed. She laughed with the joy of knowing that her feelings were returned; she laughed at the unexpected delight of seeing Merlin brought low by his own doing, and she laughed with the security of one who knows she is loved.

Merlin tugged her closer still, threading one of his hands through her hair and gripping her waist with the other.

"You're wearing too much armor," he said, looking at her darkly.

She chuckled and wrapped her arms around his waist. "You'll get over it."

Her heart galloped in her chest when he slid his fingers along her jaw line and tipped her head back.

Merlin, his fine blonde hair glittering in the moonlight, smiled at her with eyes alight with tenderness and love. "I love you, Britt Arthurs," he repeated.

Before she could respond, he kissed her, and the rest of the world faded into insignificance.

Merlin's kiss was light and warm, but it hit her with the strength of a stab to the chest. It was barely more than a caressing brush, but the chemistry it packed made Britt's mind explode. For the first time since arriving in ancient Britain, everything was right. She did not feel pulled between two times, but just existed in the moment.

When he released her, he shook his head lightly. "Are you sure you don't have some faerie blood after all, because that was..."

"Magical?" Britt suggested.

Merlin did not let her go far, but instead rested his forehead against hers. "I know magic, and it pales in comparison to that," he said in a hoarse voice.

Britt tried to laugh, but she could only airily exhale. She closed her eyes and savored the moment, committing to memory the warmth of Merlin's hug and the brush of his silken hair against her forehead. "So if you've been in love with me since our argument, that means you've been holding out a long time," she said.

"Hmm?" Merlin said, seemingly distracted as he ran a hand through her hair again. "Oh, aye."

"Which means you owe me a detailed explanation of how it all went down," Britt grinned.

"I see. That's reasonable, I suppose. Though it started when I first saw you, I don't think it set in until you called me a roadside magician."

"Ahhh. That was when Morgause visited, and you called me an ungrateful pig-child, was it not?"

"Behold, the astounding verbal exchange between lovers," Merlin said, kissing her cheek.

Laughter bubbled up from the pit of Britt's stomach, and for an evening...everything was perfect.

12
THE FIGHT FOR BRITAIN

Though she wanted nothing more than to fidget and bite her lip, Britt kept her back ramrod straight and her expression serene as she, seated on Roen's back, faced down the massive Roman army.

The two armies had gathered in what Merlin claimed was called the Vale of Soissons.

Britt didn't know why the valley had a name—it was utterly unremarkable and looked like every other valley she had seen. (Except for the Roman army positioned at the opposite end, that was.)

Though the sky was heavy with overcast clouds, Britt squinted to try and make out individual soldiers.

The Roman legionnaires were much more intimidating than Britt had imagined. They wore the uniforms Britt had seen in movies—a red woolen tunic with curved metal shoulder guards and body armor, and a skirt made of leather strips. What she had not prepared herself for, however, was the sheer *power* they radiated.

Each soldier carried a rectangular wooden shield that was more than half as large as he was, a throwing spear, a gladius sword designed for thrusting, and multiple daggers. Whether it was because of all the weaponry they carried or their training, the soldiers were built like bears but had an unnerving amount of organization and moved in precise formations.

The Roman army was not a citizen militia, as many of Britt's soldiers were. It was a trained war machine that would devour whatever was in its path.

Intermingled with the Roman forces were soldiers from King Ryence's lands, marked by the orange and green banding on their uniforms.

"Fear not," Merlin proclaimed loudly as he popped out of the ranks of the army gathered behind Britt. "Though the enemy is fierce, surely God is with us."

Britt raised an eyebrow at him. "Is that for me, or for the men?"

"For you," Merlin said. "Everyone else made their peace long ago and is eager to fight on behalf of Britain." He paused a few moments, directing his horse closer to her so he could ask in a lowered tone. "Are you all right?"

She pressed her lips together. "I'm afraid," she admitted. "The last time we had a real battle, I didn't have a clue what was going on, and I was over-confident due to my sketchy knowledge of Arthurian lore."

"And now?"

"I know better."

Merlin nodded slowly. "Then I have a question for you. Are Camelot and the Round Table—the justice, honor, and chivalry you've fought to incorporate, the lives you've changed, and the moral code you've established—are they worth fighting for?"

Britt didn't hesitate to answer. "Absolutely."

"Then rest on that knowledge," Merlin advised. "You fight so that your people may live in peace."

As she mulled over Merlin's words, she turned in a circle. Much of her tension eased when she saw her army.

Knights and soldiers alike were spread behind her in a glittering array. Banner carriers were posted throughout the mass, marking the different kings and their soldiers with colorful flags that stood out starkly against the backdrop of polished armor.

Merlin was right. Men from all across Britain, Ireland, and Scotland stood together to fight, perhaps for the first time ever, in a united front.

Britt smiled at the picture, and then at the company she was to lead—a large group of Camelot's best knights, including: Kay, Bedivere, Tor, Mordred, Gawain, Griflet, Lancelot, Lionel, Safir, Lanval, and more.

(Ywain had campaigned hard to be included in her company, but Merlin refused on the basis that *someone* had to lead the troops Laudine had sent into battle.)

"Did you see Emperor Lucius?" Merlin asked.

"No. Where is he?"

Merlin nodded at the opposing forces. "He's the one in the fancy armor surrounded by all the banners and flags."

Though he was too far away to make out the details, Britt spotted the Emperor, who wore a chestplate wrought in one solid piece, and also sported arm and leg guards—unlike his soldiers.

Britt marked him in her mind—he was the one they would have to capture to end this, or he would return to the Roman Empire, gather another army, and march it north again.

King Pellinore, who was included in Britt's company as he had dumped the responsibility of leading Anglesey's troops on Percival, broke ranks and joined her and Merlin. "Are you ready, Arthur?"

Britt nodded.

Merlin peered up and down the ranks. "It seems that all preparations are complete. We are ready for battle."

Pellinore slightly bowed his head. "Then if you would signal the troops, Arthur?"

Britt paused.

"You don't want to use the agreed upon signal, do you?" Merlin asked.

"Because it sounds *stupid*," Britt said emphatically.

"It will appear impressive," Pellinore said.

"It will make me look like one of those cheesy heroes in the movies," Britt argued.

Pellinore tilted his head. "The what?"

"Stop complaining and just do it," Merlin ordered.

Britt kept an endless grumble going under her breath as she nudged Roen forward, pulling out in front of the army so all could see her. She kept complaining as she unsheathed Excalibur—the magic sword seemed to glow in the gloom of the valley—then swung it up in the air.

As planned, Merlin hit Excalibur with a burst of magic, making it shine like an exploding star.

The little show made the British army cheer, but Roen—who was quite difficult to spook—apparently drew the line at having a beacon shine above his head and reared with a loud whinny.

Britt—a competent enough rider but *not* the natural her knights were—turned her grumblings into muffled oaths as she clung to the saddle and tried to stay seated without stabbing herself or her gelding with her bare sword.

The cheers grew thunderous at this spectacle, and Britt forced herself to smile as she returned to her company of knights.

Merlin nodded in satisfaction. "Well done," he said.

Britt watched as different parts of their army pulled out. Among the first was Ywain and his troops, moving with his father, King Urien and his soldiers. On the opposite end were Agravain and King Lot, leading Orkney troops into battle. Next, King Anguish and his army moved out, followed shortly by Sir Ector with Bonmaison soldiers, and Duke Maleagant and King Bagdemagus with their forces.

Britt watched them sweep across the vale, their weapons drawn as they descended upon the enemy soldiers with shouts.

"For Britain!"

"For Arthur!"

The Roman army moved as one, holding their formations and raising their shields against any mounted knights. The song of weapons clashing and the thump of shields being smacked filled the air, nearly eclipsing the shouts. Roman archers, positioned farther back, began releasing waves of arrows and picking off British soldiers.

Percival, leading Anglesey's forces—which were mostly archers—brought his men forward, secured behind the closed ranks of King Lot's and King Urien's troops. The Anglesey archers engaged the Roman forces and began picking off enemy archers.

Britt began last-minute checks of Roen's tack and armor as she prepped for her charge.

"Though I won't ride with you, I'll be watching," Merlin promised. "Magic isn't good for battles like this when the fights are too close to differentiate friend from foe, but if you're in trouble, I'll be able to give you a hand when needed."

Britt smiled. "I appreciate it."

Merlin glanced back at the army, then nudged his horse so close their knees brushed. "Be careful, lass." He reached out and quickly squeezed her hand, the only show of affection he dared display in front of so many who didn't know the truth of Britt's identity. He cleared his throat and rubbed the back of his neck awkwardly. "Ride with courage. But be safe."

Britt grinned. "'Course. I'm King Arthur, aren't I?" She glanced over her shoulder to make certain her knights were watching her, then waited for King Ban and King Bors—whom Sir Bors the younger rode with—to lead their charge first.

She wanted to say something to her knights, for in every movie she had ever seen speeches were given directly before war, but intellectually she knew it was a very stupid idea to try and lecture her knights in the middle of a bloodbath. So instead, she raised Excalibur and roared, "For Britain!"

Britt and her knights swept across the field, their horses eating up the ground between them and the enemy.

The red cloak Britt wore flared up behind her, and her knights roared like dragons as they descended upon the Romans, a grim picture of death and beauty with their polished armor and thundering warhorses.

The first line of Roman soldiers raised their shields, but they didn't get their spears up fast enough, so the horses plowed straight through them, breaking their ranks like a plow parting the field.

The acidic, metallic scent of blood laced the air, as did the shouts of the wounded and fallen. Britt swung her sword, downing soldiers as Roen knocked men away.

Mordred and Gawain flanked her, protecting her back when soldiers tried to encircle her. Once or twice Kay and Griflet zigzagged in front of her, trampling soldiers who hefted spears in her direction as she cut a path straight through the army. Pellinore roared as he took out a row of soldiers, and Lancelot caused chaos as he snaked his horse through the enemies' formation.

Sweat dripped down her temple, and Britt reined Roen in long enough for her company to reform their ranks. Craning her neck, she searched out Sir Ector. She spotted him fighting one-on-one with a Roman centurion, but as she watched, Bonmaison soldiers moved to support their lord, ensuring his safety.

Continuing her survey of the battlefield, she spied Ywain—whose crumpled chest plate bore the signs of a mace blow. The knight himself, though, was fine as he and his lioness roared together, frightening a number of Roman soldiers so badly they actually fled rather than hold their ranks.

The brother kings, Ban and Bors, teamed up with King

Anguish, and together they completely immobilized the right fringe of the Roman army.

Agravain had been unhorsed, but he had wrestled a war hammer away from a fallen soldier and was sending men flying left and right. As un-fatherly as he appeared to be, King Lot followed closely behind his son, keeping an eye on him even though the king himself had an arm wound that was bleeding pretty badly.

A soldier roared, and Britt snapped back to attention, swinging Excalibur with precision so its blade bit down on the muscles between the Roman soldier's neck and protected shoulder. She then kicked him in the chest so he stumbled backwards, away from her and Roen.

"Where to, Arthur?" Pellinore shouted above the din of the fight. He plucked a spear right out of a Roman soldier's hands, then used the butt of it to smash three soldiers and toss them to the ground, all while his horse kicked and bit at any soldier in reach.

"I want to reach the Emperor," Britt said.

"The Emperor? He's the dead center of his army!" Lionel roared.

"I know. But it's the quickest way to end this battle, or we will lose thousands of men," Britt said.

Sir Bedivere fought off two soldiers bearing down on Kay—who had briefly lost his horse. "I don't believe Merlin ever mentioned that in the tactical meetings," Bedivere said.

"He didn't," Britt yelled. "And I purposely didn't tell him because I knew he'd fly off the handle if I mentioned it."

Kay's charger reared, trampling an enemy before Kay vaulted onto his back. "A very appropriate reaction," he growled.

Britt grit her teeth and pushed down in the saddle stirrups as she leaned perilously out of the saddle to engage a Roman soldier. "Merlin was positive we would win, and I agree with him. But our mustered force is incredible, and I'd rather not see the majority of it laid to waste, particularly when I know that with my best knights, reaching Emperor Lucius won't be a problem." As she spoke, Roen sidestepped an attempt from the enemy to spear him, and slammed into a soldier that Britt finished off with Excalibur.

Mordred reclaimed his position at her left. "Wherever you go, My Lord, we will follow." He smiled at her, briefly flashing his dimples, then intercepted a soldier aiming to run Bedivere's horse through.

Britt glanced back at the rest of her knights. Gawain and Lancelot finished off a pair of mounted centurions, as Tor, Safir, and Lanval destroyed a cluster of archers.

"Lead the way, My Lord!" Griflet shouted. He was unhorsed, but fought admirably well on foot with his sword.

"Griflet, take a horse," Gawain shouted, indicating one of the mounts of the fallen centurions.

"Don't mind if I do!" Griflet climbed into the saddle of his new charger and hurried to join the other knights in reforming ranks behind Britt.

Britt brandished Excalibur in the air. "For Britain!"

"For the High King!" Gawain shouted.

"For Britt Arthurs!" Kay roared.

They resumed their path, aiming for the center of the Roman army.

For a while, Britt was only aware of her personal battles. Every soldier she struck down seem to be replaced by two more. Once, when she got sloppy and instead of using precise sword movements blindly swung her sword, a legionnaire managed to land a glancing blow on her side. Her armor took the brunt of it and didn't even buckle, but it still felt like she had been hit in the gut with a hammer.

Gawain made short work of the soldier that had dared to hit her, and they pressed on.

The Knights of Camelot worked together. They didn't move

in the near perfect synchronization that the legionnaires did; instead they rode together, some of them surging forward then falling back as the next line of knights pressed in to guard and then replace them.

Tor had taken a blow and began favoring his right side, but Lionel moved in with the strength of a lion to guard his weak side. After being clubbed in the head with the butt-end of a lance, Mordred was moving a little slower, and Kay's prized horse bore a glancing blow to its rump. (It was nothing endangering, but Britt would bet Excalibur the taciturn knight would get Morgan to inspect it before the day was out.) But the general lack of injuries—even though Britt and her knights were a small company in the middle of the Roman war machine—bore witness to their impassable wall of teamwork.

During a brief lull in the onslaught, when Griflet and Kay surged forward so Britt was surrounded by her men, she twisted in her saddle, searching out her allies.

Ector, it looked like, had been forced to retire from the battle by his men, who had bodily escorted him to Merlin's side where an herb woman was wrapping his head in bandages. (Based on her foster-father's flailing arms and red face as he shouted directions his troops would never hear over the clashes and clangs of battle, he was fine.)

Selfishly, knowing he was out of combat made Britt feel incredibly relieved.

Next, she searched for Ywain. He and his lioness were in the thick of things, covering for his father as he gave orders to their soldiers.

Britt nodded and squared her shoulders, returning her attention to the battle brewing around her just in time to see a Roman legionnaire spear Gawain in the shoulder, knocking him from his horse.

Her heart froze. "Gawain!"

Adrenaline took over as Britt descended on the soldiers

moving in on Gawain. She was as silent as death as she cut through their ranks, Roen arching his neck and snorting so the reds of his nostrils showed.

The angle from her charger's back was proving to be a difficult place from which to defend Gawain, so Britt halted her horse in the middle of the thunderous battle and very properly dismounted him.

One of Ryence's soldiers would have landed a blow to her back, but Lancelot darted in at the last moment, intercepting the blow. "Can't you slide or vault off like any proper knight?" he demanded.

"So sorry; my sister's riding teacher didn't cover emergency dismounts when I was a kid." Though her words were laced with sarcasm, when she faced the enemy soldiers, her expression was set in stone.

Getting into a proper stance, she whipped Excalibur through the air. The enchanted sword sang, and those closest could have sworn they saw it glitter with lightning. The sword felt hot in her hands, and Britt, working in-tune with Merlin even though there was an army between them, whipped Excalibur in front of her. It crackled, releasing an explosion of power that knocked Roman soldiers over like dominoes.

"It's the Elvenking!"

"The Red Dragon has come!"

She wasn't sure if it was her soldiers or the Roman ones who sounded the cry, but it swiftly echoed across the battlefield, reinvigorating British forces.

Britt pulled Excalibur close, then began attacking the troops as soon as they staggered to their feet. She laid into them like Ywain's lioness, wreaking destruction wherever she directed Excalibur.

Ryence's forces—having previously witnessed Britt fighting when she was incensed—fled the area, opening up holes in Roman formations.

Britt, careful not to get too far away from her knights, backed up to her company, Roen flanking her.

Gawain wheezed as he sat up on his elbows, his horse standing over him protectively.

"How bad is it?" Britt asked, swinging her sword in an unspoken promise as she eyed enemy soldiers, silently daring them to close in on her.

He coughed and shook his head. "Didn't punch through my armor, but it kicked like a mule. My arm is numb."

"You might have dislocated it," Britt said.

"I'll be fine for now," he insisted. "My aunt will see to it tonight."

Britt's expressionless mask broke long enough for her to offer him a lopsided grin. "I think you should ask Ragnelle."

Gawain blinked. "The Lady of the Lake's handmaiden? Why?"

Lancelot swung in between Britt and Gawain, his horse pawing at the air. "I hate to break up this heart-to-heart, but might I remind you we're in the middle of a battle with Roman troops all around us?!"

Gawain nodded and pushed himself to his feet. Though he grimaced as he gingerly climbed back into the saddle, his face was set with determination as he took up his sword again.

"See, Lancelot, I much prefer your snide sarcasm to that odious charm you used to ooze," Britt said. She briefly sheathed Excalibur and whistled to Roen, who trotted up to her. She waited until he was completely still before swinging up in the saddle, making Lancelot sneer.

"And I would much prefer you to actually learn battle maneuverings instead of flashy magic shows!" Lancelot shot. He cut down a spear a soldier threw at Mordred.

"It would make you a margin safer," Kay acknowledged as he threw a lance and took out a Roman centurion who had been heading a charge towards the knights.

"Very well," Britt said with a reckless grin. "When all of this is over with, you all can spend a week tossing me off Roen. Until then, however, I have a fight to pick with an emperor." She heeled Roen, who charged forward like a dark cloud. Heedless of her men's shouts of concern, Britt hunkered down against her gelding's neck and freed Excalibur from its scabbard once more.

She fixed her eye on the spot of gold armor that marked the emperor. No longer did she try to scatter the enemy; now she trusted Roen to plow through and focused on fending off any who attacked him.

We have to hurry, she thought grimly. *With every injury we take, we lose momentum.*

The knights scrambled to fall in place—Mordred and Kay now taking up her flanks with Gawain in the center.

Though the knights snarled behind her, Britt was silent, every muscle tensed as they drew closer to the emperor and his guards.

The muscles in Roen's neck popped as he and the other chargers plowed through Roman formations.

Britt's ears rang, and suddenly they broke through the army, colliding with the elite soldiers that guarded the emperor.

Knights gushed forward, falling on the soldiers with shouts. The air tingled with the clang of blade striking blade as the knights and guards fought.

Kay caught a spear and twirled it over his head before throwing it at a soldier. "Knights, open up a spot for Arthur!"

Lionel snarled and flung himself off his horse. He picked up one of the bear-like guards and threw him into his comrades. "Here!"

Gawain and Mordred surged in like water, Mordred covering Gawain's injured arm while the Orkney prince and his horse took down a string of soldiers.

"Now," Mordred barked, swinging his horse aside so the brief hole opened up by Lionel and Gawain was cleared. "Go, Arthur!"

Britt nudged Roen, who snorted as he charged through the hole, jumping a fallen soldier. She almost fell off the black gelding's side, but he crow-hopped, hefting her back into the saddle. Her balance, however, was compromised, so Britt ended up sliding off his opposite side, but managed to land on her feet with Excalibur extended.

When she straightened, the wind picked up, whipping her red cloak and her golden hair. Across from her was a figure in gold armor decorated with a red eagle, Emperor Lucius.

He smiled darkly and made no move to grab a weapon. "Welcome, Arthur...King of the Britons."

Britt said nothing as she shifted her weight into a better stance and adjusted her hold on Excalibur, trying to make observations on the emperor's fighting style.

Around them, the battle raged. Horses screamed and men shouted as the Knights of Camelot and Lucius' guards fought around them in a perfect circle. Britt and the emperor stood alone in the center.

"You've done well," Emperor Lucius said. He adjusted his helm, which was true to the Roman style and protected his skull but left an open space for his chin and face. "I didn't think *anyone* would be able to unite Britain. It's filled with a quarrelsome people who seem utterly intent on killing each other. That you were able to gather such a great army is astounding...but I'm afraid your impressive acts will end here." He unsheathed his gladius.

Britt stared at his sword. "You're not going to win."

"On the contrary, I cannot lose." The emperor's smirk made Britt's skin crawl. "And once you and your little knights are defeated, I will carve up this land and suck every tax and tribute I can squeeze from it."

Britt's expression stayed icy cold and almost unnaturally calm.

Lucius laughed. "All your knights will be slain, as will those of your line, and I will take Camelot apart brick by brick and sow the farmland with salt." He tilted his head, waiting for a reaction.

Britt didn't even blink.

The emperor frowned, his eyes hardening. "This land will regret the day you denied me my tribute and homage." He hefted his sword, resting the edge of the blade on his armor-covered shoulder. "The world will learn, little king, that no one may threaten the splendor of Rome—especially not a backwater island."

As long as Lucius spoke, it gave her the opportunity to observe him, to estimate his reach and speed, and to notice patterns in the way he shifted his weight. But now he had finally opened a hole in his defense, so she took the opportunity and struck fast.

Moving like lightning, Britt lunged with Excalibur extended, striking him on his armored belly. The blow did not injure him, but he lurched backwards to get distance between them and to chop his gladius down.

Britt side-stepped it and slid closer to him. When they were almost chest to chest, she popped him in the throat with her elbow. He choked, but before she could push her advantage, one of Lucius' soldiers swung at her with all his might, crushing her right pauldron and flattening part of her cuirass so it squeezed her chest.

She grit her teeth with pain and swiveled so she could see both the guard and Lucius—who rubbed his bruised throat. Before Britt or the guard could move, Tor clamped a meaty fist on the guard's helmet and yanked him backwards, sending him sprawling. As Britt watched, Ywain and his lioness fell upon the guard with growls.

Britt returned her attention to the emperor, discreetly testing to be certain her range of motion wasn't hindered by her aching arm and ruined armor.

Emperor Lucius sneered as he fixed his grip on his sword. "You'll pay for that," he hissed, then charged her.

As Lucius' gladius was made for thrusting, his fighting style was similar to Britt's in that he attacked ruthlessly. He rained blow after blow upon her, hitting her with enough force to rattle her teeth.

Britt stayed on the defense—a dangerous tactic for her, as her skill at the sword depended on *quickly* defeating the enemy so it did not become a test of stamina or strength—but she knew in this case, it would pay off.

Lucius was angry, and he struck her with great force but without much thought. He attempted to use his brute strength to tear through her defenses, thrusting at her cuirass-encased torso and well-covered knee joints, and shouting with every strike he made.

With his strength, he would eventually knock her to the ground…but Britt bet the entire battle on his thoughtless strikes and the fact that he, lacking Britt's superior armor, would reveal a hole in his defense.

Britt kept her movements small and did her best to dodge as Lucius chopped at her left side. Her muscles screamed in protest, and she was starting to feel weak in the knees as her ruined armor pinched her shoulder.

When Lucius raised his gladius high above his head with the intention of striking Britt in the skull, she made her move.

She rocked forward, soundless and swift where everyone else roared and shouted. She struck him in the chest with Excalibur. With his arms still above his head, the force rocked him backwards. Britt slithered after him, taking careful aim as she had only *one shot*. When she was certain of her aim, she slid her hand down Excalibur's blade and yanked it up, popping Lucius on the chin with the hilt.

His head flopped back with the force, and he pinwheeled his arms as he gurgled. Britt then swept her leg behind his and yanked them out from under him, making him topple to the ground.

She kicked his sword away, her breath heavy as she pressed

Excalibur into the skin of his neck. "Surrender," she commanded. Her heart pounded in her throat, and her muscles shook with exertion, but it was done. Lucius was defeated.

Lucius spat a wad of blood and glared at her. "Never." He hissed. "You may destroy my army, but I'll raise one up again. I'll return, and crush every man, woman, and child here. Your demise is only a matter of time, Arthur Pendragon. I will hunt you until you beg for relief, and I will rule Britain!"

His proclamation startled Britt, for she had never pictured a scenario in which Emperor Lucius would return. As she stared down into his hostile gaze, men roared, and the hot scent of blood clenched her throat.

In that moment, she could sense the truth of his words. Emperor Lucius Tiberius would never rest until Britain fell. This battle was not about the defense of their land...but *survival.*

Britt hated death. She hated wars, and she hated killing. But she would not make her people sacrifice in this way to ease the pain of being king.

Excalibur glowed silver like the moon, and Britt felt the hair on the back of her neck prickle as the sword turned icy cold in her hands. *Merlin.*

"Very well," she said. She twirled Excalibur, making the blade sing and glow brighter. "Then may God judge you himself." Britt plunged her sword into Lucius' chest. The sword, radiating magic, bit through the armor of his chestplate as though it were kindling, and she stabbed him through the heart.

Lucius shouted, but it was over swiftly.

Britt's insides heaved as she tightened her grip on Excalibur, pulling it with her as she stepped away from the Emperor's body.

The few knights that weren't fighting stared at her wide-eyed. Beyond them, the Romans began to realize their commander had fallen as Sir Lanval and Sir Safir took out the last of the honor guard.

The soldiers fled, their organized formations falling apart as they lacked the leadership of their officers and commander.

Britt ignored her knights' slack jaws as she strode towards Roen. "Pursue them," she said. "I want them run out of Britain." She tried to mount her gelding, but the muscles of her legs were trembling so badly she couldn't get her foot in the stirrup.

"My Lord," Pellinore said with a brief bow. Before Britt could react, he gave her a leg up, boosting her into her saddle.

Britt nodded in thanks, but Pellinore did not step back from her or her charger. Instead, he gazed up at her, ignoring the chaos and shouts that swirled around the battlefield as British soldiers swept across the field, chasing the Roman forces.

"Britt!" Sir Ector, riding a snorting horse, pulled his mount to a skidding stop mere feet away.

Merlin was right behind him. "You did it, lass! We've won!" he laughed as he slid off his horse. "You were—" He fell silent when he saw Britt's hardened expression.

"Britt," Sir Ector puffed as he joined Merlin at her knee. "You did the right thing. Well done." He squeezed her hand, finally getting a flicker of a smile.

Britt felt like her heart started beating again, and the horror of battle was not so stark as her foster-father beamed up at her. "Thank you, Merlin…Father." She took a breath and set her shoulders, her expression relaxing. "Now, we pursue?"

"You bet we do," Merlin snorted.

Britt caught sight of Duke Maleagant and King Bagdemagus streaking across the field, chasing off mounted officers. Beyond them, Percival was rounding up the archers and preparing to move them with King Anguish's army, and King Lot and King Urien were holding a brief conference with King Ban and King Bors before the four split up, sweeping their forces after the fleeing enemy.

She breathed more easily, though the fight was not over yet.

They had won.

And Britain was more than safe. It was united.

"Is it *really* that bad, My Lord, that you should strip down here…in the middle of a battle?" Griflet anxiously wrung his hands and walked back and forth as Mordred helped Britt shed her crumpled pieces of armor.

"Be reasonable, Griflet. We're still pursuing troops, not in battle," Britt pointed out, gritting her teeth when Mordred wrenched her pauldron off her shoulder.

Though it was late afternoon, the sun was finally peeking out through the hazy clouds. British forces swarmed the surrounding hills and valleys, flushing out the remaining Roman troops to chase back to their boats in the south.

The battle had been grueling, and the chase was scarcely less so, so after hours in the saddle with her armor uncomfortably pinching her, Britt felt bruised and exhausted, and announced she was stopping to shed her armor. (Of course, her company insisted on staying with her.)

Ector squinted and peered at Britt's shoulder as she rotated her arm. "Is it bruised?"

"It feels like it."

"Perhaps we ought to return to camp so Lady Morgan or the Lady of the Lake may attend to you," Sir Kay said.

"So it's *Lady* Morgan now, is it?" Lionel smirked as he threw a pebble into a nearby river.

Britt breathed easier when Mordred unbuckled her cuirass, freeing her torso. "I don't know that it's necessary to go back yet, though I would like to check in with Gawain." (After arguing strenuously with the Ladies' Knight, Gawain agreed to have Ragnelle administer to his wounds rather than head out with Britt and the rest of the knights.)

"Perhaps we ought to return regardless," Bedivere said as he squinted up at the sun. "As we ride with the High King, it wouldn't do for us to get caught out in the hills after dark."

"I believe Sir Bedivere's words are wise," Merlin said. "It would be best if we began the journey back to camp."

"I also believe we should return," King Pellinore said. "I ought to check in with Percival, and I'm certain the smaller units are anxious to hear from our king."

"Of course!" Griflet said, losing his worry in a moment of enthusiasm. "We won!"

Several of the other knights cheered, still exuberant from the fight.

Britt, moving more freely in her chain mail shirt, packed her gear into the empty saddle bags on Roen's rump. "All right, Merlin. We'll start heading back."

Lancelot raised an eyebrow. "You aren't going to argue?"

"I'm about at my limit," she admitted. "Lucius was a harder foe than I imagined. Fighting him took all I had."

"It was a jolly good fight to witness," Sir Tor said.

Britt swung up into the saddle, her muscles burning in protest. "The important thing is that we get the remaining Roman forces out of Britain."

"Rome is without an emperor now, Britt. As the winner against Lucius, by all rights, the throne could be yours," Merlin said slyly.

"No." Britt shook a finger at him before she turned Roen back in the direction of their camp, following the river. "Don't even start!"

Ector puffed, mussing his well-trimmed beard. "But he's right, Britt! You could be the emperor!"

"We're not marching on Rome," Britt said firmly.

"Mmhmm, we'll see." Merlin's expression was as innocent as a baby bunny as his horse picked its way around several large boulders.

Britt rolled her eyes. "For crying out loud. I'm not—"

"Death to the king!"

A crossbow arrow struck Britt, puncturing her chain mail and striking her shoulder. Britt flopped out of the saddle and hit the ground with a boneless crack.

"Arthur!"

"Britt!"

The knights shouted, moving into a protective formation around her, but it was too late.

Britt couldn't sit up, and the pain was so intense she had a hard time breathing. Ector and Kay were at her side first. Her foster-brother propped her up slightly as Merlin whirled around, looking for whoever had attacked her.

"Show yourself!" he thundered, and the ground seemed to rumble.

Vivien stepped out of the underbrush, holding a crossbow and a dark scowl. "You ruined everything!" she shouted at Britt. "I espied out your courts from the inside; I took your magical scabbard; I seduced your wizard—but you still won! How?!" Vivien's voice was little more than a shriek.

Sir Lanval growled and stepped towards her, but Pellinore stopped him. "Just wait," he said, tilting his head at Merlin.

"I was going to be a queen!" Vivien howled. "You ruined it—you ruined it all! But now you will die with my dreams." She laughed and fitted another bolt into the crossbow.

Merlin *roared*. He didn't say an intelligible word. He didn't point or gesture. He merely clenched his hands into fists and snarled with the ferocity of a dragon, and the world began burning.

White hot fire ignited in the area, consuming everything in its path. Merlin's face was a mask of anguish and rage as his magic burned like a star.

The knights of Camelot backed up, drawing closer to Britt—who gasped with the exertion it took to keep breathing.

Vivien never stood a chance.

The knights were split between staring at Merlin in frightened awe and crowding around Britt.

"It's in deep," Pellinore murmured. "And it's close to her heart."

"Britt, hang on," Ector said, squeezing her hand. "You're going to make it."

"It hurts," she hissed, biting her tongue.

"We have to get her back!"

"But can we risk moving her?"

Britt scrunched her eyes shut as pain wracked her body, leaving her too weak to scream.

Lancelot fell to his knees next to her. "I did this." His dreamy green eyes were dark with regret and building horror.

Merlin stalked over to him and grabbed him by the shoulders with shaking hands. "*What did you say?*"

"I, I told Vivien about Excalibur's scabbard." Lancelot shook his head, his expression bewildered. "I didn't think...I never meant for this to happen, Britt!"

Merlin shoved Lancelot backwards and stalked away. He kept his gaze on Britt as Kay and Ector tried to staunch the blood flow, but Britt could see the dark hopelessness in his eyes.

She was dying.

"Do we pull the arrow out?" Ector asked.

"We'll have to, but it will make the blood flow worse," Pellinore said grimly.

"Someone ride for Morgan and the Lady of the Lake!" Kay shouted.

Mordred hopped on his horse—which was still snorting and shying at the singed patch of ground where Vivien had once stood, but Merlin forestalled him.

"Wait," he said. "We can summon them here." Merlin drew Excalibur from Britt's side and handed it hilt first to Bedivere. "Cast it into the river," Merlin said, pointing to the river they had been following.

Bedivere took the sword and ran.

"But..." Britt tried to voice a protest, but the pain was too much.

Merlin crouched at her side and took her icy hand in his. "It will be fine, Britt. I promise. You're going to survive this."

Bedivere plowed through cattails and, from the sound of it, must have been at least shin-deep in the water before he threw Excalibur.

Britt expected it to hit the water with a splash, but an arm covered in a white silk sleeve plunged out of the water and caught the sword, holding it there. Everything was still for several moments, until the water beyond the arm that held Excalibur began glowing.

Britt's sight started to grow hazy as she looked from the river to her knights.

Many of them hung back, their eyes closed in prayer. Others paced back and forth—like Griflet. Mordred smiled at her when he caught her gaze, but Britt could read the fear in his eyes that shadowed every man's expression.

Only Lancelot's expression differed. Anguish wrinkled his brow, and Britt could hear his labored breathing over her own as he still sat where Merlin had shoved him.

Britt closed her eyes and fought to swallow against the pain that made her lips numb, then croaked, "Lancelot."

The handsome, charismatic knight scrambled to her side. "My Lord?"

She opened her mouth, wondering where to start.

Lancelot, however, interpreted her silence as rage. "Everything you said about me was right, My Lord." His famous control faltered, and he rubbed his face. "I let my self-centeredness push me into an act of treason. But I never meant for this to happen, you must believe me! You're my *king*!"

Even in her pain-hazed state, Britt could see the other knights moving away from Lancelot. Kay shook with barely contained rage—Britt was willing to bet if she passed out from the pain, her brother would deck him.

Just as the legends said, Lancelot betrayed Arthur. And just as the legends said, the act would rip Camelot to shreds. For Lancelot was a prince, and his father, uncle, and cousins would stand with him, even as Orkney, Anglesey, and other parts of Britain rode against them.

Britt knew she was dying, and with it, so would the dream of Camelot.

...or would it?

She licked her lips and rallied the pieces and bits of strength she had left. "Lancelot, I forgive you. You are pardoned from your part of this."

The silence of the area was so absolute, her ears rang.

"...Britt?" Ector finally ventured.

"You can't mean that," Kay said.

Britt closed her eyes. She wished she could address her foster brother and father, but she had to fix this with Lancelot.

In a way, she had done this to herself. She had always treated him with suspicion and dislike. Now was her chance to change Lancelot's future—and the future of her knights.

She struggled to focus on Lancelot—her eyes and limbs were growing slow to respond. "In combat, you are the best knight in Camelot, Lance. But you have the potential to be more than that. Please...become the knight you *could* be."

Lancelot nodded, his eyes shining with tears and regret.

Britt shifted her gaze to Merlin, who was squeezing her hand like he could keep her there through sheer will. The grim line of his mouth eased a bit when there was a tremendous splash.

"Britt!"

Nymue, Morgan, and Ragnelle ran out of the river, their wet skirts sticking to their legs as they raced in her direction.

"What happened?" Morgan asked as she and Nymue skidded to a stop next to Britt.

"Crossbow bolt to the shoulder," Mordred said grimly.

"We can see that," Nymue snapped.

"It was Vivien," Merlin said.

Morgan stilled, her face smoothing with terror. "Did she use her magic?"

Merlin helplessly shook his head.

Nymue hunkered over Britt, her long beautiful hair frizzled and snarled. "The arrow is in so deep she didn't have to."

Ragnelle tilted her head as Ector and Kay moved back to give the ladies room to work. "I do not detect any poison, either." She continued speaking, but her words sounded slurred to Britt's ears.

"Britt, hold on!" Morgan's voice swam in and out of Britt's focus. "Stay with us," she ordered as she tucked a bit of Britt's hair out of her face.

"—going into shock."

"Can you do anything?"

"No. We'll fight it, but…"

"No!" Merlin shouted, his words clear compared to the other voices that alternated sounding sharp and muffled to Britt. "She can't die! We have to do something!"

"We don't have the capabilities here," Nymue snapped. "Maybe a faerie king could heal her, but we haven't the time to get her to one!"

Merlin slumped next to Britt, still clinging to her hand.

Britt tried to squeeze his hand and smile. "It's all right, Merlin."

Merlin met her gaze, his blue eyes wide with desperation. "No. No, it's not." He snapped his attention to Nymue, Ragnelle, and Morgan. "Send her forward to her time. They have the science to deal with something like this."

"Send her *what?*" Mordred said.

"I thought you said such a thing was impossible," Ector protested.

"Strictly speaking, it is," Merlin said. "Because of the flow of time, you can only bring someone back into time, not push them forward to the unknown future."

"But Britt is already from the future; there's a spot there for her," Nymue said.

Morgan gripped Britt's free hand. "So there's a chance we can send her home."

"How did you two know Britt is from the future?" Ector asked.

"I puzzled through it when Britt asked me to alter her language spell, and I got a look at the magic coating her." Nymue's fingers skimmed around Britt's injury with care.

"Kay told me," Morgan answered.

Britt opened her mouth to say something sarcastic about keeping exclusive secrets, but another wave of pain hit her and made her clamp her mouth shut to hold in a scream.

"Why didn't we know?" Griflet yelped.

"Where she's from hardly matters as long as she ruled well. Can we send her home or not?" Merlin demanded.

"Is magic even capable of sending a person forward?" Ragnelle timidly asked.

"There's a spell. It was used by an elven warrior king," Nymue said.

"You know it?" Merlin asked.

Nymue nodded. "After inspecting the spell that pulled her back in time, I looked for one that could send her forward. I thought she would ask me about it, but she never did, so I chose not to tell her."

"Hag," Britt murmured. She would have insulted her further, but it was all she could say.

The hard lines of worry edging Nymue's eyes softened long enough for the Lady of the Lake to smile at her. "Unfortunately, it's a dangerous spell. It requires much magic—more than I have

—and the last time it was used, four people were killed in the kickback."

"If we're careful, can we manage it?" Morgan asked.

Nymue raised an eyebrow. "We?"

"I'm helping you, of course."

"As will I." Ragnelle's dark eyes were worried as she glanced down at Britt.

Britt was swinging in and out of the murky waters of consciousness. She could hear their conversation, but none of it was really settling in her mind. She hurt too much, and the numbness of sleep was a siren call she was having a hard time resisting.

"Even with the three of us, I'm not certain we'll have enough power," Nymue said, her voice tight. "If we send out a call the faerie folk of the area might hear, but we're running out of time—"

"I'll help. I'll do anything," Merlin said. "Take every drop of my magic if you have to. Just...save her," he pleaded.

Merlin's voice was the last thing Britt truly heard. After that, things started to grow fuzzy.

Pain exploded when they pulled the arrow from her shoulder, but she could barely tell when they stripped her chain mail off her, leaving her in linen underclothes.

When they gingerly picked her up to move her, Britt swooned and lost consciousness. When she came too, she was floating on water. She blinked, trying to clear her vision, but all she could make out were hazy shapes.

She knew Merlin still held her hand, though. She felt his strong grip on her fingers. Water splashed as people moved around her, and the area was filled with light.

What's happening? Britt's eyes fluttered as she tried to think straight, but her thoughts wouldn't obey, and it took too much effort to keep breathing.

"Merlin...it's time."

Merlin squeezed Britt's hand, then slipped his fingers from hers, and she was left alone.

No...Merlin!

Light was everywhere, and every pore of her body screamed as she was flooded with what felt like bottled lightning.

When the crackling fizz of the magic left, Britt could make out the hazy shapes of gravestones.

"Oh my gosh, Britt!"

"What happened? She just grabbed the sword—why is she bleeding like that?"

"How do we call 911?"

"Pardon me—I have a cellular phone. I shall call an ambulance service for your friend!"

So tired...

"Britt, hang in there! Britt!"

Britt closed her eyes, and everything went black.

13
A NEW REALM

Britt groggily opened her eyes, frowning at the sharp, sterile smell of the air. She blinked, and it took her a few moments —full minutes, really—to realize she was in a hospital bed.

The room was done up in an uninspiring shade of off-white. After being gone for so long, the plastic smell of upholstery was a sharp scent to Britt's nose, and the cotton sheets felt odd.

Where am I?

"She's awake!"

"Britt!"

Three girls scrambled around Britt's bed, their eyes wide with worry.

It took Britt several seconds to place them, as it had been *years* since she last saw Grace, Amber, and Lyssa—the three friends she had embarked on her England tour with before she touched the Sword in the Stone and was pulled back through time.

Then that must mean...I'm back?

"What happened to you?" Lyssa asked.

"We saw you get struck by lightning, but it was too bright to see what happened to you. When the light faded, your clothes had changed, and you had that big bloody wound...." Amber trailed off, and bit her lip.

"The doctors told us lightning couldn't hurt you like that." Grace pointed to Britt's heavily bandaged shoulder. "They said it looks like you'd been stabbed."

For a moment, Britt wondered if all of Camelot and her adventures in medieval Britain had been a coma-induced dream. But that was impossible. She could still feel the bruising on her arm from where the Roman soldier had clubbed her, and her butt was sore from all the riding. Above all, the memory of Merlin letting go of her hand was far too real to be a dream.

Britt rubbed her head, still trying to adjust and puzzle through what had happened. "How long have I been out of it?"

Amber offered Britt a styrofoam cup filled with water. "About a day. They kept you unconscious for the surgery."

"I wonder what happened to that really hot guy who called the ambulance for us," Grace said.

"I'm more curious to figure out what happened to the sword," Lyssa said.

Britt, who had been sucking down the water, coughed and choked. "What did you say?"

Lyssa exchanged looks with their other friends. "The sword we were posing with for our pictures...it's gone."

Britt dropped her cup of tasteless water and fell back against the pillows of her bed. *Gone. The Sword in the Stone was gone.* Of course it would be; she'd pulled the sword from the stone and left it in the church in London.

But that meant...she was here in modern times and had no way to return to medieval England, to return to the Knights of the Round Table, to return to *Merlin.*

For a moment, she didn't know what to think. Finally, she was back in modern times! She would get to see her sister and her mother! But...the loss of Camelot and everything she had known roared like a black hole in her heart.

There were so many people who meant the world to her, and she would never see them again. Ector, Kay, Gawain...and Merlin, they were lost to her.

Tears flooded Britt's eyes, and she sobbed as she realized the life she had embraced and the people who meant so much to her were gone. Forever.

"Britt, are you okay?"

"Does something hurt? Lyssa, go get one of the doctors!"

Britt shook her head, but she couldn't stop crying as the despair continued to build in her heart. Tears dribbled from her eyes, and her sobs made the stitching of her shoulder wound pull uncomfortably. But she didn't care.

Britt's life as King Arthur—King of Britain and ruler of Camelot—was over.

~

BRITT KICKED off her shoes as she entered her apartment, pinching her smart phone between her ear and shoulder as she rummaged around in her purse. "No, I haven't been in a fight with any of my friends. Why?"

"You've just been a little despondent since you took that trip to England." Her mother must've had her cell phone on speaker, for her voice sounded tinny.

"It was a tiring trip," Britt said.

"But it was over a month ago," her mother pointed out.

Britt fell silent—she knew better than to bring up her shoulder injury and use it as an excuse. (When she first received word of Britt's "accident," Britt's mother had flipped. If anyone ever mentioned the injury in her presence, she frequently went off on a tirade, verbally abusing the police for being unable to figure out what happened to Britt.)

"I'm just concerned about you, honey," her mother said.

"I'm perfectly healthy. There's no need to worry." Britt sprinkled some food in her goldfish's aquarium. "I just need some time to recover."

"If you say so.... Oh! I was going to tell you about this nice boy I met! You should meet him for coffee sometime, he—"

"No," Britt said, louder and with more force than necessary. She winced. "Sorry, Mom. I'm not really up for dating right now. I should go, but thanks for calling!"

"Of course, sweetie! I'm sorry; I know I shouldn't be poking my nose in your business, but I'm just worried. I love you. You know that, right?"

"I know, mom. Don't worry about me, I'll be fine...eventually."

"What was that?"

"Nothing. Love you, Mom. Bye!" Britt sighed as she ended the call and braced herself on her kitchenette counter.

She curled her hands into fists and shook her head, trying to ignore the tears that stung her eyes.

She thought losing her modern life when she went to medieval England was bad, but this was far worse. Back in Britain, Britt could talk to Merlin, Kay, and Ector about her old life. But here, no one even knew what had happened to her. If she told them, they'd think she was insane! After her weird, unexplained "accident" in England, they wouldn't hesitate to hospitalize her.

So Britt quietly carried her despair and loss alone.

She pinched the bridge of her nose. She missed everyone—her foster family, Bedivere, Pellinore, Gawain, Ywain, Morgan, Nymue, even Lancelot, and especially..."Merlin," she whispered.

Her apartment was silent, and the roaring darkness of loss threatened to devour her. "No." She shook her head. "They wouldn't want me to lose myself. I *have* to keep going."

Britt's phone buzzed, then whistled when she received a text from her next-door neighbor, Issie.

Are you up for laundry tonight? I have a knitting pattern I want to show you.

Britt's lips quirked in a sad smile. Seemingly since her trip to England, her neighbor had taken up knitting with a fanatical passion. But, unfortunately, she wouldn't have the time to meet up with her.

Sorry, can't make it. Thanks for the invite though!

The text sent, Britt tossed her phone on the kitchen counter, then padded into her room, rummaging around in her closet until she unearthed a carry-on suitcase.

She hadn't told her mother yet—though she had told her sister as soon as she received the offer—but she had been invited with a few other members of her sword hall to give several demonstrations and clinics in Europe on medieval swordsmanship.

In truth, she needed to look for a full-time job. But Britt's work with her sword hall had become comforting on a completely new level since she returned. So, she was going.

"I can't just survive; I have to thrive. I can't let them down." She began sorting through her clothes, taking what she would need for her trip.

Thankfully, her sword hall would not be going to Britain. Britt had been avoiding thinking of Britain ever since she had gotten back and had the chance to read up on old King Arthur legends.

None of it was encouraging. Lancelot and Guinevere were still recorded as an adulterous pair, and Mordred was credited with killing Arthur and taking over Camelot. According to history, Merlin had been done in by Vivien, and Gawain, Griflet, Kay, Percival, and all the other knights were killed with the downfall of Camelot.

Britt's greatest hope, however, is that the legends were just that, legends, and not based on historical fact. (Besides, nowhere had she been able to find even a hint that someone suspected Arthur had been a woman. That had to mean something!)

"You are too concerned with the legends of the future." Merlin's

words that he'd spoken to Britt from so long ago echoed in her mind. They were an unpleasant mix of a soothing balm and a gaping reminder that she would never see the Merlin she loved again.

Tears blurred her vision, and she shook her head again. Mustering her courage, she sucked in a shaky breath and forced herself to focus on packing.

"MAKE your stance a little wider when on defense. It will make you harder to move and better able to parry blows," Britt instructed. She leaned against a wall as she watched the teenagers who were assigned to the defense role shuffle their feet.

"Your goal is to keep your center of balance in your core. If it's too low or too high, your opponent will be able to grapple with you and knock you over easier," she continued.

Her phone chimed, signaling she received a new email. She ignored it and stared at her temporary students who had shown up for the clinic.

"Arthurs, I'll take over for you. You're on break," one of Britt's friends from her sword hall called.

Britt waved to him and weaved out of the demonstration room, muffling the clang of sword leads when she closed the door behind herself.

Several months had passed since Britt started giving demonstrations in Europe. Since then, she had traveled with several other members of her sword hall around the world giving clinics in technique.

The jobs didn't pay much, but her plane tickets, hotel rooms, and food were always covered, and Britt enjoyed it.

They had been in the states the last few weeks, which gave Britt enough time to work on her resume and send it out to a couple of nonprofit organizations. After a lot of deliberation,

Britt had realized that the time in ancient Britain had changed her for the better. She still longed to help people, as she had as King Arthur. So, she decided she would like a career path that focused on nonprofit companies.

Britt slipped into the small room they had been lent to store their gear that also served as a snack station. She still missed everyone from Camelot with an ache that wouldn't dull, but at least now she wasn't reduced to tears every time she remembered them. (Constantly moving from place to place had helped significantly.)

She grabbed a bottle of water, an apple, and a cookie, then plopped down in an overstuffed chair. She bit into her apple, then gave in to her curiosity and checked her email, furrowing her eyebrows when she saw she'd received an email from a company named Avalon with the subject of "interview inquiry."

She didn't remember applying to a company called Avalon, but she selected the email and read it over anyway. It was chock-full of the typical spiel—mentioning the company had seen her resume on various job websites, promising they felt she was a perfect fit for their organization, and so on—and finished with an offer for a job interview with one of the company recruiters—John Wayne.

The email was so nice, it had to be a scam.

Britt highlighted it, intending to delete it, then paused.

Avalon...Where have I heard that?

After taking another bite out of her apple, a quick internet search revealed the company was, in fact, not-for-profit.

It had launched out of the blue approximately three years ago, pouring massive amounts of money into water purification for developing countries, self-defense courses for girls in inner cities, an entrepreneur mentorship program, and building multiple schools in developing nations.

Apparently, it was well respected, though there was little

information on it besides the news articles and government agencies that praised the company for their philanthropy.

Britt finished her apple, then shrugged. "Why not? It's not like I've got any other job offers." Switching gears, she responded back that she would love to have an interview with John Wayne.

Perhaps, if she was lucky, her day as a wandering swordswoman would soon be finished.

BRITT TRIED to discreetly fix her dress pants so the hemline sat properly as she waited for her interview with the Avalon recruiters.

She had arrived early and was pretending to relax on the leather couch as she waited for the recruiter to come for her. In her phone interview—which oddly hadn't been with John Wayne, who had first contacted her—the recruiter had mentioned she had been sought out for a management position. Britt suspected it was probably for one of their self-defense courses for girls, though she was a little curious why they would want a *sword* instructor for that.

She fiddled with the folder that held her resume and tried not to gape too badly. The Avalon building was a work of art with its wood-paneled ceiling, floor-to-ceiling windows, and gorgeous chandeliers.

Britt was staring at a painting of a lake, which seemed oddly familiar, when her cell phone buzzed. She fumbled with it, switching it to silent mode, then checked her messages.

Her sister had sent her a text: *Cleaning out my old bedroom at Mom's place—check out what I found!*

Attached was an image of Britt at her very first sword hall. She was tiny—she couldn't have been older than seven or eight—and she was lined up with the handful of kids who were in her swordsmanship class. She could see half of a man as he stepped out of the frame—her instructor—and bolted to the wall behind the kids were several dozen different swords.

Britt smiled fondly at the copied image, which was a little blurry and tinted yellow from the bright flash. She swiveled her phone so she could enlarge the photo, and when she zoomed in on herself, her heart stopped.

Behind her seven-year-old self was one of the many swords. But this one, Britt recognized. "Excalibur?"

She stared at the photo, hardly daring to believe it could be true. Excalibur had survived for centuries?

Her heart pounded in her ears, and she barely heard when a woman dressed in a business suit called, "Miss Arthurs?"

Though Britt wanted to scream with exuberance, she forced herself to focus. "Yes, that's me." She snatched up her folder and stood with a smile.

The woman returned the smile and gestured up the hallway. "This way, please."

Britt followed her into an elevator, up to the top floor of the building. It seemed like a weird place to house HR, but Britt was too giddy with the realization that Excalibur might still be around to question the company's logic.

"I'm glad we are able to arrange an interview," the woman said.

Britt snapped herself out of her gleeful haze. "Yes, thank you for this opportunity."

The recruiter laughed as elevator doors dinged and rolled open. "Indeed, it is we who should be thanking you!" She led the way down the hallway. "They are quite eager to meet you."

"You are too kind." Britt paused as the meaning of the woman's words finally caught up with her. "...I'm sorry, did you say *they*?"

She posed the question too late, as they had already reached a set of double doors. The recruiter knocked and opened one of them. "Miss Arthurs," she announced. She then stepped back and motioned for Britt to enter.

Slightly disconcerted, for she hadn't been to many interviews, but she didn't think this was the norm, Britt slipped into the room, clutching her folder. "Thank you for inviting me to this interview."

It did not appear to be an HR office, but a rather plush meeting room that contained an obscenely large circular table, a plush red carpet, artistically rendered stone walls, and sets of old weaponry secured above a horse-sized fireplace. A number of people were posted around the table, seated in fancy wooden chairs.

Hoo boy. There must have been a mistake. Why would they recruit me, a jobless graduate, and bring me all the way up to what is clearly the executive floor?

Even so, she made herself continue with a professional smile. "Avalon is an amazing company. I admire many of your community initiatives."

Two men who were seated at the table with their backs to her stood and approached her. One had a carefully groomed mustache and a perfectly pressed suit; the other was slightly more casual with a clean-shaven face, tousled hair, black slacks, and a blue dress shirt.

They smiled at her—real smiles, not the bland gesture of professionals. Their smiles were big, and when both reached her, Britt stopped breathing.

"...Kay? Gawain?" She dropped her folder. Her resume papers fell out of it when it hit the floor and splayed everywhere.

Gawain pressed one of his arms to his chest and bowed over it. "My Lord."

Kay's mustache couldn't hide his beaming smile as he held out his hand to her. "Britt."

Britt's leg muscles gave out, and she sat down hard. She tried to breathe, but she couldn't seem to take in enough oxygen. "You're not real."

The knights crouched at her side. "But we are, Britt." Gawain spoke in a coaxing voice that was probably a sure sign she was losing her mind. (It must have been the time travel. The side effects were finally getting to her.)

Kay placed a warm hand on her shoulder. "We're really here."

She shook her head. "It can't be. It's impossible!"

"Says the brat who once posed as a legendary king and wielded a mythical sword."

Britt looked past the pair, and her lower lip trembled as she saw two women draw closer.

Morgan was recognizable with her silky brown hair piled into a messy bun at the top of her head, sporting heels, perfectly fitting black pants, and a black suit coat with a lacy blouse.

The second woman also had heels and black slacks, but she wore a kimono-like jacket made of blue silk with a lily pad pattern. Her hair was styled in a short pixie cut and dyed platinum blonde, and her features were round and oval. It was she who had referred to Britt's time as Arthur.

Britt contemplated getting up, but her legs were still too weak. "Issie? What—how do you know about this?"

Her next-door neighbor smiled and snapped her fingers. Her hair turned ink black, and her features sharpened, turning elfin. "Did you miss me?" Nymue asked.

Britt stared at her for several seconds before her brain and blood pressure finally gave out, and she began to slump in a faint.

"Catch her!" another man—Bedivere, dressed in an impeccable suit—shouted, darting forward to help Gawain stabilize her.

Morgan crouched next to Britt and Kay. "This is why I said we should have broken it to her gently."

Britt was with it enough to notice that Morgan took one of Kay's hands in her own and squeezed it.

Nymue brushed some of Britt's hair out of her face. "You have only yourself to blame," she told her. "I was going to tell you the night we were supposed to meet up and do laundry. It was going to be a touching reunion and a sweet moment between us girls. But did you agree to meet me? Nooo! Instead you ran off into the wild blue yonder, making it dreadfully difficult to track you down!"

Tears—happy tears—clouded Britt's eyes, and she laughed as she embraced first Nymue, then Morgan. Before she had released the sorceress, Kay swept them both into a tight embrace. Caught up in the exuberance, Britt then hugged Gawain and Bedivere, laughing as they all sat sprawled on the plush carpet.

When she finally recovered some semblance of control, she gazed around the room, taking in the familiar faces: Griflet, Percival, Lionel, Ragnelle, and—most strangely of all—Guinevere's good friend and the recipient of Griflet's passion, Blancheflor.

The knights all sported cut hair and stylish clothes, blending in effortlessly with modern fashion.

"Can you stand, My Lord?" Bedivere asked.

Britt nodded and stood on shaky legs like a newborn fawn. "But...how?"

Nymue snorted. "How do you think? Magic, of course."

Ragnelle glided up to Gawain, tucking her hand into his elbow. "It was all My Lady's and the wizard Merlin's doing. They constructed a spell that would allow a few people to be entombed in a small cavern. Doing so would set those inside the cave out of reach of the flow of time."

"Ragnelle is making it sound much grander than it really is," Nymue said wryly. "Faerie lands all possess similar spells; it was just a matter of making one in which the flow of time was a precise ratio to that of the rest of the world. We crafted the spell so that a day in the cave was the equivalent of a year outside it."

"It required several persons gifted with magic to power it

internally," Morgan added. "So Ragnelle, Blancheflor, and I aided the spell from the inside."

"I did not know you to be a sorceress, Lady Blancheflor," Britt said.

"Actually, I'm not," Blancheflor confessed. "I am one of Lady Nymue's handmaidens. I was sent to watch over you in Camelot."

Britt stared at Nymue, who innocently studied her nails. "You didn't stay in there with them, Nymue?" she finally asked.

The Lady of the Lake laughed. "Hah! You must be jesting. You founded Camelot centuries ago. Even with a year outside equaling a day in the cave, they were locked up in that small, enclosed space for approximately two years. Never would I put *myself* through that sort of misery."

"You didn't have a problem ordering me to endure," Blancheflor said sourly.

Britt felt as though her brain were leaking out of her ears. She was having a hard time gathering her scattered thoughts. "But... What became of Camelot? Where's Mordred, and..." Afraid to speak the name that burned in her heart, she found she couldn't utter it.

Their smiles took on a sad edge.

"Mordred," Kay said gently, "stayed behind to rule in your place."

"He was going to come with us," Griflet ran a hand through his slicked-back hair as he leaned against a wall, and his eyes were filled with pain, "but eventually we realized that out of those in your service, only Ulfius and Bodwain were remaining behind, as Bedivere and Kay had sworn to come. Ulfius and Bodwain would rule Camelot well...but they were older, and they didn't have an ounce of royal blood."

"Mordred said he swore to you that he would remain with you because you needed knights you could trust in your own castle," Percival said. "So he stayed...because he knew your heart was with Camelot, and it would break you if your legacy of a united Britain were to fall."

"It grieved him." Nymue said. "I cannot begin to tell you how much it grieved him that he could not see you again. But he ruled Camelot well. Under his reign, the practices you put into order expanded and flourished."

"You weren't entombed with the others, so you got to see him? You got to see the rest of my Knights?" Britt asked.

The Lady of the Lake nodded and gracefully seated herself on one of the wooden chairs pulled around, Britt now recognized, a smaller version of the Round Table. "Your lionhearted Ywain stayed behind and was known as a force to be reckoned with, as well as a devoted husband. He, along with King Pellinore, frequently visited Mordred in Camelot and were his staunchest allies. Agravain became King of Orkney after Lot—though whenever he visited Mordred in Camelot, he griped that he should've been allowed to come with Gawain. Gaheris and Gareth became excellent knights in their own right, and they served Mordred all their lives with Sir Tor, Sir Lanval, and Sir Safir. Sir Bors stayed in Camelot until his father's health started failing, then he returned to Gaul—though he remained Mordred's ally."

"And Guinevere?" Britt asked, worrying for the kindhearted blonde princess.

Nymue threw her hands up. "It is inexplicable to me, but she fell in love with Mordred, and the two married and had many spawn of their own." Folding her arms across her chest, she grumbled, "They were always sending their brats to my lake."

"You enjoyed it," Morgan chided as Kay slipped an arm around her shoulders. "With two thirds of the Lancelot Hate Club unavailable, you had no friends around."

"I object to that conjecture!" Nymue declared.

"So there was peace?" Britt's heart almost hurt with the hope that built up inside of it.

"There was peace," a voice said from the shadows of the room.

"Mordred was a great king because he was loyal to you...far more than I was, My Lord."

Some of the tension in Britt's chest eased as the speaker stepped out of the shadows. "Lancelot."

Lancelot was dressed the most casual, wearing a green sweater and khakis. His black hair was cut short, and his expression was more subtle now.

The sight of him made Britt smile because it meant the legends were wrong. Lancelot's betrayal hadn't ended Camelot. The Round Table was still whole.

Lancelot bowed his head. "I apologize, Britt, for my part in your injury."

Britt smiled reassuringly at those clustered around her, then slipped from their grasp and approached the somber knight. "I told you back when it happened I forgave you."

"I know. I remember well." Lancelot met her gaze, his usual good charm and charisma stripped away. "You were right about me. About everything. And I will spend the rest of this age making sure that I prove you right about my potential."

Britt tilted her head and studied the knight. "You don't have to prove anything, Lancelot," she said, "because you came."

He blinked. "How is my presence here at all noteworthy?"

"It would have been easier to stay behind where your name was renowned and your pedigree meant something." Britt smiled and clasped his forearm. "Your actions say a lot. I'm glad you're here."

Lancelot's smile grew charming. "As am I, My Lord."

"Are you still angry about my sadly lacking knowledge of emergency dismounts?" she asked teasingly.

"Angry? It's his fault you didn't learn as a child!" Griflet snorted.

Britt cocked her head. "What do you mean?"

"Here." Morgan pointed to two framed photos that hung on the wall.

One was nearly a twin copy of the photo Britt's sister had just sent her. The only difference was that the teacher was still in the frame. Britt's jaw dropped as she stared at the instructor.

As a child, she could remember very little besides the fact that he had a mustache, she worshipped the ground he walked on, and he had taught her the basics of swordplay. But now, Britt was easily able to place her teacher…as Kay.

The other photo was of Britt's sister and herself, posing with her sister's riding instructor…Lancelot.

"You two were our teachers!?" Britt squawked.

Kay bowed. "We created the sword hall solely for your sake. I was given the honor of teaching you because I best knew your sword fighting style."

Lancelot frowned, and for the first time since Vivien had shot Britt, she saw a glimmer of his vain self. "I also wanted to be part of the sword hall. Unfortunately, Lady Morgan, Lady Blancheflor, and Lady Ragnelle all insisted I be the riding instructor because they could use my face for marketing purposes."

"We got quite a few clients that way," Blancheflor reminisced.

Lancelot's frown turned into a smile that held hints of smugness. "Although, I was given the honor of being the one to call the ambulance when you arrived back in modern Britain."

"That was only because we had no idea when she was going to get sucked through and then come back," Griflet said.

"Now, now," Lionel said. "You're just sore because you missed the chance by one shift."

"Once we had the approximate timeline down of when we knew you would visit Britain, we all took shifts watching the graveyard for you," Percival said for Britt's sake.

Britt, her jaw hanging as she still tried to process that Kay had been her teacher, stabbed a finger at her foster brother. "It was you who taught me to hate Lancelot!"

"Of course," Kay rumbled.

Morgan rolled her eyes. "In your case, dear, Kay thinks pretty much any male is the enemy."

"I don't understand. How did you pull this off? And where's..." She hesitated yet again. No one had mentioned Merlin, besides crediting him as the source of the spell. Her throat closed uncomfortably for a moment, but Britt shook her head and made herself speak. "Where's Merlin?"

Everyone abruptly looked away from her. Kay stared at his fancy watch; Nymue went back to studying her nails; Percival actually pulled out a cell phone. Britt's breath came slowly, as she feared the worst.

Britt pivoted so she faced Gawain, instinctively knowing he would tell her.

Gawain scratched the back of his neck "Merlin is..."

The sound of someone running up the hallway tapped out a steady beat. Whoever it was sprinted full-bore and slammed into the door rather than stopping. The double doors were nearly flung off their hinges, and when Britt swung around to see who it was, she sprinted.

"Merlin!"

Merlin, who was usually impeccably dressed, was flushed and a little sweaty. The coat of his charcoal gray suit was flung over one arm, and the sleeves of his blue dress shirt were messily rolled up. When he set his brilliant eyes on Britt, a glowing smile lit up his features. "Lass!" He dropped his suit coat and took a step into the room, only to be bowled over by a massive, apricot-colored dog from behind.

The dog loped up to Britt, wagging its tail merrily. Britt laughed and caressed Cavall's head, but she kept running to Merlin.

By the time she reached him, he had recovered and swept her up in a tight embrace. Britt clung to him and hoped he would never let her go. She laughed and cried at the same time, clutching Merlin around the neck as he wiped tears off her cheeks.

"You came," Britt cried. "Even though Britain was united, you came."

Merlin leaned forward so their foreheads touched. "I told you, Britt. I met you, and you changed everything." He smiled, then kissed her deeply.

Once again, all was right with the world. Yes, perhaps she would eternally be in limbo between the stories of knights and the skyscrapers of modern life. But the legends of the past had joined her, and Merlin had moved time itself to be with her.

It was more than she could have ever hoped for.

The kiss stretched on, and Britt could hear Kay tap his foot and grunt, "Humph."

"Let them have their moment, Kay," Morgan said. "This has been centuries in the making."

Britt couldn't help but giggle when Merlin finally ended the kiss, though he did not loosen his tight grip on her waist.

"Thank you," she whispered.

He kissed her cheek and under her ear. "I couldn't lose you."

Nymue stabbed a finger in their direction. "You are horribly late. You were supposed to get here before Britt."

"I got caught in traffic whilst picking the monster up from his daycare facility." Merlin eyed Cavall with great reservation.

The mastiff licked his chops, then pressed his face into Merlin's side, leaving a wet smudge behind.

Britt was almost distracted by the thought of Merlin hauling Cavall around and dropping him off at doggy daycare, but more important matters pressed to the front of her mind. "I still don't understand how this all works," she said. "How could Kay be my teacher if you were all entombed in a cave? How did you even find me?"

"We had to reset the spell periodically," Nymue said. "So every few centuries, everyone piled out of the cave. While the ladies and I reworked the spell, your sideshow-hack and knights went off on adventures, trying to figure out and piece together history."

"If you search history, there are multiple times when King Arthur and his knights became a popular topic and had a renaissance of sorts," Morgan said wryly. "That would be the time when we let them loose, and they caused havoc with their zeal."

"We were mostly working blind for the first few centuries," Bedivere said with a smile. "Thankfully, you did leave us a few hints!"

"Like what?"

"We found your backpack and the British travel book in your room in Camelot," Gawain said. "It took a while for us to decipher modern English, but at least then we had the year."

"And we had the iPod you gave Merlin," Kay added. "When we knew we were coming close to the time, we popped out of the cave more frequently to inquire if Apple was yet a corporation."

Lionel laughed heartily. "As soon as it was available to the public, Merlin heavily invested in it from some of the gold horde we stored in the cave with us."

"It was one of several investments we were able to make that turned out well due to the loose historic timeline we were able to piece together from your travel book," Lancelot added.

"That and Nymue is a real-estate guru," Morgan added.

"But how did you find *me*?" Britt asked.

"You certainly didn't make it easy on us, Britannica Arthurs." Merlin used her full name—which she had never gone by and had certainly never told any of them. He leaned closer and whispered into her ear. "Britannica, from the root word Britannic, which means '*of Britain.*' No wonder the sword chose you."

Kay began tapping his foot again.

Merlin cleared his throat and inched his head back, but he still did not loosen his hold on her waist. "Blaise was able to pinpoint a general time before we left, but as I knew your approximate age, and we had the travel book, we popped out of the cave a few years early just to be sure."

Britt frowned slightly as she looked from Merlin to the rest of her friends. Though they looked different, it was mostly in appearance only. Gawain still looked like he was barely twenty, as did Griflet and Percival. "So...why haven't you aged, then?" She asked.

Merlin smiled triumphantly. "It's a side-effect of the spell. Even mortals will have the same lifespan of a faerie if they spend enough time on faerie land."

This revelation shocked Britt almost as much as knowing that her friends were still alive. "Does that mean…?"

Merlin smiled and kissed her cheek. "Yes. All of us are ageless with you."

This proclamation made Britt burst into tears, which caused Cavall to bark and made everyone fuss. There was another round of hugging; this time Britt embraced everyone present, ending with Kay.

The room was filled with laughter and good cheer, and Britt felt so happy she could almost burst…. But there was still one person missing. "Kay…Did our father stay behind?"

Kay's smile dimmed, and he retreated to the round table. "I'm sorry, Britt. He couldn't leave Bonmaison, or mother. But, he gave me this letter to give you." He handed Britt a binder filled with laminated pages. Some of the pages were covered with script, old English Britt couldn't understand. But others were written on Avalon-themed stationary. "I laminated the original to save it, then translated it so you could read it yourself."

Merlin guided Britt over to a chair so she could sit down as she read the letter from her foster-father.

To Britt Arthurs,

If you're reading this, then Kay and the others have successfully found you. I regret that I cannot come with them, for more than anything I would like to be there for you. I would love to see what you do and the new goals you accomplish! But I am needed here, in this time. And as much as I would wish it, my place is not with you in the future.

But that does not change how proud I am of you, or how much I love you. Camelot is strong, and Britain is great because of your court and because of you. I know you can do it again, in your time. Though it is a different situation, I know you will continue to do many great things, and you will change the world for the better.

So please, Britt. Remember me, and know that I love you, and I will always think of you with a parent's pride and joy. You will ever be my Britt, my daughter, and my King.

With all my love,

Your father

It took Britt several minutes before she could stop crying. Kay, Morgan, and Merlin stayed with her, and Gawain hovered just behind her chair.

Though the letter tore her heart, it soothed her soul. For Britt knew just as she had changed Britain after becoming king, the knights who served her had changed her. She would miss Ector, the man who had been, and still was, her father. Though he had died hundreds of years ago, she would still love him and try to make him proud.

The same was true for the loss of Mordred, Ywain, Pellinore, and all the other knights who could not come with her.

Now, as little more than a jobless graduate, she didn't know what kind of impact she would have.... But in their memory, she would do her best.

Britt took the Kleenex that Kay offered her and smiled through her tears at her foster brother. "Thanks, Kay."

Kay nodded and suspiciously rubbed his eyes.

"If I might, perhaps, brighten the occasion," Bedivere said as he and Percival slowly approached Britt now that her tears were gone.

Britt laughed. "I'm sorry. I'm so happy everyone's here. It's just…"

"We understand, Lass." Merlin took Britt's hand and intertwined it with his own.

"Yes, but it's about time we hand off your official position in Avalon," Bedivere said.

"Right. What did you guys call me in here for?" Britt asked.

"It was my idea to lure you in with the promise of an interview," Nymue said. "You are a jobless millennial, after all."

"Not any longer," Bedivere said with a big smile. "Percival, if you would."

Percival gave Britt a wooden nameplate with a shy smile.

Britt flipped it around, her brain flatlining when she read it.

Britannica Arthurs, CEO

"What?" Britt asked dumbly.

"You are the new CEO of Avalon!" Lancelot crowed.

"Between reading your travel book and investing in Apple, we've actually managed to multiply our wealth," Bedivere said.

"Indeed," Merlin said. "We actually have more assets in monetary value than you did as King of Camelot. And it's all yours."

"You can't just give me all that money," Britt protested, with an unamused look.

"Of course we can," Morgan said firmly.

"And our first Lancelot Hate Club reunion meeting will be to go shopping," Nymue announced.

Griflet snapped his fingers at Britt and winked. "Yeah, the ladies have made it a rule that if you work here, you got to look on peak."

"It's point. On point," Merlin said flatly.

"Going through so many centuries, your knights have found it hard to adjust to modern slang," Nymue said. "So I wouldn't let any of them handle your PR stuff if I were you. We ladies, however, excel at it."

"But I don't get it," Britt said as Merlin pulled her from her chair. "What do you expect me to do?"

Lancelot shrugged his shoulders. "Does it matter what you do? You are our King. We will follow you wherever you go."

"We can invest in and work on the issues you think important," Kay said. "The initiatives we started with Avalon are merely the beginning."

"Though we did fund what we thought you would be interested in," Griflet said. "The water purification venture was my idea!" He sidled up to Blancheflor and batted his eyes at the faerie lady. She rolled her eyes, but Britt didn't miss the way she minutely shifted closer to him.

"You can't just throw all this money at me," Britt protested as Merlin led her around the Round Table. "I'm not a business person—I won't know what to do with it!"

"Most of our funds aren't liquid, so we are incapable of physically assaulting you with it," Gawain pointed out. "Except for your crown and armor, of course."

"I saw your statements online. Avalon is a multi-billion-dollar organization," Britt said, preparing to hold her ground on the issue. "You can't be so calm and nonchalant about passing it off to me!"

Bedivere blinked at her, wide-eyed as if he were shocked with her reaction. "Why not?"

"Because, because you can't!" Britt said.

"Britt," Merlin said, stopping her tirade.

"What?" She snapped.

Merlin tilted his head at the wall. Still feeling overwhelmed and snappish, Britt, scowling, turned to face the wall, and her anger faded away.

Excalibur, mounted on a wooden plaque, was bolted above the fireplace. Britt reached out and brushed the hilt, which still felt as if it were made especially for her and hummed in her grasp.

Touching it made some of her protests die. "But.... You...." She sighed. "We'll have to make a new goal," she said finally. "I mean, we can't do anything with the British government. I'm not a citizen, and it's not just a monarchy anymore."

Merlin helped her lift Excalibur from the wall, freeing it. "Oh, I wasn't thinking about Britain this time."

Britt snorted as the sword practically hummed in her hand. "Then what *were* you thinking of?"

"How about...the world?"

THE END OF KING ARTHUR AND HER KNIGHTS

DATE NIGHT

Britt didn't know what to expect when Merlin said he would pick her up for their date that night—their first date ever, really. It had crossed her mind that he could arrive in a horse-drawn carriage, a Mercedes-Benz, or anything in between.

So she was somewhat surprised when he pulled up on the street in front of her apartment complex in a silver Toyota SUV. It was a nice car. It still sported the new car smell, and it had a leather interior and heated seats. But it was surprisingly...practical.

"So you really have a driver's license?" Britt asked as she buckled her seatbelt.

"Indeed," Merlin said. He waited until she was situated before shifting the car into drive. "All of us are certified citizens of the United States. We all pay taxes, and we all have our driver's license. Well, excluding Morgan, that is. She keeps failing her driver's test, but that's because she drives like a maniac."

"How did you manage to get IDs?" Britt asked.

"The Lady of the Lake," Merlin said. "A number of her hand-maidens work for the US government.

"I don't know if that's reassuring or terrifying," Britt said.

Merlin made a turn, navigating through the maze of city streets. "Oh, the US is not the only pie she has her thumb in. Most of her power lays in her real estate holdings and in the great number of favors the various faerie royalty throughout the world owe her."

"I'm starting to think *she* would've made a wonderful High King of Britain," Britt said.

"I'm forced to disagree with you," Merlin said. "She doesn't care a jot for anybody in whom she is not emotionally invested."

"That's true," Britt chuckled.

Merlin spared her a soft smile, but Britt noticed he held a death grip on the steering wheel. *Perhaps he isn't as comfortable driving as he appears to be?*

Three weeks had passed since Britt had set foot inside Avalon's office building. Though she and Merlin had spent days together, much of it was spent adjusting to changes. (They moved Britt into a new apartment closer to Avalon's offices that would also allow dogs as big as Cavall, plus all of the knights insisted on meeting her mother and sister, and already she had begun to take over some of the non-profit's projects and chat with Kay about the company's financial position.)

It was Merlin who had insisted in taking her on a date. ("I want you to myself," he had said. "Everything else can wait.")

Recalling how Gawain and Ragnelle—Cavall's sitters for the evening—had arrived a few minutes before Merlin with the promise that the wizard would be along shortly, Britt asked, "So everyone lives together in one big mansion?"

"Almost everyone. Nymue floats around in whatever matter suits her, but yes. Everyone else lives under one roof. I'm afraid that's a habit from Camelot we won't ever break."

"I think it's fun."

"I don't," Merlin muttered. "I had a wretched difficult time leaving the house without being nudged and winked at every other step."

"Will I get to move in with everyone?" Britt asked.

"Eventually," Merlin said evasively.

They continued to chat—Merlin explaining some of the finer details of how the Knights of the Round Table had kicked up their heels, waiting for Britt to grow older and travel back to ancient Britain—until they pulled up at a quaint Italian restaurant.

The restaurant smelled tantalizingly of garlic and butter, and Britt's stomach growled painfully as the hostess led the way to the table Merlin had reserved.

After Merlin pulled her chair out for her, Britt stared at the wizard as he seated himself. His clothes—black slacks and a dove gray sweater—made his blue eyes appear even more brilliant than usual, and his fine blonde hair was almost white in the dim light of the restaurant. He'd been carrying his coat oddly, and instead of hanging it up, he carefully arranged it on an open chair pulled up to their table.

She shook her head. "I know it's been three weeks, but I'm still having a hard time wrapping my head around this."

Merlin tilted his chin up. "Around what?"

"That you're here. With me. In the future." Britt awkwardly rested her hands on the table surface. "It's so…different."

Merlin leaned back in his chair. "The clothes we are wearing are more modern, and the setting is far more hygienic, but we're still the same people. I'm still your sideshow hack magician, and you are still the legendary High King of Britain."

Britt licked her lips. "Are we really still the same? For me it's been about a year. But Nymue said you were stuck in the cave for nearly three years, and that doesn't count all the time you spent outside the cave tracking me down and then waiting for me to grow up."

Merlin reached across the table and took one of her hands in his. "Nothing has changed. I still love you with every inch of my being and drop of magic I possess, and I am confident enough in your love for me that I know you still feel the same way."

Britt grinned and raised an eyebrow. "Cocky, are we?"

"Not at all. I know you; you love wholeheartedly. You would not so easily set your feelings aside. But even if you had, I would have the foreseeable future to beguile my way back into your affections."

She fought a blush. "You are right."

Merlin smiled arrogantly, but he sweetly intertwined his fingers with hers. "If anything has changed, it is only that *I* now also bear a grudge against Lancelot."

Britt grinned as he squeezed her hand. "I told you all to let it go."

"Forgive me if I find it exceedingly hard to let that prig skip around like an innocent sheep after being at least partially responsible for your gravest injury—and for my separation from you," Merlin said wryly.

"Although I'm glad you listened to me, I have to say I'm a little surprised you let him come forward in time with you," Britt said.

"It was a close thing," Merlin said. "We were evenly divided on leaving him behind and opting to bring him with us. The bleeding hearts of the group—Griflet and Percival—were in favor of letting him come with us from the start. In the end, Kay was the swing vote."

Britt gaped. "*Kay*? The man who taught me to hate Lancelot ever since I was a child?"

"Indeed," Merlin said. "He was afraid if we left him behind, Lancelot would cause the demise of Camelot. That was something he would not abide as he knew of your love for the place. So Lancelot came with us."

Britt smiled fondly. "That's so sweet of him!"

Merlin raised his eyebrows, but they were interrupted.

"Good evening, and welcome to our establishment! I will be your waiter for the evening."

Britt and Merlin shifted their attention to their waiter.

Lancelot, wearing a white dress shirt and black slacks, held a small notepad and beamed down at them.

Merlin cursed under his breath.

Britt stared at the charismatic knight. "You've got to be joking."

Lancelot tipped his head. "I'm afraid I don't know to what you are referring."

"You're not the waiter, Lancelot. Get lost and send the real guy out here," Britt said.

Lancelot smiled brightly. "Oh, but you see I am your waiter for tonight! Lionel and I paid off the wait-staff."

"That can't be legal," Britt said.

"We weren't really sure how much to give them. I assume $1,000 is a day's wages?" Lancelot asked.

"That money better be from your own funds," Merlin said sourly.

"It was," Lancelot said. "But I shall need an advance on next quarter's stipend."

"That's not happening," Merlin said.

"Whatever," Britt said, trying to move past the budding argument. "Can you just tell us what the night's specials are?"

"I have no idea," Lancelot said. "I don't even know what I'm supposed to do besides carry this," he said, holding up the notepad. "But Lionel may know." Lancelot turned to shout across the sparsely populated restaurant. "Lionel! Do you know what tonight's specials are?"

Lionel, wearing an identical white dress shirt that seemed to be bursting at the seams due to his muscular shoulders and chest, strolled across the restaurant. "I reckon there's some kind of soup? That seems to be a normal special. And probably a pasta dish or two." He, at least, had the decency to give Britt and Merlin crystal glasses of water.

"I had forgotten how helpful the two of you are," Britt said.

Merlin scowled up at the pair. "How did you figure out where I was planning to take Britt?"

"Morgan hacked your phone and found it on your recently called list," Lancelot said.

"She almost didn't tell us." Lionel folded his arms across his chest, making the buttons of his shirt pull even tighter. "She thought it was cute that 'Britt' was your password to swipe open your phone screen."

"I should have guessed that hag would be behind this," Merlin muttered.

Britt picked up the restaurant's menu with her free hand. "If you don't know what the specials are, you should at least go see to the other customers."

Lancelot shrugged. "There's only one other couple here right now, and they're fine."

"I think she meant for us to get lost," Lionel said cheerfully.

"Exactly," Britt said.

"But we ought to stay," Lancelot said. "Being attentive is a good waiter's job. And I want a good tip—paying off all the waiters cost more than I expected."

"Go!" Britt ordered.

"Fine, fine." Lancelot flipped his little notebook shut. "You can take the King out of England, but you can't take the King out of the girl."

Merlin scowled after the cousins with unusual fire as they sauntered off.

Noticing he was twisting his cloth napkin as if attempting to decapitate it, Britt asked, "Is everything all right?"

Instantly, he was all smiles. "Yes, everything is fine."

"I would apologize on his behalf," Britt said, "but for starters, I don't want to enable him. And truly I don't think he really is sorry."

"No, this is definitely deliberate." Merlin still hadn't released her hand, so he squeezed it. "It's nothing compared to some of the shenanigans the other knights pulled over the years."

"They did things worse than crashing dates?"

"Much worse," Merlin assured her. "We had to renew the spell that tethered the cave's passage of time to the world's passage of time sometime in the 1890s. Griflet and Bedivere slipped from our control and attended a performance of the musical, *King Arthur and the Knights of the Round Table*. While there, they met a couple who owned a company that distributed flour. Bedivere cajoled them to rename their business, and the King Arthur Flour Company was born."

"You're joking," Britt said.

"Unfortunately, I am not," Merlin said. "Kay, on the other hand, is responsible for being the catalyst for just about every legend that mentions Lancelot's disloyalty in love." He grunted. "He, likely, was able to cause more damage and bring King Arthur back in fashion more so than any other knight. I had thought Morgan would keep him on a tight leash, but I forgot she was almost as absurdly fond of you as he was. By the time I realized their actions, they had already frolicked through centuries of King Arthur renaissances as we were forced to pop in and out of the cave to check on the passage of time."

"You mean you didn't stay in the cave the entire time?"

Merlin shook his head. "As I mentioned, there were several occasions in which we had to renew the spell. But also I did not know the exact year you were born, and we did not want to miss it. So, every so often we left the cave to inquire if America was yet a place, or to make investments."

Britt flipped her menu over to check out the appetizer list. "Wow, so that means you probably spent more than a few years with everyone."

Merlin stared at his menu and said in a deadened tone. "Correct."

Britt's phone buzzed. "Sorry." She pulled her hand from Merlin's grasp and picked up the phone.

"No trouble at all." Merlin eyed the glass of water Lionel had provided before daring to take a sip from it.

Britt intended to shut her phone off, but when she swiped the screen of her smart phone, she saw the text was a message from Kay. Concerned, Britt opened it up.

You should order the spinach artichoke dip. I believe you will enjoy it.

She stared at the message, and her phone buzzed when another text message arrived.

And tell Merlin to stop holding your hand.

Britt twisted in her seat and gazed around the nearly empty restaurant. The only other customers were a couple seated across the restaurant. The woman wore a hat that covered her brown hair and shaded her eyes, though she smiled and waved when Britt saw them. Her companion hadn't even bothered to try and disguise himself. It wouldn't have mattered anyway; Britt would've recognized his mustache a mile away.

"It seems Lancelot and Lionel weren't the only ones who decided to crash our date."

"Hmm?" Merlin looked up from the menu, then dropped it on the table when he saw where Britt was looking. "Kay and Morgan. Of course, the overprotective brother wouldn't let me take his darling sister out without looming in the background."

Britt laughed and returned her attention to her menu. "And Morgan?"

"She would never miss a chance to see me squirm," Merlin said dryly.

Britt furrowed her eyebrows and was about to ask why he would squirm over a mere date, when they were interrupted.

"Smile!" A light flashed and a camera clicked.

Britt blinked stars from her eyes and peered up at the newest arrival. "Percival, Bedivere?"

Percival smiled widely and held up a camera. Bedivere was a little behind him, fussing over his cellphone. "Yes, My King!"

Merlin growled and took another swig of his water.

"What are you doing here?" Britt asked.

"I'm here to record this momentous occasion and take photos for instant-gram!" The knight proclaimed.

"Instagram," Britt corrected mindlessly.

Bedivere finally looked up from his phone. "Which filter would you prefer on this update, My King: Crema, Lark, or Valencia? Mind you, I can't post this picture with the filters on Facebook," he said.

"You have *Facebook*?" Britt asked.

"A few of us do," Bedivere said with a guileless smile. "We were quite relieved you kept your profile as public and did not switch it to friends only, for it would have made watching you much harder."

"I thought you two were going out with Griflet and Blancheflor tonight?" Merlin asked.

"We are!" Percival smiled. "They're here as well."

Merlin stiffened. "What?"

"My King!" Griflet, walking arm-in-arm with Blancheflor, charged through the restaurant's front doors. "Fancy meeting you here! Why, what could the chances be that we would pick the same restaurant as you?"

"I'm fairly certain the act is not needed," Blancheflor said as she looked from Kay, to Percival, to Lancelot.

Britt was tempted to pinch her eyes. "I'm beginning to think it's a good thing I don't live in the mansion with all of you."

"You have no idea," Merlin said.

Blancheflor waved off the hostess as Griflet chose a table that did not block Kay's view of Britt and Merlin.

Lionel bustled over to their table and gave them waters.

"Thank you, but I believe we'll all want a round of wine soon," Griflet said.

Lionel raised an eyebrow at him. "You better get it yourself then. I'm certainly not hauling out all those glasses."

While viewing Griflet's pursed lips, Britt's frustration began to melt into amusement due to her affection for all those present. "Well, so much for alone time." She sighed. "But it's not bad for a first date."

She glanced at Merlin, surprised to see that he glared at his water glass as if he could melt it with his gaze. She reached across the table and squeezed his hand. "Is it really that upsetting?"

Merlin scowled still, though he intertwined his fingers with hers again. "Normally it would not be, and I would only consider this a mild inconvenience. But tonight I was going to… And they all know…"

"You were going to…?" Britt prompted.

Merlin flattened his lips and refused to respond, but it didn't matter, as the door banged open once again.

In came Nymue, completely ignoring the hostess as she made a beeline for the table next to Britt and Merlin's. "I believe I made a mistake in failing to invest in parking garages. Finding a parking place on the street is a quest worthy of your best knights," she announced.

Merlin squinted at the faerie lady. "Is it really necessary for even *you* to crash this evening?"

Nymue shed her jacket. "No one was home, and I was bored."

"I can't believe Gawain and Ragnelle are the only two who refrained from crashing our date," Britt said.

"Don't you let that boy's sweet exterior fool you," Nymue said.

"Indeed." Morgan saluted Britt with a water glass. "The only reason he is not here is because he thought it would be shameful to so directly spy on you. Why else do you think he offered to watch Cavall, if not to force you to tell him of the night's events when you return home?"

"Other diners will soon arrive," Merlin predicted.

"No, they won't!" Lionel said cheerfully. "Kay rented out the place for the night."

Kay frowned slightly at the brawny man. "I did, and I can assure both of you that I'm not paying you anything for your service on top of what I already paid the restaurant."

Britt glanced across the table and patted Merlin's hand. The anger seemed to have fizzled out of him as he slumped in his chair and stared forlornly at the table top. When she stood, Merlin tried to tug her back into her chair.

"Where are you going?" he asked worriedly.

She laughed. "I'm just going to use the restroom. Does anyone know where it is?"

Lancelot shrugged. "Nope."

Britt rolled her eyes. "Of course you wouldn't."

"It's past the bar and down a short hallway near the employee exit," Kay said.

Britt smiled at her brother, then slipped through the pattern of tables, making for the restroom.

As she escaped into the ladies room, she could hear the roars of laughter as Lionel began ripping Griflet for the first date he had taken Blancheflor on.

After using the bathroom, Britt washed her hands, checked her makeup, then stepped into the back hallway, where she was abruptly yanked away. She opened her mouth to yelp, but someone slapped a hand over her lips.

"It's me," Merlin said as he tugged her along. He removed his hand from her mouth so he could juggle his jacket and hers as they hustled down the hallway and slipped out the employee exit.

"It's not necessary to leave," she said after the door shut behind them.

"But it really is," Merlin said sourly.

Britt ignored his sarcasm and continued, "I would love to spend time with just you, but we do have a *long* life ahead of us. I missed you all so terribly…"

"On any other night, perhaps I wouldn't be quite so selfish. But tonight? Not a chance. I'm going to have this night with you, even if it kills me. And *they* are not going to stop it!" Merlin declared.

Britt's heart throbbed in her chest as she and Merlin made their way back to his car. She was glad it was dark, for it hid her blush, and she gratefully rested her head on Merlin's shoulder as she clutched his arm. "Where are we going, then?"

Merlin opened the car door for her. "A hiding place, and one of the trump cards I was hoping to use the next time you get mad at me."

Britt was more than a little curious as they drove toward the outskirts of town, stopping only to pick up cartons of take-out at her favorite Chinese restaurant. When Merlin turned onto a gravel road, Britt recognized it as the long driveway to the mansion where everyone lived.

"Good thinking," she said. "No one would suspect we would come back home."

"We're not going into the house." Merlin parked his car in the impressively large garage. He carried the plastic bag of their take-out and insisted on awkwardly cradling his jacket.

Amused, Britt trailed him as he trundled across the mansion grounds, following a brick pathway around a copse of trees, and popping out next to a beautifully lit, wooden stable.

Merlin flicked on the inner lights of the barn, revealing gorgeous wooden stalls complemented with brick archways, cobblestone flooring, and more impressive architecture than Britt's apartment. The familiar smell of hay and horses brought a prickle of tears to Britt's eyes as memories from Camelot briefly surged in her mind.

"Welcome to the stables," Merlin said. He put down their food and grunted as he dragged a few hay bales into the middle of the aisle, then covered them with a pristinely clean horse blanket.

"Many of the mounts belong to your knights, but this one is yours. His name is Camelot."

A large, golden-colored buckskin—with a perfectly combed black mane and tail and a fuzzy black muzzle—blinked his liquid brown eyes at Britt and pushed his muzzle against the bars of his stall. Camelot was quite large, even larger than Roen had been. As Britt stepped closer to the stall, he breathed out of his nostrils, and the ache to ride and race the wind filled her heart. "Thank you." She paused. "For being so thoughtful about everything."

Merlin smiled faintly and patted the blanket-covered hay bale next to him. "I had a long time to plan for it."

Britt planted a kiss on Camelot's muzzle, then joined Merlin. She opened a carton of sesame chicken and picked at it with her chopsticks. "Selfishly, I'm glad you brought me here. When I first got back, there was so much I missed about medieval England that it was easier to push it all away and ignore the pain. I didn't even know how much I missed horses." Britt cleared her throat, trying to dislodge the lump that had taken up residence there.

Merlin set his food aside and wrapped an arm around Britt's shoulders, scooping her against his chest. "You've given up so much, lass. More than anyone should have to." He kissed her forehead sweetly.

Britt also put her chicken aside and leaned into Merlin, wrapping her arms around his waist. They sat there for several quiet minutes, Merlin combing his fingers through her hair as Britt listened to the beat of his heart through his tailored shirt.

When he awkwardly cleared his throat, Britt pulled back and picked up her food again. She paused, her chopsticks raised halfway to her mouth, when Merlin went down on one knee in front of her hay bale. "Merlin?" She asked wonderingly.

Merlin held his oddly bundled jacket across his knee, his shoulders set, and his expression serious. "Britt Arthurs, as you know, I am wildly and madly in love with you, so much so that I will ruin the fabric of time itself to be with you. I ask, would you tie yourself to me forever and marry me?"

Britt gaped, and her chopsticks fell from her unfeeling fingers.

Merlin forged on. "I know this is all rather sudden—for you anyway—but when I nearly lost you, I promised myself I would never let the chance escape me again. And no matter how much time we have together, I know it will never be enough for me. So, would you do me the honor?" He hesitated in the silence, then started speaking a little too quickly. "If you wish to delay the wedding and not get married for some months, I completely understand. But if you are willing, I would still like us to be spoken for as the knights of Camelot would speak for their lady loves. Although, I suppose, in this case, perhaps I'm in the role of the lady?"

He's babbling again, Britt thought. *He must do that whenever he's really nervous.*

Merlin opened his mouth to continue, but Britt leaned forward and silenced him with a kiss. She tried to fill it with all the love she felt and the joy that had colored her life since she realized he was still alive.

Merlin seem to appreciate it, for he tugged her forward until she tumbled into his lap, breaking their kiss.

"I hope you don't mind," Merlin said, a faint blush heating his cheeks. "But I decided to depart from tradition."

Britt tucked a strand of her blonde hair behind her ear and tried to shift so Merlin's jacket didn't jab her back. "What tradition?"

"The engagement ring. I thought long and hard about it, and in the end I decided a silly little rock had no way of representing everything our love is. So instead, I got you this." Merlin tossed his jacket aside, revealing a scabbard gilded with gold. The leather surface was buttery smooth, and the goldwork was styled into miniature pictures—one was a sword in a stone, another was a perfect representation of Camelot, and another showed two horses and a stag.

"It's sized to fit Excalibur, and it's enchanted—not anything as strong as Excalibur's old scabbard was, though."

Britt ran her fingers across the golden horses and deer. "How is it spelled?"

Merlin cleared his throat. "It's enchanted so I'll be able to find it—and you—no matter where you are. Past, present or future, I will know." He shifted slightly. "I did the spell work myself, but Nymue checked it over. If you like, I'm certain if we work with her and Morgan, I can attach some stronger enchantments to it."

"No." Britt shook her head. "It's perfect."

"Are you certain?" Merlin asked. "If you like, we can still pick out a ring…"

Britt finally tore her eyes from the scabbard. "It's perfect, Merlin," she repeated. "And it proves to me just how much you know me and how much you love me. It's *exactly* what I want."

Merlin's shoulders heaved, and he took a great gulp of air. "Good! I didn't want to mess this up." Without further ado, he renewed their kiss, wrapping his arms securely around Britt.

Britt clung to him, her heart welling over with the knowledge of his love. When they finally parted, she rested her head on his shoulder. "So I take it everyone else knew you were going to propose tonight?"

"Yes," Merlin said sourly.

Britt laughed as she pressed her forehead against his neck and clutched her engagement scabbard.

Centuries ago, Blaise—Merlin's mentor—had said the modern day legends of Camelot weren't about her Kingdom—at least, not in its entirety.

At the time, Britt hadn't quite believed him, but now she could see it.

No legend could ever convey Kay's steadfast care or Gawain's faithful loyalty. In particular, no story could *ever* properly express the depth of love between Britt and Merlin. Neither wars nor time itself could part them.

So now, she finally understood what Blaise was trying to tell her. Britt was forevermore the founder of the Round Table, the love of Merlin, and the High King of Camelot. Long Live King Arthurs!

THE END

THE NEW HIGH KING

"Once the giant was defeated, it was quite simple to free the lady. Sir Lanval did most of the work, but it was a jolly good adventure!" Sir Tor beamed at the Knights of the Round Table, in a in a cheerful mood as usual.

Mordred rubbed his chin. *At least that hasn't changed.*

"Yes, thank you, Sir Tor," Sir Ulfius said. "I believe that brings this meeting of the Round Table to an end. Unless you wish to say something, My King?"

Mordred pushed his shoulders back and smiled. "Only that I'm exceedingly proud and happy with the Order of the Round Table, and I would like to thank every one of you for making Britt's vision of Camelot carry on. That is all."

Various emotions flickered across the knights' faces—sadness, affection, and pain at a wound that still ached.

It had been a year since Merlin and a number of Britt's closest knights sealed themselves in a cave in hopes of meeting Britt in the future. It had been even longer since Britt had left, but the gaping hole of her absence was still felt, though it had dulled to an ache rather than the stabbing sensation that had plagued everyone in Camelot for months.

As knights began standing and taking their leave, Sir Ywain trotted up to Mordred. "My King, I wish to tell you that I shall return to my lands in a week."

Mordred smiled. "You miss your wife, do you?"

"Like a thirsty man misses water," Ywain agreed.

"I shall be sad to see you go, but please pass my greetings on to Lady Laudine, and tell her we are grateful she could spare you from her courts."

"Spare me? That's a pretty way of putting it," Ywain grumbled. "She kicked me out of the castle and said if I didn't return after completing three quests, she wouldn't let me back in!"

"Your lioness tearing up her tapestries might've had something to do with it," Mordred said lightly.

"She was just playing!" Ywain insisted.

"That's an excuse to make for a kitten, not a lioness, cousin," Sir Agravain said as he and Sir Bors joined the conversation.

"Exercising your big cat, though, will make a wonderful excuse for excursions in the future," Sir Bors said. "I have plans to visit the Lady of the Lake in a month's time. Would you care to join me?"

Mordred tilted his head. "I thought I'd heard the Lady of the Lake banned you from her presence."

Bors laughed. "So she claimed. But ever since Lancelot and Lionel departed, I've been allowed into her halls."

"The Lady of the Lake has a hall?" Agravain asked, furrowing his eyebrows.

"Indeed. It is located under her lake," Bors said

"Underwater? Please, Sir Bors. Come up with a more believable idea," Agravain scoffed. "I am not some green knight you can try to feed exaggerated tales to!"

"I'm surprised with you, Agravain," Ywain said. "Knowing our Aunt Morgan, I should think you would more readily understand the use of magic."

"I do," Agravain insisted. "It is merely that I also know Sir Bors is related to the biggest boaster Britain has ever seen."

Mordred chuckled. "Now you are starting to sound like Britt."

There was a pained pause, but Sir Bors was the first to recover. "I have a proposal to make. As you are leaving soon, Sir Ywain, I think we should hold a hunt before your departure."

"A hunt!" Ywain's eyes lit up. "Yes—if you do not mind, My King?"

"I think a hunt might be just what we need," Mordred said.

Even Agravain began to smile. "Wonderful! I have a new bow I should like to try for the occasion."

"Is it the one the faerie lady gave you on your last quest?" Ywain asked.

"Yes!"

"If that is the case, you had best start praying we hunt deer, and not boars," Sir Bors said.

"It doesn't matter what we hunt, it will certainly be an entertaining time!" Ywain said. "Here now; I'll go tell Tor. Will you clear it with your seneschal and counselors, My King?"

"I will, but I've no reason to think they would object," Mordred said.

"I should think not," Agravain snorted. "With Kay-the-tight-fisted gone, there's no one to halt our festivities."

"Sir Kay was a genius at treasuries," Bors said. "I appreciate it more now that I have been looking over the financial records of my father's kingdom."

The trio of knights bowed to Mordred, then moved on, the promise of entertainment mingling with their newfound responsibilities.

Britt was not the only one who left a hole in Camelot. Kay, Gawain, Lancelot, Merlin, and all who had shut themselves into the cave were sorely missed, and their absence had caused great changes in Britain's political landscape.

Agravain was now the heir to the Orkney throne, and it

seemed that Bors would inherit his uncle's kingdom, as well as his father's.

Mordred pinched his eyes shut. Britt's breathtaking smile was still fresh in his memory, but what he most missed were her sarcastic jokes, and the quiet moments in which he witnessed her astute emotional observations. "She always knew what to say," he murmured.

"Perhaps, but you certainly take after her in that area."

Mordred jumped in his chair, smiling when he realized it was King Pellinore who addressed him. "While the compliment warms my heart, I must disagree. Britt had great understanding of the power of words and wielded them perfectly. Even if I see a situation, I struggle to find the words to say."

"That's because you're not Britt," Pellinore said. Though his words stung a little, he softened the blow with an understanding smile. "It is a good thing that you fight to uphold the principles and morals she established, but you must do so in your own way. I'm the same. I haven't that golden voice or enchanting smile Britt had. But I have my honor, and my vassals know they can trust me. So that is how I rule."

Mordred rested his fingers on the scratched surface of the Round Table. "Truthfully, I don't feel like I can rule as a true king. The men here are my friends. Who am I to give them orders?"

Pellinore shrugged. "Men followed Britt because she made them think they could be better. They fought for her because they believed in her. But wouldn't you fight just as hard, if your friend asked you to?"

Mordred frowned as he thought. "I see your point."

Pellinore grunted. "Just don't spend your time thinking of how the previous High King casts a long shadow. It's a waste of time, given that she came from such a radically different place that you could never emulate. And I believe if she were to know how you felt, it would sadden her."

Mordred nodded. "Thank you, for your advice and your continued presence in Camelot."

The older king smiled. "I'm glad I can be of service. If you ever need any encouragement or advice, I would be honored if you were to confide in me."

"I will," Mordred promised.

Pellinore clasped his shoulder, then left.

Mordred stood, groaning a little as he stretched his arms above his head, then made for the door. *I'll be holding court this afternoon, but since I have a few extra minutes, perhaps I should make an early inspection of the armory...*

When Mordred left the hall, he found Guinevere waiting for him in the passageway.

"My King," she said with an elegant curtsy. "The ladies have finished sewing and hemming the banners for the summer festival. I spoke to the seneschal, but he requested that I pass the information on to you as well."

"Thank you for your hard work," Mordred said as he ran a hand through his hair. "You finished far more quickly than expected. Isn't the festival not for a number of weeks?"

Guinevere smiled. "It is to be held in two weeks, my King."

Mordred stiffened his shoulders to keep from hunching them. "Two weeks?" *I had forgotten it was so soon. Blast! That means the preparations are running behind.... I'll have to speak to Sir Bodwain after dinner tonight and look over the accounts.* He shifted his attention back to Guinevere and smiled thinly. "It is fortuitous, then, that I spoke to you. Thank you, Lady Guinevere."

Guinevere nodded, but she squinted slightly and wrung her hands. "My King, if I could be so presumptuous..."

"Yes," Mordred prodded when she did not continue.

"May I speak to you, elsewhere?"

"Of course. Did you have a location in mind?"

Guinevere nodded, and she led the way down the hallway.

Mordred followed her all the way outside the castle, across the courtyard, and up a staircase that spilled out onto the castle walls.

Some of the tension eased in Mordred's frame as he stared out at the green lands surrounding Camelot. "So what is it that is weighing on your mind, Lady Guinevere?"

"In truth, I must confess there was not any one thing I wished to speak to you about," Guinevere admitted. She sheepishly looked down at her hands, nodded once, then pushed her chin up and met his gaze. "It appeared, to me anyway, that you needed a moment of quiet. Britt frequently walked the walls when her duties were too much for her to handle, so I thought perhaps you would find comfort in it as well."

Mordred felt a real smile warm his lips. "You're right.... I had nearly forgotten. Britt frequently walked the walls at night—or after a particularly aggravating encounter with Lancelot." He chuckled.

"Perhaps," Guinevere tactfully said, smiling.

He smiled as he leaned against a crenel in the sawtooth pattern of the wall, and watched a farmer drive by in a wagon pulled by two oxen. "I must extend my thanks and gratitude for the new role you play in Camelot."

"'Tis nothing," Guinevere said.

Mordred shook his head. "You have organized the ladies and become the social driving force behind Camelot, all without using your rank as Leodegrance's daughter or Britt's close friend as a crutch."

His praise brought a slight blush to her cheeks. "I'm thankful you have allowed me to stay here, my King."

"It is I who am thankful! You have been invaluable."

Guinevere giggled, but her smile was soft as she joined him at the wall. "Britt always seemed to expect more of the ladies of Camelot, and more of me. Her belief in us was…freeing. Now, I wish to test the limits of my abilities and see what kind of person

I can become." She paused, and her face turned nearly as red as her red gold hair. "I apologize, saying such silly things."

"No, I know precisely what you mean. I witnessed it many times among the Knights of the Round Table. Britt could move a stone wall if she tried." Mordred glanced speculatively at his companion. He knew Britt had enforced many of her new rules to protect women and give them more options, but since her exit, it had become apparent that very few women were comfortable taking up the reins of their newfound freedom. In fact, Mordred doubted any would've done it at all if Guinevere had not remained in Camelot and followed in Britt's footsteps by breaking the previously ironclad expectations of society.

The noble-blooded lady had proven on multiple occasions that she was an excellent ally to have in the castle, and Mordred was forever thankful that she was willing to corral the ladies of Camelot.

"Do you have a riding horse, Lady Guinevere?" Mordred asked on an impulse.

Guinevere bit her lip. "No, My King has been kind enough to allow me to use his personal stables."

"How would you like a horse of your own?"

The young lady blinked. "Of my own?"

"Llamrei—Britt's white palfrey has not had a rider since she left. It's a shame for such a magnificent horse to be without an owner. But while I ride Roen, I've no use for a palfrey trained as Llamrei is."

Guinevere slowly nodded. "I should very much like to accept her. Thank you."

Mordred rested his thumbs on his sword belt. "Consider it my thanks for all you do."

"No thanks are necessary. It is my pleasure," Guinevere said simply. She turned on her heels and glided towards the stairs. "I shall leave you, for I am certain you need a moment of silence." She paused at the top of the staircase. "But, my King…please do not over-extend yourself. You are in a very difficult position, and I know you wish to see Camelot thrive for a multitude of reasons. Britt, if she could see you, would be very proud of what you've done. But neither she, nor any of us in Camelot, wish to see you drive yourself to an early grave."

Lacking the courage to view her expression, Mordred stared at the forest surrounding most of Camelot. "Do you really think she would be proud?"

"I know it," she said simply. "And, perhaps it is presumptuous of me to say so, but I greatly admire you and admire your loyalty for remaining here when you could have easily left with the others."

Mordred turned around just in time to see Guinevere bob a curtsy and disappear down the staircase. Feeling lighter than he had in days, he rested an elbow against the crenel and watched the men and women scurry back and forth across the courtyard of Camelot…through his city.

~

AFTER BOTH THE hunt held in Ywain's honor and the summer festival, Mordred finally had a few days to himself. He informed Sir Ulfius and Sir Bodwain of his plans, and then set out for Baron Marhaus' lands with a number of guards to serve as his escort.

The festival went well...though Sir Ector did not attend. Not that I blame him. Camelot is, I imagine, a reminder of his children.

"If you'll excuse the interruption, milord," the captain of the guard said, disrupting Mordred's thoughts. "The front scout has returned."

The scout that had been sent ahead was a giant Scotsman who smiled frequently and tended to call Mordred "laddy."

"All is well—no signs of blackguards or bandits," he reported.

"Thank you," Mordred said to both the captain and the scout. "How far ahead is the village?"

"You ought to start hearing grazing sheep soon," the Scotsman said. "Once we pass the herds, the village is just a short ride away."

"Perfect." Mordred shifted in his saddle, then flicked a thatch of his horse's black mane back into place. His horse, Roen, nickered happily. "We'll spend the day with the village, camp there for the night, and return to Camelot on the morrow."

The guard and captain exchanged looks.

"Forgive me, milord, but is that possible?" the captain finally ventured.

"What do you mean?" Mordred asked.

"Won't Baron Marhaus press us into accepting his hospitality?"

Mordred frowned, more than a little puzzled. "Why would he?"

The Scotsman raised a bushy eyebrow. "Because you are the High King of Britain?"

"Ah. Yes." *I had forgotten about that.* This was the first time Mordred was visiting this particular village as King of Britain. Previously, he had always come as a mere knight—and with the Knights of the Round Table swarming the area on quests, he wouldn't have been at all noteworthy.

Mordred shifted in his saddle. "If he finds out about our visit, I suppose we will hear from him. But we haven't come here for the Baron, but for a shepherd who goes by the name of Arth."

The guards nodded and began to settle back into place, but Mordred felt excessively awkward. *How many kings go about paying social calls on shepherds?* He cleared his throat. "Sorry. I know it is rather…eccentric of me."

"Kings—good kings anyway—associate with all sorts of folk. Hermits, sons of cow herders, guards, and even shepherds, milord," the captain said.

"By good kings, you mean Britt," Mordred said.

The captain didn't even blink. "She is one example. But you are another."

Mordred twisted in the saddle to study his guards, his gaze flickering from man to man.

They had been Britt's private honor-guard, handpicked by Sir Kay himself. Mordred knew them from the hours he would spend with Britt on the castle walls at night. *I expected they would treat me differently. But they've continued with their air of familiarity and watchfulness.*

Several of the guards met his gaze and smiled, then bobbed their heads in bows.

Mordred faced forward once again, their painless acceptance buoying him.

When they reached the village, it was near midday, and the man Mordred was particularly seeking out—his long-time childhood acquaintance and friend—was mending the wooden fence of a small pen.

Smiling, Mordred nudged Roen into the village. "Arth—Arthur!"

The well-built man looked up and smiled. "Mordred, you blackguard! Finally gave your responsibilities the slip, did you?"

Mordred dismounted and slapped the shepherd on the back. "Indeed. It has been too long since I managed to visit you last."

"Let us stable your horse, and come in! My wife is out with the children, but she will be back not an hour from now." Arthur began to stride off, then paused. "I apologize, but I don't think we have room for *all* your horses," he said, nodding to the guards.

The captain of the guards smiled and bowed slightly. "It is no problem at all. We will begin pitching our camp at the outskirts of the village—if it pleases milord."

Mordred waved to him in agreement. "That would be perfect; thank you." The guards parted as Mordred led Roen into a small stable, which he would share with goats and various poultry.

As he settled Roen into his stall, he grinned at Arthur—Sir Ector's foster son who was meant to become King of Britain but had run off, married a shepherdess, and gone by the name Arth ever since. "I forget, you have two offspring now," Mordred said. "I hope they do not take too much after you and are not driving their mother insane?"

Arthur laughed from deep in his chest. "My daughter shows signs of my temper, but thankfully, our son seems to have inherited his mother's sweet disposition. Even so, I know she will be grateful for the help when we leave."

Mordred slipped Roen's bridle off his head and patted his velvety black neck. "You're leaving? Where will you go, and why?"

"I apologize. I forgot I hadn't yet told you—I planned to send word when we were settled in. After a lot of thinking, my wife and I decided to move back to Bonmaison lands. We will live with Sir Ector and his wife."

"So you've told them where you've been all these years since you ran off with your wife?"

Arthur slipped the saddle from Rowan's back and snorted in laughter. "My father has known almost as long as I've been gone. He discovered my location the summer King Britt was crowned."

Mordred had to pause to allow the new information to make sense. "You didn't tell me so when I approached you about Britt before I entered Camelot's courts."

Arthur raised an eyebrow. "How else did you think I knew King Arthur was really a female? Or that I knew as much about her as I did?"

When Mordred had been sent to Britain under his brother's orders, Mordred had more or less figured out that the Arthur on the throne was not, in fact, the true Arthur who was a foster son of Sir Ector. Though he had never met Sir Ector in a formal setting, he had spent much of his youth in Britain with various lords that were allies to his father and had several run-ins with Kay and Arthur.

Kay did not remember the episodes, for both Mordred and Arthur had been young boys, allowing Mordred to continue with his anonymity. But before approaching Camelot, Mordred had sought out the real Arthur and learned as much about King Arthur, Britt, from his childhood acquaintance as he could.

Mordred was too embarrassed to admit he hadn't thought much about the method in which his friend had acquired such knowledge, so he changed the topic. "May I assume Kay knew as well?"

Arthur shook his head. "No, and that is something I regret. He was my brother, but in my selfishness and worry that he would be angry with me, I lost my chance to say goodbye.... That's why we are moving back to Bonmaison. Ector has been nothing but the best of fathers, and in a short amount of time, he lost his eldest son and his much-beloved daughter. He, and my foster mother, need support. I was afraid I lost the right to be that support due to my brash conduct, but over the past few months, I've realized that even if I have, my foster parents still deserve every comfort that can be afforded to them."

"I am glad, for I know how you loved your family," Mordred said. He paused for a moment, then grinned. "Does this mean I can expect to see you in Camelot's courts?"

"No!" Arthur said sourly. "I've no use for prancing knights and pretty ladies. You know that!" He eyed him and looked like he might smack Mordred with a wooden bucket if further provoked.

Mordred looked around the stable for listening ears before turning again to look at Arthur. "You know, it is your fault I am in this position. The throne really is yours, and while I never would have let Britt stand aside for you, I am perfectly willing to return the throne to you, the rightful son of Uther Pendragon."

Arthur draped an arm over Roen's neck. "No. I may be the son of Uther Pendragon, but it is in blood only. That angel-faced woman, Britt Arthurs...She was the true High King of Britain." Arthur smiled at him. "And now, you are."

"But I'm not even British," Mordred said.

"Neither was Britt," Arthur pointed out.

Mordred said nothing.

Arthur walked around Roen so he could slap Mordred on the back. "You are a good King, Mordred. I'm happy it is you on the throne."

Mordred finally cracked a smile. "It is my honor to watch over Camelot." He paused, thinking of his friends that remained with him—Ywain, Bors, Pellinore, and more. And for a brief moment, he thought of Guinevere with her beautiful hair. "And I know it will forever be my home."

"Amen," Arthur said in all seriousness. "Come, you must be hungry after your ride. I'm no cook, but my wife, Edla, has managed to teach me a thing or two about food preparation."

Mordred followed his friend, but he was still deep in thought.

It was as Arthur had said, he was now the High King.

Mordred would very likely miss Britt for the rest of his life, as would everyone in Camelot. But he was coming to accept his position and find contentment. It was the same for all the loyal knights who remained in Camelot. The land continued to prosper; the valiant knights were still riding out on quests, and peace reigned.

And while everyone would make certain that Britt was never forgotten, Mordred knew she would want most of all for everyone to be happy.

Perhaps that should be the goal of my kingship. Not to imitate Britt, but to see that everyone thrives.

THE END

ACKNOWLEDGMENTS

This is it, the end of a series or—as it is in my mind—a saga. I started the King Arthur and Her Knights series in 2013—my first full year as a writer—and finished it in 2017. Writing *Endings* was a bittersweet experience. I was excited to finish the series and deliver a final story that my readers and Champions deserved, but I knew I would miss Britt and her boys.

I've received a lot of fan mail praising the series for its characters' conduct and the approach I took to knighthood. But King Arthur and Her Knights is an example of chivalry and friendship because of the source material—the original ballads and legends. Yes, some of their actions and the things they did never made sense (I still don't understand the black armor = Sable Knight thing) and at times they were completely over the top in the emotional ways they would react.

However, when I devoured books about King Arthur as a kid, teenager, and adult, I never doubted that Arthur was given Excalibur and ruled over Camelot because he was a just and good king, and that his knights had good hearts.

So this isn't so much a thank you as it is acknowledging all the King Arthur lore and legends that inspired me and served as a building block for my series. It is my hope that Britt, Merlin, and the Knights of the Round Table can one day do the same for you.

OTHER SERIES BY K. M. SHEA

The Snow Queen

Timeless Fairy Tales

The Fairy Tale Enchantress

The Elves of Lessa

Hall of Blood and Mercy

Court of Midnight and Deception

Pack of Dawn and Destiny

Gate of Myth and Power

King Arthur and Her Knights

Robyn Hood

The Magical Beings' Rehabilitation Center

Second Age of Retha: Written under pen name A. M. Sohma

ADDITIONAL NOVELS

Life Reader

Princess Ahira

A Goose Girl

ABOUT THE AUTHOR

K. M. Shea is a fantasy-romance author who never quite grew out of adventure books or fairy tales, and still searches closets in hopes of stumbling into Narnia. She is addicted to sweet romances, witty characters, and happy endings. She also writes LitRPG and GameLit under the pen name, A. M. Sohma.

Printed in Dunstable, United Kingdom

66811384R00170